Identity and Everyday Life

HARRIS M. BERGER AND
GIOVANNA P. DEL NEGRO

✳

Identity and Everyday Life

ESSAYS IN THE STUDY OF FOLKLORE,
MUSIC, AND POPULAR CULTURE

✳

WESLEYAN UNIVERSITY PRESS
Middletown, Connecticut

Published by Wesleyan University Press, Middletown, CT 06459

Printed in the United States of America

5 4 3 2 1

The publishers have generously given permission to reprint the following copy-righted works. Chapter two of this book is a revised version of an article entitled "Theory as Practice: Some Dialectics of Generality and Specificity in Folklore Scholarship." It is reprinted by permission from the *Journal of Folklore Research,* volume 36, number 1. © *Journal of Folklore Research* (1999). Chapter four is a revised version of an article entitled "Bauman's *Verbal Art* and the Social Organization of Attention: The Role of Reflexivity in the Aesthetics of Performance." It is reprinted by permission from the *Journal of American Folklore,* volume 115, number 455. © American Folklore Society (2002). An earlier version of chapter five appeared as "Identity Reconsidered, The World Doubled: Identity as Interpretive Framework in Folklore Research" in *Midwestern Folklore,* volume 28, number 1 (2002), pp. 5–32.

Library of Congress Cataloging-in-Publication Data

Berger, Harris M., 1966–
Identity and everyday life : essays in the study of folklore, music,
and popular culture / Harris M. Berger and Giovanna P. Del Negro.
  p. cm. — (Music/culture)
Includes bibliographical references and index.
ISBN 0–8195–6686–1 (cloth : alk. paper) — ISBN 0–8195–6687–X (pbk. :
alk. paper)
1. Folklore—Study and teaching. 2. Folk music—Study and teaching.
3. Culture—Study and teaching. 4. Identity (Psychology).
5. Group identity. I. Del Negro, Giovanna. II. Title. III. Series.
GR45.B47 2004
398'.071—dc22   2003026215

For Ruth, Dick, and Sandy

Contents

*

Chapter Five
Identity Reconsidered, the World Doubled   124
GIOVANNA P. DEL NEGRO AND HARRIS M. BERGER

Preface

*

In the social sciences and humanities, it would seem that the methods and techniques used in research are the means by which the researcher's underlying theoretical orientation is made concrete. One may be trained in Marxism or post-structuralism, Birmingham school cultural studies or phenomenology, and in one's theoretical essays or the opening chapters of monographs, one may state a theoretical commitment to an intellectual tradition and elaborate the fine points of theory. However, a critic may argue, it is only in empirical research—in participant/observation fieldwork, interviews, archival work, or textual interpretation—that one's real theoretical commitments are revealed. Following this line of thinking through, a person might even be tempted to say that methodology is theory in practice, theory made flesh.

There is certainly some truth to these ideas, but the reality of human research is more problematic than such a perspective might suggest. "Theory" does not refer to a static collection of concepts that regulate research behavior but a set of practices in its own right: practices of reading and writing, listening and speaking, publishing and gatekeeping, and all of the social and political dynamics that these practices entail. Such practices constitute one's engagement with the lived world of ideas, and their relationship with the practices that one performs in the field, the archive, or the office is dialectical and complex. Situated between the social world we study and the social world that employs and pays us, one's research is undoubtedly informed by one's theoretical orientations and theoretical practices; that theory, however, never fully dictates one's research. The mass of ideas that we possess can never have complete internal coherence, nor can it be fully articulated by even our most strenuous explicit theorizing. Even if we wanted to directly enact a research method dictated by a fixed theoretical system, we would at least occasionally be confronted by novel field situations or data that would force us to adapt our methods to fit our study object. And ideally, the content of our empirical research impinges back on our theorizing, shaping and informing the very ideas that are supposed to guide it. If this were not the case, it is not clear what the point of empirical research might be.

This collection of essays is the product of our recent theoretical practices. Trained in folklore, ethnomusicology, and performance studies, and addressing ourselves to an interdisciplinary audience that includes cultural studies scholars, anthropologists, and sociologists, the focus of our work has always been on expressive culture. As our research interests and perspectives on basic questions developed in recent years, it became clear to us that a set of theoretical and programmatic beliefs was beginning to emerge in our work. The first part of this study articulates that program by analyzing two fundamental methodological topics in the humanistic social sciences, and the second part applies our basic approach to gain new insights into the related problems of self, reflexivity, and identity in performance.

Often, our programmatic thinking has been inspired by our dissatisfaction with the ways in which research into expressive culture is presently carried out. For example, we have in recent years become uncomfortable with heavy handedly politicized research into expressive culture that ignores aesthetics or that dismisses local perspective and lived experience as nothing more than ideology or false consciousness; thinking dialectically, we are equally uncomfortable with studies that focus on creative artistry to the exclusion of power, and relativistic work that, in an effort to give voice to the voiceless, ignores the possibility that an individual could misunderstand the social world in which he/she lived. While the concept of "folklore" and the field of folklore studies have often played a key role in drawing scholarly attention to overlooked or disparaged forms of artistic behavior, we feel strongly that the notions of folklore, high art, and popular art do not correspond to any natural or transhistorical typology of expressive culture and that these ideas are often a hindrance to human research. Following longstanding traditions in our home disciplines, we exclude aesthetic criticism from our project and instead seek to understand how expressive culture is made meaningful by the people who use it. Likewise, we focus on the expressive life of a given social world and avoid a genre approach that would prejudice analysis by disengaging individual expressive forms from the matrix of social practices in which they are enmeshed. Against scholarship that treats text as its primary study object, our work focuses on practices of producing and receiving texts and lived experiences of meaning. Drawing on practice theory and elements of folklore studies, we treat such practices as emerging from the complex interplay of agency on the one hand and larger social forces and expressive resources on the other; likewise, we view expressive culture neither as parsley on the plate of social life nor as an artistic template that shapes and controls subjectivity and society but instead as one domain among many that informs social structure. Though our ethnographic background makes us cautious about the universalizing tendency found in some forms of phenomenology, we rely heavily on that tradition to unearth patterns of organization in the interpretive processes by which expressive culture and other types of social conduct are made meaningful. Viewing interpretation as practice, we see a thread that connects all of the elements of expressive culture—expressive culture is created in practices of production, received and made meaningful in interpretive practices, and tied to the rest of social life as one of many domains of practice through which society is constituted.[1]

All of the essays in this collection draw on this programmatic orientation. Articulating these ideas most fully, the essays of the first part of the book apply them to basic methodological and theoretical issues in the study of expressive culture. Chapter one takes as its focus a term that has become ubiquitous in contemporary scholarship: "everyday life." Examining selected thinkers and intellectual traditions from the vast array that employs this concept, we sketch out the gains that have been won by everyday life scholarship and reveal the subtle but important difficulties that this concept produces. Arguing that "everyday life" does not correspond to any particular sphere of social life, we show how a practice-oriented approach to expressive culture can carry forward the humanistic advances made by past everyday life scholarship without the theoretical fuzziness and difficulties of romanticization sometimes associated with this term. Chapter two focuses on the relationship between theory and data in the study of expressive culture. Treating theory and theory building as social practice, Berger suggests that the emergent nature of artistic behavior makes the search for broad generalizations about culture an inherently complex and problematic (though necessary) endeavor and argues that social insights are best gleaned when scholars take a flexible and dialectical approach to the relationship between theory and data. Though explicitly addressed to scholars in folklore studies, this chapter explores ideas relevant to anyone interested in expressive culture.

The chapters of the second part of the book build on the general orientation of the first part to examine the related concepts of self, reflexivity, and identity. While our analyses explore the intellectual history of these terms and the differing ways in which they are used in contemporary scholarship, our primary goals throughout are to gain insights into the forms of lived experience to which these words point and to shed light on the role of these phenomena in the politics and aesthetics of expressive culture. Both the structure of experience (that is, the organization of the parts of experience relative to one another) and the meaning contents of experience can produce a lived sense of self or other, and across the span of the second part of the book our focus shifts from the former to the latter.

The notion of "the self" is perhaps the most all-embracing of the concepts dealt with in the second part of the book. In chapter three, Berger explores this phenomenon and examines its role in the aesthetics of performance. In the first half of the essay, Berger uses the phenomenological notion of the horizon (the edge or limit of an element of experience) to discuss the ways in which the fine grained features of melody emerge in the experiences of musicians and listeners. The manner with which one attends to melodic details is culturally specific, and Berger shows how one's practices of focusing attention on such details inform one's experiences of musical meanings. In the second half of the essay, the issue of horizons is made to speak to the larger topic of the self in performance. The essay is largely built on the work of philosopher José Luis Bermúdez, who argues that one's consciousness of oneself is a richly multilayered affair, with foundational types of self-consciousness emerging in sense perception and additional types coming about in reflexive thought and other abstract forms. Bermúdez's ideas are examined from a phenomenological perspective and applied to the domain of artistic behavior. Berger illustrates how audience members and performers foster or diminish the various forms of self through practices of organizing attention; such practices are informed by both culture and agency, and it is shown that differing forms of self may be given differing meanings in differing expressive traditions. Addressing larger political concerns, the essay concludes with the idea that contemporary scholarship must move beyond the naive celebration of the loss of self in performance to understand the complex ways in which the self emerges in the experiences of audiences and performers.

The theme of chapter four is reflexivity and its fundamental role in expressive culture, and Richard Bauman's groundbreaking study *Verbal Art as Performance* serves as the touchstone of our discussion. Building on Bauman's penetrating analysis, we observe that in any given social interaction, an individual may have a varying amount of reflexive awareness of him/herself as a participant in an interaction and may engage in a varying amount of reflexive metacommunication about his/her conduct. But while specific acts of thinking or metacommunication are optional for any given interaction participant at any given moment, the *issue* of reflexivity, we argue, is always on the table in interaction and always plays a role in the overall meaning of the conduct. Grounding our discussion in a close reading of Edmund Husserl's fifth *Cartesian Meditation,* we show that for interaction to occur at all, individuals must be aware of themselves and others as subjects (entities that have experience); as a result, even the absence of reflexive self-awareness or metacommunication plays a role in participants' experiences of their own or the other's conduct. Turning our attention specifically to performative interactions, we argue that each culture, subculture, and scene possesses an aesthetic of reflexivity—specific ideas about what forms of reflexivity are desirable or undesirable for performers or audience members. We provide a close analysis of performance events from our primary field sites—the popular music scenes of northeast Ohio and the *passeggiata* (ritual promenade) of central Italy—and examine how practices of organizing attention, constructing reflexive self-awareness, and signaling that self-awareness in metacommunication are both creatively enacted by performers and influenced by situated and larger social contexts. We also examine how audiences draw on an aesthetic of reflexivity in their interpretive practices, reading the performers' metacommunication together with other elements of their conduct to produce complex meanings. Viewed as a whole, the essay presents a set of intellectual tools that scholars may use to interpret performances more richly.

Identity is the theme of the fifth and final chapter. We begin with an intellectual history of the notion of identity, and we select examples from the ethnographic and historical records to illustrate a few of the many conceptions of identity that have existed in human cultures. Exploring how this notion is used in folklore studies, anthropology, and allied disciplines, we present a typology of Western scholarly approaches to this concept in order to make sense of the confusing welter of meanings and functions that this term has in academic literature. Moving beyond the analysis of existing scholarship, we argue that the concept of identity is best understood as an interpretive framework, a web of ideas that people use to make sense of expressive conduct. For an individual to read another's behavior in terms of identity, we argue, he/she must read it twice—give that conduct meaning, and then inject that meaning into his/her vision of the social world. The notion of identity need not guide an individual's interpretive practices, but in cases where it does, a complex but tractable set of interpretive dynamics can be identified. We then present a detailed hypothetical example to illustrate the various ways that identity interpretations can emerge in performance, and we conclude by exploring how the notion of identity can be combined with other interpretive frameworks when audiences read performances and make them meaningful. By unearthing the interpretive dynamics associated with this crucial and pervasive concept, we hope to provide scholars with a conceptual apparatus for making more sophisticated readings of performance, and to map out the pitfalls associated with undertheorized visions of identity.

The shift of emphasis from the analysis of the structures of lived experience to the dynamics of interpreting meaning contents is a theme that both connects these chapters and differentiates the types of phenomena referred to by the terms *self, reflexivity,* and *identity.* Our discussion of the self in chapter three focuses primarily on the ways in which embodied subjects become aware of themselves through the horizonal organization of their perceptual experiences. Here, the structure of visual and auditory perspectives produces a sense of self, and the chapter concludes with an examination of how such structurally based forms of self-experience are made meaningful in performance by historically and culturally situated agents. In the discussion of reflexivity in chapter four, we explore a domain where the structure of lived experience and its meaning contents play equally important roles in constituting a sense of self. Here, Husserl's rich phenomenological description of embodiment and lived space shows that the meaning content "other subject" emerges from fundamental structures of experience. Though in chapter five we examine the specific ways in which identity interpretations may emerge for a person (embedded in perceptual qualities, made explicit in reflexive thought in words, or shared in metacommentary), the center of gravity for the notion of identity is in meaning contents, experiences of self or other that come about when one reads another's actions as tied to a dimension of social reality such as race, class, or gender. Allowing our analysis to explore both the structures and the contents of lived experience, we seek to gain new perspectives on the nature of the self and related phenomena.

A second interplay of opposing concepts that unites the various themes of the book is that of theory and data. Throughout these essays, we tack back and forth between social theory or philosophy on the one hand and ethnographic or historical examples on the other, and our larger programmatic goals are as dialectical as our methods. We believe that an analysis of fundamental notions like self, reflexivity, and identity can help ethnographers come to richer understandings of the social lives of their field sites and avoid interpretive problems like the over-reading that results when all types of artistic behavior are seen as expressions of identity or the romantic celebration of the loss of self in performance. Likewise, we believe that ethnographic or historical case studies in performance can open up new perspectives on questions often explored from a strictly theoretical angle. The unique phenomena revealed by our own field research on American and Italian performance events and those of the case study literatures we cite do not merely exemplify elements of self-experience already discovered by theorists. To the contrary, such phenomena challenge theory and force us to reconsider the taken-for-granted elements of our arguments. By exemplifying a method for treating theory and data, we hope the essays of the second part of this collection illustrate and carry forward the program articulated in the first part and help to develop new insights into expressive culture and social life more generally.

H.M.B.
G.D.N.

Acknowledgments

*

Harris M. Berger and Giovanna P. Del Negro would like to thank Richard Bauman, Jeff Cohen, Sylvia Grider, Alan Houtchens, Deborah Kapchan, Nathan Light, Jack Santino, Keith Sawyer, Greg Schrempp, and two anonymous reviewers for Wesleyan University Press for reading drafts and making comments on the writings in this collection. We would also like to acknowledge Gerald L. Pocius for initially sparking our interest in the topic of identity and Luciano Del Negro for his helpful perspectives on Quebec cultural politics.

Over the years, conversations with mentors, colleagues, and friends have helped and supported us. In this regard, we would like to thank Gage Averill, Richard Bauman, Eduardo Bonilla-Silva, Michael Carroll, Sandra Dolby, Donnalee Dox, members of the Ethnography/Theory working group (Mary Bucholtz, Barbara Finlay, Christie Fox, Sarah Gatson, Kathryn Henderson, Mary Hovsepian, Tazim Jamal, Joseph Jewell), Cornelia Fales, Claire Farrer, Kathleen Ferrara, Heather Gert, Paul Greene, Sharon Hochhauser, Greg Kelley, Kate Kelly, Jimmie Killingsworth, Doreen Klassen, Elaine Lawless, Patrick Leary, Sabina Magliocco, Chris Menzel, Marilyn Motz, Peter Narváez, Mary Ann O'Farrell, Sally Robinson, James Rosenheim, Jill Terry Rudy, Jack Santino, Patricia Sawin, Paul Smith, Susan Stabile, Ruth Stone, Jan Swearingen, Kati Szego, Lynne Vallone, Jeremy Wallach, and Deena Weinstein. We would like to extend special appreciation to Robert Walser and the other editors of the Music/Culture series, George Lipsitz and Susan McClary, for their support of our work. Suzanna Tamminen, editor-in-chief at Wesleyan University Press, also deserves our thanks for her guidance during the various stages of this project.

The Melbern G. Glasscock Center for Humanities Research at Texas A&M University provided each of us with fellowships that aided us in different stages of our work on this project, and we would like to express our appreciation for this support.

PART ONE

*

EVERYDAY LIFE IN
THEORY AND PRACTICE

CHAPTER ONE

New Directions in the Study
of Everyday Life
Expressive Culture and the
Interpretation of Practice

*

Giovanna P. Del Negro and Harris M. Berger

Since the early 1960s, the notion of "everyday life" has become increasingly important in the humanities and social sciences. For folklorists, cultural studies scholars, and sociologists, as well as philosophers, historians, and students of literature, a concern for the role of expressive culture in "everyday life" has signaled a set of strongly felt, but often undertheorized, intellectual commitments. For researchers primarily interested in aesthetic questions, such commitments include a view of expressive culture as an integral part of social life, a populist emphasis on folk or mass culture, and a critique of structuralist or formalist approaches that see texts as independent from lived experience or social context. For scholars more interested in political questions, such commitments include an awareness that "art" does not merely reflect "life," but that the arts are one of the chief media through which ideas about race, class, gender, or other dimensions of identity are inculcated, debated, and resisted. Yet for all the concern with everyday life, few scholars have presented a detailed analysis of what the term itself means. In most discussions, scholars have assumed that the definition of everyday life itself is unproblematic, and they have instead focused their energies on arguing for the importance of the everyday or illustrating its significance for problems in social or cultural theory.

Our first goal in this essay is to explore the programmatic implication that this term is meant to signal. As Rita Felski (2000, 15) has recently suggested, a search in any major bibliographic database for the term "everyday life" will yield literally thousands of hits, and a comprehensive review of all of this material would be a Herculean project. Here, we will critically review the explicit theorizing of everyday life that has occurred in three distinct bodies of work—American folklore studies, the French theoretical tradition of Henri Lefebvre and Michel de Certeau, and the British cultural studies scholarship of Paul Willis. We have focused specifically on these traditions and thinkers in order to demonstrate the similarities in their otherwise distinct programmatic visions and to illustrate how the notion of everyday life has served as a focus for their goals and projects.[1] Reexamining this concept, we suggest that there is no phenomenon, domain, or process in the social world that can be considered essentially "everyday." To the contrary, everyday life is best understood as an interpretive framework defined in dialectical opposition to the notion of special events and used by both scholars and non-scholars alike to make sense of practice. Our second goal is therefore to explore the interpretive dynamics that these processes involve, and ideas from performance theory will be used to shed light on the complex relationship between expressive culture and constructions of everydayness. Synthesizing these ideas, we will conclude with a series of programmatic statements on the analysis of expressive culture in everyday life.

Three Traditions of Everyday Life Scholarship

American folklore studies is a particularly apt place to begin our discussion. Many of the populist themes we mentioned above can be found in the work of folklore's eighteenth- and nineteenth-century founders, and since the disciplinary upheavals of the 1960s, the term "everyday life" has been frequently used in American folklore theory. Seeking to expand the disciplinary focus beyond the study of rural or premodern expressive culture, Barbara Kirshenblatt-Gimblett (1983), for example, defined folklore as "the aesthetics of everyday life." Espousing similar themes, a range of folklorists in what Giovanna Del Negro (1999, 2004) has called the neo-romantic tradition (see also Bauman 1983) have retooled their interpretive apparatus to embrace as folklore small-scale, non-institutionalized expressive culture wherever it is found, rural or urban, traditional or contemporary (Dorson 1959, 1978; Dundes 1965; Ben-Amos 1972; Brunvand 1978). The frequent but somewhat casual use of the term "everyday life" in folklore studies does not mean that the notion is insignificant to the field. To the contrary, it is so basic that most folklorists feel no need to discuss it at all, and the notion pervades every specialization in the discipline.[2]

For folklorists who study expressive genres that are typically integrated into the routines of the workplace or the home, the aesthetics of everyday life is a programmatic call. To scholars of material culture, foodways, proverbs, or legends, to do folklore is to hold a range of populist positions — that "everyday people" (rather than elites) are creative, that "everyday spaces" (rather than concert halls or museums) are the social sites of the expressive, that the pragmatic activities of everyday life (rather than the "fine arts") may be richly aesthetic, and that the boundary between instrumental and expressive practices is a highly fluid one. In many ways, the folklife movement was the ultimate expression of this approach (see, for example, Yoder 1963, 1976; Glassie 1982; Roberts 1988; Pocius 1991). Building on older European roots, American folklife scholars since the 1950s have argued that the discipline's longstanding focus on traditional genres of verbal art (folktales, folksongs) gives a lopsided view of human creativity. Many folklife scholars were primarily students of material culture, and, expanding their theoretic vision, they urged folklorists to take a synthetic, cross-generic approach and explore the interplay of "everyday practices, artifacts, and expressions" in a given social world (Bronner 1996, 282). While early folklife scholarship often gave limited attention to power and invoked romantic visions of the rural, its interest in the expressive significance of quotidian acts and holistic consideration of everyday practices foreshadowed many of the themes in today's cultural studies.[3]

The notion of everyday life is not only basic to folklife scholars, it is also foundational for those folklorists who work on expressive genres distanced from the routines of the workplace or home. For scholars from Svatava Pirkova-Jacobson (1956) to Beverly Stoeltje and Richard Bauman (1989) to Sabina Magliocco (1993), highly marked genres such as ritual, festival, or celebration are tied to everyday life, either as a critical discourse about daily practices (Singer 1972) or through formal features that link in-frame activity to out-of-frame activity (Briggs 1988). "Toward an Enactment-Centered Theory of Folklore" (Abrahams 1977) is perhaps the richest theoretical statement on this relationship. In this paper, Abrahams develops his notion of "enactments," a broad category of marked behaviors that stretches from play and festivity to rituals and performances. Sounding tones reminiscent of Erving Goffman (1959), Abrahams argues that enactments and the typical situations of everyday life are premised upon similar structuring principles (social roles, norms of behavior, and so forth). As a result, there is both a "continuity and a dialectic between everyday activities and these heightened events" (1977, 200). Abrahams critiques the normalizing tendencies of functionalist scholarship that see enactments as nothing more than a statement of social values or a venting of social pressures; likewise, the aestheticizing tendencies of traditional humanities scholarship are faulted for treating enactments as spheres of discourse autonomous from the rest of the social world. Articulating the best visions of folklore studies, Abrahams shows how expressive practices are grounded in everyday life and urges scholars to attend to the complex relationships that exist between these different realms.

On an abstract level, many of these ideas are echoed in the work of the two primary French theorists of everyday life, Henri Lefebvre and Michel de Certeau. Informed by the more humanistic early Marx and foreshadowing the 1970s practice theory of scholars like de Certeau ([1974] 1984), Anthony Giddens ([1976] 1993, 1979), and Pierre Bourdieu (1977), Henri Lefebvre's *Critique of Everyday Life,* Volume 1 ([1947] 1991) and *Everyday Life in the Modern World* ([1967] 1990) argue, somewhat briefly, that society does not exist apart from human activity. Lefebvre asserts that, to the contrary, society is produced in and by human activity, and that everyday life is the site where that production takes place. Critical of simplistically economistic social theories, Lefebvre is at pains to emphasize that expressive culture is not insignificant to social relations. Developing his critique of alienation, Lefebvre suggests that all activity can and should have an aesthetic component and that everyday life is the place where culture informs the organization of society. While the former idea echoes folklore's concern for the aesthetics of seemingly instrumental behavior, the latter notion presages contemporary work in cultural studies, which sees expressive culture as informing and regimenting a society's gender roles, class relations, and racial dynamics. Though the discussion of everyday practices and aesthetics is present in Lefebvre's work, he devotes the bulk of his writing to a critique of alienation in consumer capitalism and expends copious energy criticizing what he sees as the terror and mindless tedium of everyday life in the modern world. The force of this critique is somewhat blunted by the fact that he uses the phrase "everyday life" in two opposing senses. Lefebvre usually uses it to mean the alienated, bureaucratized, and, most importantly, de-aestheticized mundane existence of modernity, and of this he is almost relentlessly critical. However, he also uses the term in a neutral sense, simply to refer to day-to-day activity, and in his discussion of the premodern world, the lifestyles of particular neighborhoods in Paris, Milan, and New York, and the utopian "City" of the future, he suggests that everyday life has the potential to be richly aesthetic, creative, and spontaneous. In such an ideal world, he argues, work and culture are not opposing spheres, and productive labor is simultaneously creative and practical.

Michel de Certeau's *The Practice of Everyday Life*, Volume 1 ([1974] 1984) is programmatically consonant with Lefebvre's work.[4] But while Lefebvre focuses more on the alienation of everyday life, de Certeau is largely concerned with the problems of reproduction and resistance, and Lefebvre's often bleak appraisal of modernity contrasts with de Certeau's almost buoyant focus on everyday acts of resistance—what he calls "tactics." Exploring social phenomena overlooked by Michel Foucault, de Certeau attends to the ways in which social regimentation is subverted by "anti-disciplines," situated acts that oppose institutional forces. In de Certeau's view, domination is never complete, and while everyday practices may reproduce power relations, they also may resist and transform them. Further, everyday behavior has an aesthetic component, and this is expressed in a wide variety of ways. A precursor to the reader response theorists of the 1980s (for example, Radway 1984), de Certeau argues that the oppressive and ideological texts of the mass media are not passively consumed by audiences; to the contrary, such texts may be cleverly reinterpreted and actively employed in everyday life. Moreover, the tactics of resistance in the workplace and the school are themselves creative and aesthetic, rehumanizing routinized everyday life as well as producing instrumental, practical gains for the worker or the student. Discussing the novel uses of marketing structures, the active reading of popular literature, and everyday tactics of subversion, de Certeau emphasizes the potential significance of even the most seemingly trivial practices. Working with Luce Giard and Pierre Mayol, de Certeau develops his ideas on the aesthetic and creative dimensions of everyday life in the second volume of *The Practice* ([1980] 1998), a data rich ethnography of the Croix-Rousse neighborhood of Lyons. In their discussion of "the nourishing arts," for example, de Certeau, Giard, and Mayol show how the homemakers of this neighborhood do not merely apply recipes; instead, they skillfully adapt pre-existing culinary techniques, stocks of cultural knowledge, and aesthetic standards to create their own individual cooking styles and serve the needs of varying situations. Applying language traditionally associated with aesthetics to everyday practices (the art of living, styles of action), de Certeau, Giard, and Mayol find a complex balance of tradition and innovation in the practices of everyday life.[5]

These themes are also present in one strain of Birmingham school cultural studies, and Paul Willis's *Common Culture* (Willis et al. 1990) is perhaps the most cogent and powerful statement of this orientation. Willis's work focuses specifically on expressive culture in everyday life and reflects many of the populist themes we have explored above. Like the neo-romantic's notion of folklore, Willis's concept of "common culture" involves both the expressive behavior of small-scale groups within mass societies and the unofficial and "informal" culture within institutions. Most importantly, *Common Culture* situates microlevel activity in larger social contexts and focuses strongly on the problem of reproduction.[6] Willis is no romantic, and he strongly emphasizes that "the informal often provides accommodations to and reproductions of power" (1990, 130) and can construct its own patterns of domination and exclusion. He is at pains to show, however, that what he calls "the best side of the informal" (1990, 130) may be both humanizing and progressive, and that politically engaged scholarship can help to articulate and foster such liberatory tendencies. Perhaps his most productive notion is the idea of the "grounded aesthetic"—a set of expressive practices woven into the fabric of the everyday activities of a particular social group. Echoing folklife scholars, Willis emphasizes that it is not only traditionally conceived artistic practices that are aesthetic (music, painting, literature), but all forms of behavior (drinking, fighting, dressing, courting) may have an expressive component. The creative reception of mass-mediated texts and the reappropriation of consumer goods play key roles in the grounded aesthetic, and cultural studies' longstanding concern with youth cultures is reaffirmed as Willis draws our attention to the "multitude of ways in which young people use, humanize, decorate, and invest with meaning their common and immediate life spaces and social practices" (1990, 2). Not only does Willis stretch the boundaries of the aesthetic, he also argues for the social significance of expressive practices. As essential for human survival as "necessary work" (labor that serves basic biological needs), "symbolic work" refers to the production of meaning through the employment of a repertoire of signs and other devices (see Willis 1990, 9–10). "Symbolic work" is important not only because people have a fundamental need to communicate but because it serves as a vehicle through which individuals may reflect upon and critique the social order. In Willis's view, mastery of symbolic resources helps the individual gain a sense of control and perspective about the social world and can thus serve as a rehearsal for social change.

Everyday Life as Interpretive Framework

As scholars in the tradition of folklore and cultural studies, we are programmatically committed to the practice theoretic and populist themes present in these literatures. But, for all of the air time that the phrase "everyday life" has been given, it has, we believe, been strangely undertheorized. Often times, it is deployed by writers to critique other concepts and approaches; in the process, however, the notion of "everyday life" itself remains unclear. In a recent article, Rita Felski has rightly argued that "everydayness is not an intrinsic quality that magically adheres to particular actions or persons (women, the working class)" (2000, 31), and she goes on to equate the everyday with the routine and the process of routinization. The main advantage of Felski's work is that it emphasizes that everydayness is a concept with a strong ideological significance, one tied specifically to the issue of gender. We will shortly incorporate this important insight into our overall theory of everyday life as an interpretive framework. At this point, however, it is important to see that, while the routinized is often equated with the everyday, there are several ways in which these two concepts are distinct in academic and popular discourses. While the "everyday life" of many people in the industrialized world is controlled by schedules and routines, many others lead highly variable lives that are still experienced as "everyday." Marxist and other social theorists have long argued that modernity is characterized by clock time and routinized work behavior, and this is certainly not the place to inquire into the validity of these broad generalizations. We can suggest, however, that many in the premodern West and those living in contemporary non-industrialized societies lead lives that are far less routinized—but just as "everyday"—as those caught up in the repetitive, scheduled existence of modernity. Likewise in the industrial world, many of those with highly mundane jobs do not have strictly repetitive schedules. Workers with flextime, the unemployed, the retired, and those with jobs whose tasks are open and variable (insurance detectives, troubleshooters of various kinds) do not have strictly regimented routines but still lead lives they experience as everyday and mundane. We suggest that the notion of everyday life is so protean and flexible that defining it in terms of some structurally basic social process—Felski's "process of becoming acclimatized to assumptions, behaviors, and practices" (2000, 31), Lefebvre's "set of functions which connect and conjoin together systems which might appear to be distinct" (1987, 9)—will lead inevitably to difficulties. We can begin to gain purchase on the notion of everyday life by considering the way the term is in used within academia but outside the theoretical traditions that have taken it as a focus.

In the contemporary intellectual scene, the term "everyday life" is often invoked in a casual, programmatic, or polemical manner to critique the approaches and perspectives of others.[7] Attacking reification, some thinkers see the focus on everyday life as a critical corrective to scholarship that conceives of its study objects as autonomous artistic texts, abstract systems of thought, or social structures independent of human activity. Critiquing elitist art, others see the emphasis on everyday life as a corrective to work that looks only at "high art," sees mass audiences as nothing more than passive cultural dupes, and views scholars as the only valid interpreters of culture. The difficulty with these programmatically laudatory usages is that, if we wish to see all of society as constituted through practice, and if all expressive culture is produced through acts of production and reception, then the notion of "everyday life" seems to be little different from the notion of "practice" or "activity." The problem with assimilating everyday life to these more abstract concepts is that it strips the term of its rich set of associations and connotations—everyday life as oppressive or resistant, mechanically routine or artful and creative, and so forth. We do *not* wish to argue that everyday life inherently possesses any of these features, but we do believe that the highly contested meanings that surround this concept deserve greater scrutiny. Rather than making everyday life commensurate with practice, we wish to treat practice as a superordinate category and everyday life and its implicit opposite, special events, as two dialectically related subcategories used in various discourses to interpret practice. Our goal in what follows is to explore the processes by which both scholars and non-scholars employ these concepts as an interpretive framework. Taken in this way, the conceptual dyad of everyday life/special events is one of the primary devices through which lived social experience has been made meaningful in the Western world, and the analysis of this dyad can serve as a source of important insights.

Considering these concepts in terms of concrete processes of thinking, speaking, and writing, we see that whether or not an activity is interpreted as part of "everyday life" or "special events" is highly contextual. One of Paul Willis's examples illustrates the shifting nature of these categories. In *Common Culture,* he describes the Saturday night drinking sessions of young working-class men and women as a pleasurable escape from the mundane and humdrum routine of everyday life. Is Saturday night partying part of everyday life or a departure from it? If we are thinking in terms of concrete practices, it is clearly a kind of human *activity,* and we suggest that Saturday night partying can be seen either as a part of everyday life or a special event depending on how it is contextualized by the person considering it. Placed in the routine cycle of the work week, Saturday night partying is a special event; placed in the context of the yearly cycle, Saturday night is part of everyday life, and only once-a-year calendrical rituals like holidays or festivals are special events. The relative weighting of a practice as everyday or special operates on smaller and larger time scales as well: the coffee break is a minor special event when considered from the perspective of an afternoon's work; it is part of everyday life when taken in the context of the workday or work week. One's birthday is a special event when considered in the context of the year; placed in the context of the life cycle, most birthdays (turning 26, say) become part of everyday life (an "everyday" celebration), and only once-in-a-lifetime events (births, deaths, coming of age rituals) are considered special events. Even the most unique events in the life of an individual or a society can be taken as everyday if properly contextualized. Weddings and funerals can become highly mundane for clergy and morticians, and, flipping through a historical atlas, even highly consequential events like the founding of a nation state or the breakup of an empire become seen as just one more event in the all-too-repetitive flow of history. Of course, such individual or collective births are far from insignificant to the people experiencing them, and our point is that the everydayness of an occurrence depends not on the occurrence itself but on how it is interpreted.

We wish to suggest that three types of factors determine if an event is interpreted as part of everyday life—contextual factors, ideological factors, and factors of economics and practice. The category of contextual factors is a dual one, involving both the analytical context in which the interpretation is made and the cultural context of the event that is interpreted. The analytical context refers to the time scale in which the interpreter places the event—the day, the week, the year, or the life cycle as a whole. But human practices are culturally specific, and whether or not an event is considered to be everyday also depends on the frequency with which it is carried out in a given social group. Formalized storytelling, for example, was a frequent occurrence in the family life of traditional Italian society, while in contemporary Italian American ethnic communities it occurs only once or twice a year. Thus, formal storytelling must be considered on the time scale of the full life cycle to be seen as "everyday life" for Italian Americans, while it need only be viewed in the context of the work week to be "everyday" in traditional Italy. Viewed from the dual perspective of contextual factors, the interpretation of an event as everyday or as special depends equally on the frequency of its occurrence in a given society and the time scale in which it is considered by its interpreter.

Such contextual factors are deeply informed by what we call "ideologies of everyday life"—the significance (political, religious, aesthetic) that everyday life is given in the worldview of an individual or society. For example, in societies in which the divine is conceptualized as distinct from the world, sacred rituals are often seen as sharply separate from everyday life, no matter how often they occur. Conversely, those religions that see the divine as immanent in the world will tend to emphasize the everydayness and ordinariness of worship, even—or especially—in the context of yearly rituals or major rites of passage. Similarly, the everydayness of expressive culture may be interpreted in a wide variety of ways. For those who construct "art" as a domain of autonomous forms and structures, the viewing of "great paintings" or the performance of canonical works of music will always be seen as distinct from the everyday, a transcendent moment sharply set apart from the mundane world. As we shall suggest below, such ideological factors are reflected in the discourse surrounding the event and in its level of markedness. Further, the "everydayness" that is read into a type of event varies among its interpreters and can be made into the object of consensus or dissent within a community.

The notion of everydayness is highly political. On a basic level, certain groups within society are directed into particular kinds of practice—women are channeled into domestic tasks, the working class into the field and the factory, and so forth. More importantly, the concepts of everydayness and specialness are used to give meaning to practice, and the ideological weights of these interpretations can vary significantly. The everyday may be viewed positively as a realm of authentic, productive labor and celebrated as a site of resistance; conversely, it may be disparaged as the domain of tedious, uncreative repetition or a place where power relations are mindlessly reproduced. In sexist or classist discourses, practices typically ascribed to women and the working class (domestic or manual labor) may be associated with everydayness in its pejorative sense and depicted as uncreative or mechanical. Alternatively, conservative discourse may romanticize the "everyday" practices of these groups in order to justify or obscure underlying inequities—the cheerful factory worker happy to do his job, the good wife working away in the kitchen. Progressive discourses may deny the pejorative everydayness of women or the working class by recuperating their important political, artistic, or scientific deeds. Conversely, such discourses may transvalue the pejorative everydayness of the social roles and activities thrust upon these groups, as when progressive scholars argue that working-class labor is responsible for the industrial achievements that capitalist discourses attribute to "great men." These dynamics play themselves out in the politics of expressive culture as well. In conservative views of art, the expressive behavior associated with women or the working class (the decorative arts, folk music, and, to a certain degree, popular music) may be associated with pejorative everydayness and depicted as lacking in individuality, innovation, or formal complexity. Progressive thinkers may either try to reveal the overlooked technical sophistication in such "everyday" expressive practices, or they may critique the standards that value the manipulation of "autonomous" or "pure" formal structures over communicative efficacy in an "everyday" social world.

Finally, the economic and practical features of a practice itself have a large impact on its interpretation as everyday or special. These can be defined as the amount of capital and labor resources necessary to engage in an activity relative to the available resources of the society and the interpreter's own position within it. For example, television production is hugely labor and capital intensive, and yet for wealthy, technological societies, television is widely seen as part of everyday life. In the United States of the early 1950s, television viewing was only an everyday activity for the wealthy, while the rest of the public saw it as an extremely special event. The influence of economic and practical factors upon the interpretation of practice always operates in conjunction with the contextual and ideological factors we have outlined above. For example, even though some forms of experimental theater may be neither time nor labor intensive, their often transgressive themes make them less likely to be interpreted as everyday in mainstream society. Likewise, the economic and practical factors themselves may be given meaning in reflexive and unexpected ways. To the busy professional, for example, TV watching may be seen as a special-event activity marked nostalgically as an everyday life activity from the leisurely days of youth.

Shifting our focus from the factors that influence the interpretation of everydayness to the objects of those interpretations, we suggest that it is not just practices that may be read as everyday or special. Categories of persons, times, or places may be abstracted from the holistic gestalt of concrete practice and associated with these attributes. As above, the interpretation of everydayness is always ideologically construed and locked in a dialectic with various kinds of opposites, and we can only begin to catalog the different ways in which this idea is employed. For example, Felski has observed that for writers like Lefebvre, women—traditionally consigned in the West to the private sphere and domestic work—represent the category of persons most closely associated with the everyday. In other discourses, the term "everyday people" refers to the working or middle classes (as opposed to the wealthy), and money is often depicted as an escape from everyday life. Such visions may be inverted, as when the mass media represents the rich in a maximally mundane fashion to dampen class antagonisms and confect for them a humble, "down home" image. This approach has its roots in the well publicized stories of the regular, workaday routines of early-twentieth-century industrialists and extends to the folksy media constructions of Sam Walton in the 1980s and H. Ross Perot in the 1990s. While the category of the celebrity is, in its unmarked sense, constructed as the polar opposite of the everyday person, the representation of fame in media discourses is also highly flexible. In entertainment news programs, movie actors and musicians are alternatively depicted as glamorous stars, happily free from the tedious and constraining bonds of everyday life, or as devoted parents and spouses—just regular, everyday people—raising children and trundling off to the studio for a solid day's work.

At higher levels of abstraction, even lifestyles, sensibilities, or entire worlds may be interpreted through the lens of everydayness. Mike Featherstone (1995) has argued, for example, that the notion of everyday life is often constructed in opposition to the "heroic life" (see note 7), and nowhere is this dialectic more evident than in fantasy literature. While all fantasy worlds provide for their readers with an element of escape, the relationship between the everyday and the non-everyday, here, is surprisingly fluid. In traditional fantasy like C. S. Lewis's *Chronicles of Narnia*, the everyday is represented as a world of tedium and constraint, and magical portals like enchanted wardrobes hide just out of view to whisk bored children into special places and heroic adventures. Here, the everyday is strictly opposed to the heroic. More richly dialectical, works of magic realism revolve around ordinary people whose lives are transformed when they discover the operation of magic lurking in mundane settings. In these works, the heroic is represented not as a separate world but as a facet of the everyday world waiting to be discovered. So-called reality television shows like *Big Brother* or Andy Warhol's six-hour film on sleep problematize that boundary by making maximally mundane activities the focus of intense mass-media attention.

In sum, everyday life is an interpretive framework, and the reading of any social practice as everyday or special depends on a complex interplay of factors and the interpreter's own meaning-making process. The significance of this analysis, we believe, is that it clears away the fog that surrounds the notion of everyday life and can help to focus research on concrete human practices and reveal the differing ways in which everydayness is constructed.

Performance, Expressive Culture, and Everyday Life

In popular discourse, everyday life is frequently associated with pragmatic, instrumental, and means-oriented behavior, and all of the literatures we have explored have been at pains to insist upon its expressive dimensions. In fact, the difficult relationship between expressive and instrumental behavior has been one of the defining features of these discourses. But if everydayness is an interpretive framework rather than a structural feature of the social world, how are we now to understand the insights into the aesthetics of everyday life offered by folklore theory, Lefebvre, de Certeau, and Willis? The notion of framing in performance theory can help to make this problem more tractable. Grounded in the work of Erving Goffman, theorists such as Dell Hymes (1975a) and Richard Bauman (1977, 1989) have defined performance as a special mode of behavior in which the performer takes responsibility for a display of competence. Here, acts of keying or framing cue the audience to watch with greater intensity and to read the performance in a heightened or nonliteral manner (see Bauman 1977, 9). The notion of performance has allowed these scholars to view a wide range of expressive genres (from highly marked events like rituals or festivals to everyday conversational genres like urban legends or proverbs) through the same lens and find common social dynamics in practices as seemingly disparate as front porch storytelling in Texas (Bauman 1986) and political oratory in Micronesia (Parmentier 1993).

At first blush, it may seem that the notion of performance is equivalent to special events and opposed to the everyday, but there are two key problems with such a reading, and examining these difficulties can allow us to better understand the relationship between expressive culture and everyday life. The primary difference between performance and special events is that performance is defined by reference to structural features of the behavior itself—as a mode of behavior marked by specific acts of framing and keying. To the contrary, our notion of everyday life/special events is defined relatively; there is nothing absolute or definitive about any stretch of behavior that will mark it as "everyday" or "special," and the classification of an activity in one category or the other is a highly variable phenomenon depending on both the interpreter and the interpretive context. The second and more significant problem with equating performance with special events and non-performance with everyday life is that it recapitulates the opposition of expressive and instrumental behavior that authors from Lefebvre to de Certeau sought to overturn. In sum, performance in particular and expressive culture in general can be smoothly integrated into the most mundane day (as in common joke telling) or sharply separated from it (in the performances of weekly or yearly rituals), and any given performance may be interpreted as either everyday or special, depending on the contextual, ideological, and economic factors we have outlined above.

If performance and everyday life are not simply two opposed domains of practice, the relationship between them is nevertheless important. Performances can be found in any culture. The meanings given to performance, however, vary widely across cultures, and the differing constructions of everyday life in a given society (by critics or lay folk, elites or disenfranchised groups) deeply inform the ways in which performance is understood there. This relationship is expressed in two ways—the physical relationship between performance space and spaces constructed as everyday, and the explicit and implicit ideologies about the relationship of performance and everyday life. At one extreme are expressive practices guided by an art-for-art's-sake aesthetic and performed in dedicated spaces—for example, highly formalist music performed in the concert hall or studies in abstract painting displayed only in the art museum. In the middle of this range are forms of expression intended as a commentary on society but set apart in specialized venues—for example, romantic nationalist music performed in the concert hall. Here, art is still seen as a distinct realm of endeavor, but it is also meant to comment on everyday life. Moving to a more intimate relationship between performance and the unmarked world, we see expressive practices situated in the home or street (TV viewing, radio listening) that are meant as "entertainment," that is, meant as nothing more than a mere diversion from everyday life. Finally, we can find a range of expressive practices that are both situated in everyday spaces and intended as a comment on everyday life. For example, in a classic passage from Barre Toelken's *The Dynamics of Folklore* (1979, 93–103), Toelken describes a quiet evening at home for a Navajo family. Here, the mother weaves in a corner of the room, children play at making string figures, and, later in the evening, the family's grandfather tells a story about the supernatural figure Coyote. The weaving, string games, and tale telling are framed as expressive activities, but they achieve their specific meanings at least partially because they are situated in the home. More important, the Coyote narrative is not only meant to be entertaining, it is also intended to provide moral instruction for the everyday lives of the children.

Other examples from performance literature show how ideas about the relationship between performance and everyday life can become intentionally blurred or inverted. In his analysis of a performance by the experimental dramatic company Squat Theater, Richard Schechner (1985) describes how the group's director replaced the back wall of the stage with a window, thus allowing the audience to overlook a busy New York street while the play proceeded. Actors posing as pedestrians would walk down the street and engage in various kinds of outrageous behavior, causing the audience to question the boundary between performance and non-performance space and the relationship between these spheres and everyday life. In a quite different vein, Daniel Cavicchi's *Tramps Like Us* (1998) illuminates the aesthetics of performance found among Bruce Springsteen fans. Rather than seeing performance as a special event cut out of everyday life, the fans take Springsteen performances as the focus of their existence and see everyday life as the negative space that intervenes between concerts. Perhaps more importantly, Springsteen fans use the in-frame behavior of the concerts as a lens for interpreting everyday events and situations. Here, performance transforms non-performative practice, and everyday life is made meaningful by references to the experiences of special events.

The politics of everydayness in expressive culture is complex and highly reflexive. On a basic level, it is a truism of both academic and non-academic discourses that elite expressive culture is associated with dedicated performance spaces and an aesthetic of autonomous formal complexity, while the expressive culture of disenfranchised groups is characterized by "everyday" performance spaces and an aesthetic based on relevance to a tradition or community. A range of scholars has produced examples in which these associations may be inverted—the incorporation of quilts or graffiti into the world of art galleries and museums, or, alternatively, the broadcasting of "high art" to the masses on public television or radio. It would, of course, be a mistake to ignore the development of sophisticated formalist traditions within the expressive culture of oppressed groups or the existence of highly "everyday" expressive culture among elites (family lore, personal experience narratives, heirloom recipes, TV viewing). But we wish to critique the standard associations in a different way and emphasize the diverse and culturally specific ways in which genres of expressive culture may be taken up into discourses of everydayness and given varying valences and meanings.

The formal promenade of Sasso, a small town in central Italy, can help to illustrate the differing ways in which everydayness and performance can be constructed.[8] Involving almost all of Sasso's three thousand residents and performed daily in the public space of the town's central piazza, the formal promenade (or *passeggiata*) might seem to be an ideal example of everyday expressive culture. Contrary to the discursive truisms about expressivity and everydayness, the *passeggiata* has traditionally been associated with the gentry, not the common people. In the period before World War II, Sasso's old aristocratic families would spend their Sunday afternoons promenading through the piazza, demonstrating their elegance and civility through displays of fine clothing and stylized greetings and gestures. Peasants and artisans could rarely afford the expensive attire necessary for this event, and it was not until the economic boom of the late 1960s that the *passeggiata* became a daily activity for a broad spectrum of Sassani citizenry. Based on participant observation fieldwork and in-depth interviews, Del Negro (1999, 2004) explored the wide range of ways in which townsfolk of different social positions (working-class residents and local elites, women and men, young and old) interpret today's *passeggiata*.

No one in Sasso doubts that the *passeggiata* is an example of everyday expressive culture, but the meanings given to this concept vary widely among the participants. In the official perspective (voiced most loudly by the local political elite), the *passeggiata* illustrates a Sassani sensibility that views expressive culture as the domain of all people and aesthetic experience as a necessary part of everyday life. This liberal vision is not shared by everyone in the region. Sasso is the economic center of a cluster of hilltop communities, and the citizens of the rival towns of Flavio and Roccaspina often depict Sasso's *passeggiata* in the opposite way. Only the foppish Sassani, they argue, would need to convince themselves of their value by daily parading up and down in fine clothes. For Flaviani and Roccaspinese, it is ostentatious to trot out public performance on a daily basis, and these forms of expressive culture should be reserved for special occasions rather than everyday life. Differences in interpretation also can be found across gender lines. While both women and men participate in the *passeggiata,* the event is most frequently seen as a female sphere. Men may choose either to stroll the piazza or observe from the sidewalk cafes, but women are expected to participate regularly and conform to higher sartorial standards. Teenage women are especially encouraged to participate in the *passeggiata,* as it is a socially sanctioned realm where young women may find a mate. In interviews, many of these young women described the *passeggiata* pejoratively as a *passerella* (fashion runway)—a gauntlet of prying eyes in which the pressure to be poised and beautiful is an onerous burden. To them, performance is an ordeal and its incorporation into everyday life a nagging reminder of traditional gender roles. Townsfolk of different class positions also voiced varying perspectives on everyday expressive culture. Claudia, for example, was a working-class woman from a communist family in Sasso. Unable to afford fine clothing and marginalized by her political affiliations, she expressed feelings of exclusion when discussing the *passeggiata.* If the official line depicts everyday life in Sasso as a democratic sphere in which the pleasures of expressive culture are open to all, Claudia felt that everyday life is a place of inequity, and performance an arena in which class distinctions are drawn and redrawn. Significantly, many wealthy Sassani have become disenchanted with the *passeggiata* for the exactly opposite reason. Now that the event has become a routine affair populated by everyday people, some affluent families have begun to avoid the *passeggiata* and seek recreation in a nearby city. Coming full circle, we find here the traditional construction in which the expressive culture of everyday life is pejoratively associated with "the common people."

The *passeggiata* example illustrates the constructedness of the notions of everyday life and expressive culture and the complex ways in which these concepts can inform one another in a given social world. While everyday expressive culture can bring great pleasure to both audiences and performers, it may also be interpreted as a source of social pressure or an arena for the ostentatious display of power. It may be associated with either the elite (as in the pre–World War II period) or the "common people" (as in the contemporary perspectives of the wealthy), and the performance itself may be seen either as a privilege or a burden. Of course, these oppositions represent just one possible constellation of meanings, just one way of construing the politics of everyday expressivity, and what is needed is an empirical investigation into the construction of everydayness—both our own construction and the constructions that occur in the social worlds we study.

Studying Everyday Life

If everyday life is not a domain of the social world but a framework for interpreting practice, then how are we to understand the everyday life literatures from folklore studies to Lefebvre to Willis? On the one hand, we must take a critical approach to the notion of everyday life by exploring the varying ways in which this concept is used and teasing out the complex relationships it has with other important themes and ideas. On the other hand, we must capitalize on the insights of the existing everyday life scholarship by taking this work not as a series of theses about a domain of practice but as an attempt to problematize dominant discourses about expressive culture, situated activity, and power. What the various scholars of everyday life have provided for us is a humanizing critique of practice, a set of guideposts and warnings signs for research into the social world, and we would like to conclude with a series of programmatic statements that consolidate and forward these diverse insights into the study of expressive culture.

In line with the diverse literature we have discussed above, we reaffirm the following. (1a) *A populist perspective on expressive culture.* That all people, not just the talented elect, the educated, and the powerful, are capable of creative activity; that expressive culture can be found in both common and exalted places and among all social groups; that both the production and the reception of texts have the possibility to be creative; that any type of behavior can have an expressive dimension; and that expressivity is basic to social life, not merely icing on its structural cake. (1b) *Practice orientations.* Against scholarship that reifies value systems, texts, or social structures, we urge scholars to conceptualize their study objects as value systems embedded in practice, situated acts of producing and receiving texts, and the production, reproduction, and transformation of society by human action. Further, both highly marked expressive practices and the aesthetic dimensions of instrumental behavior in the workplace or the home may be consequential for the reproduction of social relations. (1c) *Ethnographic methods and the concern for non-academic perspectives.* In this context, ethnography is a crucial—but certainly not the only—method for the study of expressive culture. Not all research topics lend themselves to ethnographic methods. But in projects where interviews and participation/observation fieldwork can be employed, ethnographic techniques such as these allow the scholar to see how actors engage with texts and make meaning in their situated social contexts. Ethnographic methods are but one component in a larger orientation that seeks to understand a given social world by taking seriously the diverse perspectives of the actors within it. Such an orientation need not abandon critical work or naively accept everything the participants say. To be sure, individuals can passively misread or actively misinterpret both their own experiences and the larger society in which they are embedded. Here, ethnographic engagement can, at the very least, show us how people read the texts of their social world and use them in their lives. At the most, however, ethnographic attention to participant perspectives can provide us as scholars with interpretations we never would have seen, point out the flaws in our own readings, and help to pull us back from the paternalism that sometimes mars critical research.[9]

Scholars like Abrahams, de Certeau, and Willis have decried the simplistic interpretation of expressive culture as either a realm of autonomous formal technique or as nothing more than a passive and mechanical response to larger social forces. Forwarding this tradition, we urge (2) *scholars of expressive culture to explore the complex dialectics of the expressive and the instrumental dimensions of practice.* It is the overwhelming instrumentality of expressive culture, the fact that artistry can be yoked to such a wide variety of ends, that makes the acquisition of expressive skills so important in so many cultures; likewise, the endless instrumentality of artistic behavior drives home the fact that expressive competence is a field of activity with its own techniques, processes, and dynamics. The dialectics we are concerned with apply equally to the expressive dimension of instrumental practice and the expressive performances woven into the activities of the workplace and the home; likewise, they speak to the interests of both scholars concerned with the politics of culture and those focused on matters traditionally labeled as "aesthetic." Certainly the notions of expressivity and instrumentality are problematic, and there may be social worlds in which they are wholly inoperative; where these concepts are applicable, however, we can gain real insights by exploring their dialectical interplay. It is only a starting place in our dialectics to recognize the fact that the forging of a rich artistic life is a political achievement for members of oppressed groups; and it is equally a starting place to observe that the political instrumentality of expressive culture, its rhetorical and social power, comes from its artistry—its ability to induce pleasure, to evoke and satisfy desire, and to persuade. The richest analyses of expressive culture forward our understanding of the dialectics of the expressive and the instrumental in any given situation, revealing how the social actors in question conceptualize their expressivity, and illustrating the consequences that their pleasures have for the politics of their social lives.

We can see some of the complexity of this dialectic when we consider the relationship between the expressive and the instrumental in material culture. At what point does an object—a chair, a plate of stew, a haircut—stop being instrumental and start being expressive? Grounded in the study of material culture, folklife studies was spearheaded by a group of scholars who saw the folly of drawing a sharp boundary between instrumental and expressive behaviors, who wished to explore the expressive and instrumental dimensions of all of the practices in a community, and who saw the tightly woven web of everyday life as a unified whole. Material culture challenges the student of everyday life to discover how objects in any social world are produced, received, and experienced—expressive or instrumental, hegemonic or counterhegemonic, important or trivial—and to explore the boundaries between objects, their uses, and practices. By going beyond the standard array of artistic genres (music, dance, verbal art), we can open ourselves to the indigenous categories of expressive practice at play in a given culture and attend to the complex social dynamics and rich worlds of experience that would otherwise be missed.

As we have already suggested, the programmatic call to focus on everyday life has often been sounded as a critique of elitist scholarship that only takes so-called "high art" seriously. A converse pitfall awaits everyday life scholars. Criticizing the treatment of the quotidian by cultural studies, Felski suggests that we must focus our attention on "everyday life without idealizing or demonizing it" (2000, 13); focusing specifically on expressive culture, we therefore urge scholars (3) *to avoid romanticizing or disparaging either the expressive practices of everyday life or those of special events.* If we are indeed committed to a practice theory approach—the view that practice produces and reproduces society—then there is no kind of expressive culture that should, a priori, be excluded from study. Understood in this way, the categories of "high culture," "popular culture," and "folk culture" are historically emergent ideological labels for different expressive practices; however they would be traditionally categorized, all types of artistic behavior can be taken as the focus of analysis.[10]

Privileging the expressive behavior of special events or everyday life is equally problematic, however those terms are construed. As Abrahams has suggested, past scholarship on rituals, festivals, public displays, and other highly marked spheres has tended to assume that these events act as templates for culture, serving as instruction for mundane behavior and shaping or even controlling the society in which they exist; such a perspective treats everyday practice as the robotic enactment of pre-existing scripts. But if this approach is problematic, it is equally wrong to assume that large-scale display events are mere reflections of more fundamental social processes. What is required is a detailed empirical investigation into the relationships between the practices of highly marked events and those found in the rest of the society. A related argument applies to the study of those forms of expressive culture that exist outside highly marked spheres. One of the advantages of the literatures on everyday life has been to draw our attention to forms of expressivity that have been undervalued or neglected. The danger to which such scholarship is sometimes susceptible comes in naively celebrating any given practice, overplaying the resistant capacity of a given type of act, or attributing a weight and profundity to a form of expression that it does not possess in the experience of its practitioners. This is not to say that "everyday acts of resistance" cannot be highly subversive or that "everyday expressive behaviors" cannot be profound. It is, however, to argue that we must discover, rather than assume, the links of concrete consequentiality that connect expressive practice to the rest of social life. Similarly, we must look to the lived experience of situated actors to discover the profundity of expressive practice and not assume, a priori, that any particular form, either so-called "high art" or "low art," is trivial or profound.

Scholarship on everyday life has drawn our attention to practice in general and overlooked practices in particular. If we can no longer say that everyday life is a unique domain of practice, we can instead use this scholarship to highlight the expressive dimensions of activities that have been dismissed as merely pragmatic, mechanical, or insignificant, and the markedly expressive behaviors integrated into other types of practice. For those wishing to build upon the traditions of everyday life scholarship, there can be no limits to the types of practices that may be taken as the focus of analytic scrutiny. To further these programs, we must rethink our traditional notions of "folklore," "common culture," "l'art de faire," and "the aesthetics of everyday life," and embark upon a critical inquiry into the ways in which everydayness, expressivity, and practice itself are constructed by us and by the people and texts we study. If the terminology were not so awkward, we might say that such work could lead to the development of a kind of "post-everyday life" studies. Keeping ourselves open to all forms of human expressivity, maintaining a rigorous focus on practice, and searching for the concrete relationships between different types of situated activity in a given society, we can use expressive culture to gain powerful new insights into social life.

CHAPTER TWO

Theory as Practice

Some Dialectics of Generality and Specificity in Folklore Scholarship

*

Harris M. Berger

All research is motivated by curiosity and discontent. Whether one studies butterflies or ballads, curiosity about the world and discontent with one's present state of insight are the driving forces behind inquiry and debate. In folklore, these forces simultaneously pull in two different directions. Our curiosity motivates us to examine individual items of folklore, genres, and expressive traditions (that is, data), but at the same time we also seek perspective on the nature of folklore in general (that is, theory). This essay is motivated by a curiosity about the phenomenon of theory itself and a discontent with our current understanding of the process of theory building, an area of concern that could be referred to as "metatheory." The last thirty-five years has seen a substantial growth in folklore theory, but metatheory in folklore has been somewhat less abundant. While all theoretical inquiry involves the analysis of conceptual frameworks and underlying scholarly assumptions, metatheory is distinguished by its explicit examination of the notions of theory and data per se. The range of questions that metatheory addresses is broad. For example: can theory explain the phenomena of expressive culture, or does each individual item of folklore have a particularity that transcends generalizing theoretical frameworks? How are we to reconcile the search for broader social insights with the inevitable specificity of individual items of expressive culture? What is the relationship between a theoretical program and the particular ideas that emerge from it? What is the data in folklore research and how is it constructed? What is the value of archival collectanea and other pieces of decontextualized data brought together by past collecting? How can data that have been integrated into research from one scholarly orientation be examined from the perspective of other theoretical orientations? Here I will only examine the first two of these questions, but I hope to make clear the importance of this area of inquiry for the discipline as a whole. Though this discussion is oriented specifically toward the field of folklore studies, the underlying issues it addresses are relevant, I believe, to scholars from any discipline interested in expressive culture.

Most metatheory in the last thirty-five years has focused on the processes by which folklorists construct and represent data. For example, the series of exchanges between Kenneth Laine Ketner and Anne and Norm Cohen in the mid-1970s (Ketner 1973, 1975; Cohen and Cohen 1974, 1975) focused on the role of hypothesis in field method. There, Ketner's important observation that hypotheses help us to transform the motley of field observations into discrete items of data was nicely challenged by the Cohens' insight that novel field situations may offer crucial opportunities for observation often unpredicted and unpredictable by a priori research designs. Shifting the focus from the construction of data in fieldwork experiences to the representation of data in academic writing, ethnopoetic scholars throughout the 1970s and 1980s sought to expand the definitions of what counts as data and what could be represented in a folklore text (for example, Tedlock 1972, Fine 1984, Sherzer 1987, Woodbury 1987). Charles L. Briggs (1993a), building on work done with Richard Bauman (Bauman and Briggs 1990), shows how folklorists in general, and ethnopoetic scholars in particular, employ the discursively situated practices of editing, framing, and intertextual linking to imbue their data with authority. Operating at a similarly metatheoretic level of analysis, an important 1995 article by Jeff Todd Titon traces the various ways that folklorists have construed the notions of data and text and examines the connections between intertextuality and cognition.

Much of this metatheory uses insights from the analysis of data construction to shed light on the relationship between theory and data, though this relationship is sometimes of secondary concern to the scholars involved. For example, a short passage in Ketner's article suggests that the emergent and nonrepeatable nature of particular folklore performances can be accounted for in hypothesis and theory (1973, 120–121). Titon (1995) and other scholars (for example, Narayan 1995) take the opposite view, suggesting that the interpretation of text is an ongoing, openended process. Despite intense disciplinary self-examination in the 1960s and 1970s and extensive theoretic discussions of definitional issues, little metatheoretic work in folklore has examined the nature of theory itself; my goal here is to examine the relationship between theory and data by taking theory, rather than data, as a focus. Such a topic is, I believe, of the greatest importance for the discipline. With the enormous growth of theory, the need to understand the process of theory building has become acute. Some folklorists have become wary of glittering theoretical trends and unfamiliar interdisciplinary linkages, and it has become proverbial in the discipline that, "Theories come and go, but the stuff of folklore will always remain." While this hoary wisdom is occasionally voiced with anti-intellectual undertones, I believe that such a distrust reflects a basic problem in the field: we crave broader insights, but we still wish to respect the particularity of the expressive act, and we are unsure about how to pursue both ends. In sum, the relationship between theory and data has been undertheorized.

I hope to address this problem by showing that there is a rich dialectic between the unique totality of particular experiences or historical situations and the broad applicability of theoretical insights. The machinations of this dialectic are complex and have broad implications for how we plan projects, carry out fieldwork, and analyze data. As an approach to this dialectic, I will begin by treating theory as the outcome of theory building, a set of social practices that includes reflection, reading, and writing. Next, I will connect the phenomenological concept of *eidos* (or experienced essence) to the practice of theoretical reflection and show that such reflective practices can be understood as attempts to reveal the *eidos* of a particular domain of social life. The theorist's pursuit of *eidos* is a valid and desirable activity, I will argue, but our full experiences are always a gestalt of *eidos* and contingent details. While the dialectic of theoretical generalizations and the particularity of specific expressive forms is probably a chronic feature of folklore theory, the relationship between the two can be treated as a positive problematic—a set of difficulties that sustained inquiry can convert into richer understandings.

Let us begin with the vision of theory as the outcome of theory building. The utility of viewing theory not merely as the uncovering of truth but as the result of a social activity should be reasonably clear and intuitive in the contemporary scene; scholars as diverse as Michel Foucault and Thomas Kuhn have articulated this vision in different ways, and I need not dwell unduly on this idea here.[1] Beginning with this perspective and applying concepts from social theorist Anthony Giddens ([1976] 1993, 1979, 1984), we can say that practice encompasses three elements: social context, which both constrains and enables the practice; social consequences, which can be intended or unintended; and the practice itself, which is influenced by context and oriented toward consequences, but itself depends at least partially on agency, a person's active involvement in the world.[2]

On a most basic level, the practices of theory building are reflection, talking, and writing. I sit on the bus going to campus, pace about in my study, or chat with my colleagues, and ideas about the workings of folklore tumble forth (or fail to do so). I send e-mail, tap away at my word processor, or scribble in a noisy coffeehouse, and, eventually, a paper is written that, it is hoped, others read. The theory thus "built" is the set of ideas that passes through my experience and is partially shared by readers and interlocutors through face-to-face social interactions, networked computers, or the printed page.

The past and present contexts of these practices are legion, and those contexts both constrain and enable my theory-building practices. One crucial context for present acts is the thought of other scholars, past and present. These ideas may be mediated through the printed page, the lecture, the conversation, or the electronic mailing list, and each medium has its own convolutions. We well know, for example, that the politics and contingencies of intellectual history deeply affect which scholars are read or forgotten; the language translator's craft adds another level of mediation, as does the historically and culturally specific rhetoric that the writer employs and the present theorist's interpretive practices. Such interpretive acts of reading or listening are themselves informed by a legion of social contexts—society's support for humanistic scholarship, the politics of canon formation in graduate schools, the limitations of reading and thinking imposed by the body, and so on. Because the context of present practice is often past practice, a practice theory approach, if diligently pursued, could lead us to inquire into the contexts of contexts. An appreciation of the fact that the act of theory building is nested within nearly endless levels of potentially significant context is all that is necessary for the present purpose.

Beyond the dynamics of practice in intellectual history, other social contexts inform my theory building as well. My everyday life, my experiences with the "stuff" of folklore, and my past all provide for me an intuitive image of the social world; this tacit context is the bedrock on which I build my basic definitions of terms, my ideas of how the world works, and my broader programmatic goals. The immediate performative context of folklore theory building (the distractions and facilitations of the word processor, the pen, and the work space) subtly shape the work. My understanding of the possible venues for scholarly writing and the politics of ideas in academia and in the society at large shape my theoretical practices. And as any good materialist will remind us, theory building depends upon the theory builder's economic support and is hedged in by all of the other calls on the builder's time.

In the same way that past and present contexts converge from the most distant horizons to influence the act of theory building, the consequences of theory building may lead to endless possible futures. One consequence of theory building is that the academic apparatus moves forward. Professors inch toward tenure or promotion, or don't, and students receive grades; trees are knocked down, and libraries are filled up. Those from different theoretical traditions have different visions of the broader consequences of theory. The vulgar Marxist tells us that folklore theory does nothing more than divert attention away from the more pressing issues of social base. The traditional humanist tells us that folklore theory gives us a richer understanding of the nature of expressive culture and what it means. The cynic says that, outside of the academy, folklore theory is almost completely inconsequential. Almost everyone agrees that changes in folklore theory have some consequences for the methods used in folklore research, although how theory impinges on the practice of fieldwork is not fully clear. The cynic aside, any one of these consequences may in turn yield an ever-increasing crop of broader social effects. Many of us, for example, work with the hope that a more enlightened citizenry will elect saner leaders and support more humane policies. Though hotly debated, the consequences of theoretical practice are potentially endless.

This brief discussion presents one way of conceptualizing theory building as practice. While a variety of large-scale studies could explore the interplay of contexts, agency, and consequences that make up this process, the germ of a more circumscribed study is entailed in this discussion as well. I will return to the topic of multiple and nested levels of social interaction in the conclusion, but for now we can focus on one very simple observation—the basic act of theory building is reflective thought, the constitution of ideas. Clearly, any insights that can be garnered about the act of reflection, however it is contextualized, will have important implications for our understanding of folklore theory. Though the notion of *eidos* in Edmund Husserl's *Ideas I* ([1913] 1962) is problematic in some ways, a brief and somewhat informal discussion of this concept can help lead us to such insights. Throughout, my interpretation of Husserl has been informed by Erazim Kohák's excellent discussion of *Ideas I* (1978), especially his emphasis on the experiencing of *eidos* as a "seeing" or "seeing as" (xi).

Phenomenology begins with the idea that our theories about the world must be grounded in our experiences, and it asks us to return to those living experiences and describe them without the prejudices of any particular philosophy or ideology. To illustrate the point, I will take the example of viewing the table at which I am writing this passage.[3] When I see this table, I see its color (brown), the material it is made of (wood), and its texture (flat and slightly rough). These are all particular factual details of this individual experience. But my experience of this thing has another aspect as well. When I look at an object—and when any subject views any object—I don't merely see the physical features of the object. I directly *see* relationships between parts, as well as uses and meanings; I see objects as examples of a type, and these features are all part of the *eidetic* aspect of experience. Thus I see this assemblage of wood and metal *as* a table, and the essence "table" is just as much an aspect of my direct experience as is its color or material. An *eidetic* phenomenology of tables would seek to describe the table *eidos*, and, as a first approximation, we could say that the *eidos* of table is that it is a thing that can be used to rest objects on or to divide the social space in a room. If this table were plastic, smooth, and painted blue, I would still see it as a table. Of course, this "seeing as" is done not just by me but by all experiencing subjects. When we carefully attend to our experiences, we realize that both contingent details and *eidos* are present in immediate experience. In fact, this "seeing as" is a necessary condition of having an experience at all; even the most random reality before us is brought into experience by organizing its aspects into meaningful wholes—if only by "seeing them as" random and formless.[4]

The *eidos* that we see, therefore, is a relationship of parts organized by meaning, categorization, or potential use. As we encounter our experiences, we are constantly confronted with coherent forms, and we see both facts and essences.[5] The image of a boy lazing on a summer hillside, alternately finding butterflies and lions in the clouds above, provides the simplest (though not, perhaps, the most accurate) illustration of the *eidetic* dimension of experience. Unlike the idle child in this example, in the common run of our lives, the *eidē* (plural of *eidos*) that we find in our experience are usually motivated by practical concerns. Thus, the same child could grasp the assembly of metal, cotton, and wood in his bedroom by focusing on the bouncy springs, seeing and using that object as a trampoline. Tired after a long day's romp, however, the boy will most likely foreground the warmth of the object's blankets and the supportive—rather than projective—possibilities of its springs; in other words, he will see it, and use it, as a bed.

The vagaries of translation make the concept of *eidos* ripe for several kinds of misinterpretations, and these must be carefully avoided. First, we must be aware that while I may be able to see the factual givens of any situation in several different ways, *eidos* is neither purely subjective nor fantastic; the *eidos* that we see is constrained by the situation before us. Thus, for example, we may view the famous Rubin's Goblet drawing as either a pair of silhouettes or a goblet, but we cannot organize its parts to form the map of Connecticut. Indeed, one might say that the goblet and silhouettes are *eidetic* possibilities, but the map of Connecticut is excluded as an *eidetic* arrangement by the empirical givens.[6] Second, we must avoid thinking of *eidos* as something outside of experience. *Eidos* is the ancient Greek word for "form," and Plato employed that expression to refer to his famous "forms" or "ideas." In a related fashion, the English word "essence" carries with it the implications of a mind-independent reality approachable only through some mysterious path. Husserl's notion of *eidos* runs completely against these usages. In his thought, the *eidetic* is neither obscure nor otherworldly; it is there for the perceiving subject in the same way that specific factual details are there—as a part of directly lived experience. Third, we must keep in mind that while the *eidetic* is a dimension of all experience, we may have difficulty providing an explicit description of its organization. This may seem paradoxical, but any ninth grader who has clearly understood a written sentence but had great difficulty producing the requested sentence diagram in English class will understand the sense of this observation. In fact, it may take great intellectual work to describe in reflection what is completely clear in immediate experience, and one of the main projects of transcendental phenomenology is to describe the *eidos* of various domains of experience.

The relevance of all of this for the study of folklore theory building is that in most cases theory building is *eidetic* description—the isolation of a domain of experience and the description of the *eidos* of those experiences in reflective practices of thinking, writing, or conversing. By viewing folklore theory building as the act of *eidetic* description, we can problematize theoretical practice in a unique and productive manner. The examination of three well-known approaches—Karl Marx's ([1867–94] 1974) analysis of profit, Richard Bauman's (1977; 1989) work on performance, and Vladímir Propp's ([1928] 1968) work on folktales—will illustrate the point. Since my broader goal is to explore the dialectics of *eidos* and factual particulars in folklore theory building, this initial illustration will be brief.

At the center of his discussion of capitalism, Marx seeks the essence "profit" in the capitalist/worker relationship. In the Marxist interpretation of industrial capitalism, the capitalist owns the means of production, which includes any technology or contrivances necessary for the production of goods; workers are hired to use the means of production and produce goods, which are later sold for a price. The capitalist determines the price by adding together the cost of the raw materials, the wage paid to the worker, the depreciation of the means of production, and an extra sum—

the profit—that the capitalist keeps. In this view, the worker's labor power transforms the raw materials into the product, and the capitalist's contribution to the process has been only the ownership of the means of production. Marx's critique of profit rests on the observation that the capitalist has done no work and yet has extracted value from the effort of others; in short, profit is unpaid labor. Interpreting Marx, we can say that his analysis is an *eidetic* description—a description of the structure, there for anyone analyzing the situation, of the capitalist/worker relationship. While one may agree or disagree with the ideas, we can see that Marx's critique is an attempt to reveal the inner logic of profit, the *eidos* of the capitalist/worker relationship. That Marx's critique is an *eidetic* description is clear from the broad and formal nature of the argument. Marx seeks to describe (and, additionally, to criticize) the abstract structure of these human relationships, independent of the concrete particulars of any individual situation or immediate cultural context. Whenever this meaningful relationship of parts is present—capitalist, means of production, workers, labor—then profit, says Marx, is unpaid labor.

Similarly, performance theory in our field can be seen as an attempt to describe the essence of experiences of expressive interaction. Take Bauman's 1989 definition of performance—heightened, aesthetic action oriented toward an other in communication. What is performance? Performance is a type of social interaction in which one person is orienting his/her action toward the perceptions and responses of another, and in which the performer is paying special attention to the aesthetic dimension of the action undertaken. Viewed as *eidetic* description, Bauman's theoretical work is an account of the structure of experiences of performative interactions, an attempt to depict the relationship of parts during any experience one would call a performance. Dan Ben-Amos's 1972 "artistic communication in small groups" is a more specific *eidetic* description, a claim about the structure of experiences of folklore performances in particular. Here, the *eidos* of folklore performance is only present when the performance is occurring in the context of a small-scale group. And again, it does not matter if the participants of the interaction are conceptualizing the event as a performance or not. Just as we need not be able to construct a grammatical diagram of a sentence for the structure it describes to be present in our experiences, the participants in an interaction—or the folklorists—need not be actively thinking "this is a performance" for each to be orienting his/her action toward another with special attention to the aesthetics of their acts. *Eidetic* descriptions describe the structure of immediate lived experiences, independent of any accompanying awareness of the situation.[7]

Turning to structuralist theory, we can see Vladímir Propp's *Morphology of the Folktale* ([1928] 1968) as *eidetic* description as well. Working in a culturally specific sphere, Propp sought the essence of the Russian fairy tale, the meaningful relationship of parts present in any experience of those stories. Where the experienced "parts" in Marx's critique of profit or Bauman's description of performance are people involved in productive or aesthetic interactions, the "parts" that Propp concerns himself with are narrated events in stories. Interpreting Propp, we can say that a Russian—or anyone properly acculturated—hearing a Russian fairy tale does not merely experience the teller's tale as a description of a series of disconnected actions by the characters; to the contrary, the events relate to one another in series and, taken together, make up a narrative. Further, the properly acculturated listener does not merely hear the events in this story as the unique actions of these characters in this situation. The events in all of the tales, Propp argues, form a pattern, and the story's audience experiences the abstract set of relationships between the narrated events as well as the particular activities of the characters in this particular story. Thus, for example, each of the stories begins when one member of a family absents him/herself from the home; listening to a tale in which a prince leaves for a journey or one in which a child's parents die, the listener familiar with Russian fairy tales grasps this particular narrated event (the prince's leaving, the parents' death) as the absenting of the family member. In this sense, Propp reveals the *eidos* of Russian fairy tales, a reflective description of the structure of the folktales there to be grasped by any listener.

Even though none of these thinkers were phenomenologists, we may nevertheless understand their various theories as *eidetic* descriptions. All three seek to describe the abstract relationships of the elements of a domain of experience—productive actors in an economic relationship, aesthetic actors in a performative interaction, and a series of narrated events in the web of a tale.[8] While the relationships in an economy or the events in a story have the autonomy of objective reality, they have their existence for us when we grasp them in experience. This is not to say that, because we are describing the nature of relationships or narrated events in experience, those relationships or narrated events become infinitely malleable or merely subjective. If we claim to be describing experiences of profit or performance, then we are bound and limited by the social relationships themselves. If we claim to be describing the structure of a fairy tale in experience, then we are bound and limited by the fairy tale itself. While our experiences may differ greatly, all social subjects share a common world, and to say that theory building is *eidetic* description is to say that most theory builders seek to find the structures of the world that are there for any person trying to bring that part of the world into focus in his/her experience.

In sum, we may understand theory as *eidetic* description and say that the main practice of theory building is a kind of reflection, the attempt to depict the *eidos* of a particular domain of experience. Theory building in folklore is important because it redeems the field from pure collection and seeks to make clear what is present but not clearly grasped in experiences of expressive culture. With only a small amount of thought, it is evident that much folklore theory seeks to explain the diverse methods by which people establish the *eidetic* structure of experiences of expressive culture; that is, much folklore theory seeks the *eidos* of the constitution of *eidos* in folklore performance. For example, from a number of different perspectives, folklore theorists have observed that any one piece of folklore may be grasped in a variety of ways to yield experiences with a variety of meanings; that the way in which one constitutes a given experience depends on the culture and social history from which one emerges; that the experience of a particular body of folklore may change over time; and so on. On these points, I feel that the idea of folklore theory building as *eidetic* description is relatively straightforward and intuitive.

It is, however, fundamental to Husserl's transcendental phenomenology that *eidos* and particular factual details are distinct from one another. Transcendental phenomenology, long critiqued by existential phenomenology and other branches of continental philosophy, seeks grand structures and universal necessities and tends to focus less attention on (and assign less importance to) the contingent. But, as folklorists, we are interested in the particular as well as the general; we are interested in the machinations of individual cultures as well as general descriptions of humanity; we care about the particular people we work with as well as the search for broader insights. And after a generation of writings by postmodernists, some doubt that the theorist can ever escape his/her acculturation sufficiently to tease apart the necessary from the contingent. Setting aside these vexed questions, we can be certain of one thing: while any one experience may be retrospectively decomposed into *eidos* and particular factual details, as it is lived, experience is a gestalt of the two. As we experience the world, each individual experience is a unity of form and fact that is greater than the sum of its parts and is itself contingent and particular. This does not dissolve the distinction between *eidos* and particular factual details, nor does it make those terms invalid—it points to a rich set of dialectics between the two. By dialectics, I do not mean a situation wherein two abstract concepts oppose each other across a smooth continuum along which concrete particulars are variously arrayed. A dialectic is a complex and dynamic set of relationships in which the members of the dialectical pair may define, oppose, delimit, complement, interact, or transform one another. In sum, the positive problematic of *eidos* and factual particulars displays in sharp relief the dilemmas of theory building in folklore, and any new insights we can garner about this situation will help us to gain a fresh perspective on the practice of folklore research. Such an approach follows in the well-established tradition of existential phenomenologists such as Maurice Merleau-Ponty and Jean-Paul Sartre, who emphasized dialectics and the fundamental importance of contingent factual particulars for *eidetic* analysis (or any other type of generalizing work) in all fields of inquiry.[9]

The advances of contemporary neo-Marxism can serve as a starting point. The allure and the difficulty of Marx begins with his critique of profit. I find Marx's critique to be rigorous and compelling; his description reveals the *eidos* of the worker/capitalist social relation, and as *eidetic* description, his theory is valid and unassailable. In lived experience, however, we never have a pure type "worker" and a pure type "capitalist." Instead, we always have a particular worker and a particular capitalist, each interacting in a particular time and place, each with his or her own particular history that colors and affects the gestalt of the situation. This observation, the fact of context, in no way invalidates Marx's critique—profit is still unpaid labor—but neither does that critique capture the richness of any particular economic situation or the full meaning of lived economic experiences. For specific people in specific places, the culture and the history of production relations in their own particular societies are crucial elements of the economic situation. As moments in a dialectic, the critique grounded in historically unique particulars does not overwhelm the powerful *eidetic* insight; it compels us to push the dialectic forward. We must use the particularist critique to transform and give nuance to the *eidetic* analysis.

Allan Pred and Michael John Watts's *Reworking Modernity: Capitalisms and Symbolic Discontent* (1992) illustrates this kind of approach with clarity. Sensitive to the basic unfairness of unpaid labor, Pred and Watts reveal how local religious beliefs and traditions of expressive culture interact with the general, *eidetic* form of capitalism to produce complex social situations. In Pred and Watts's view, such situations are not radically unique and isolated moments in history, incomprehensible to outsiders and incompatible with all theories of historical change, social structure, or justice; nor are they simply examples of a universal and abstract form, mere instances of a larger social theory. In one chapter, Watts's discussion of recent Nigerian history reveals how local forms of Islam and pre-existing ethnic tensions have interacted with the boom and bust cycles of the petroleum markets in oil-rich Nigeria to produce complex social situations. Here, profit is still unpaid labor, but the inequitable social situation that it engenders is distinct from European and American capitalisms and cannot be reduced to the status of mere example. In another chapter, Pred discusses the folklore of place names and neighborhood narratives in the rapidly expanding Stockholm of the late nineteenth century and shows how working-class Stockholmers interpreted and responded to the rapid transformation of their city. In a third chapter, Pred examines labor newsletters, strike placards, and union handbills in a labor conflict in late-1980s San Diego to show how folklore becomes the terrain upon which workers interpret the tensions between regional, national, and class identities. In each of these examples, Pred and Watts show how the cultural particulars in each affair—religion, identity, ethnicity, folklore—become entangled with the *"eidetic"* production relations; the resulting situations entail, but cannot be reduced to, the inequities of capitalism that Marx's analysis critiques. While capitalism in fluctuating Nigeria, expanding Stockholm, or transnationalizing San Diego includes capitalists profiting from the unpaid labor of workers, the particular history and culture of each society plays a huge role in the local responses of the participants to these conditions and the meanings they make of them. Most importantly, the meaning of profit in production relations cannot be understood without considering these historically and culturally particular elements. While retaining the *eidetic* insights of the critique of profit, neo-Marxism seeks a richer understanding of the interplay of productive relations and culture.[10]

I believe that analogous dialectics occur in folklore, and our scholarship should attend to them. In Propp's work, for example, the narrative structure of the decontextualized tales is the object of the *eidetic* analysis, while the performance event is elided, set aside as contingent detail. Certainly, any performance of traditional Russian fairy tales will entail the structure of narrated events—the *eidetic* relationship of parts—that Propp describes. But the full situation will always be a gestalt of the *eidetic* relationships of the narrated events, this particular teller's unique performative features (constituted by the narrative event), and the situated and broader social contexts. Thus, a tale told sweetly by a prosperous Russian to her child during a period of relative social stability will not have the same meaning as the same tale told with menacing body language and rushed delivery at a Russian-American center during the turbulence of the post-Soviet social transition. The context and style of performance form a gestalt with the generically fixed morphological structure to produce a unique constellation of meanings for the participants. The audience's and performer's experiences of the narrative structure of such fairy tales may be accurately described by Propp's *eidetic* account, but they are not merely examples of that form. The particular factual details of the performance and the *eidetic* narrative structure form a unified whole, a gestalt whose fully situated meaning can neither be reduced to narrative structure nor fully escape it. As partners in a dialectic, the particulars of performance transform, but do not erase, the meaning of the *eidetic* structure. Decontextualized, the generic consistency of the narrative form of Russian fairy tales may, for example, conjure an impression of reassuring stability. Performed during the period of the purges, the stability of the narrative form might appear as a kind of depressing inevitability, an icon of the inevitability of repression in Stalinist Russia; performed during the attempted military coup of 1991, the same stability of the structure may be grasped as a cruel parody of the contemporary scene, a nostalgic survival of more socially predictable times. In any case, the *eidos* and the factual particulars of specific performances interact in a dialectical fashion, coloring and informing one another without destroying each other's integrity.[11]

This vision can be elaborated in a variety of ways. For example, there can be numerous dimensions and levels of *eidos,* and different participants may focus on different levels of *eidos* or particular factual details in their experiences of the event. A listener just learning about the Russian fairy tale may foreground the narrated events of this particular tale and background the *eidetic* narrative structure of the genre, the performative features of today's telling, and the *eidos* "performative interaction." A listener familiar with the generic form may background the details of this particular story and attend to the pleasant familiarity of the tale's narrative structure—an *eidetic* structure that all of the Russian fairy tales share. A rival storyteller may listen critically, foregrounding the performative features of this particular telling and backgrounding the events of the individual tale, its narrative form, and the fact of interaction. A graduate student newly awakened to performance theory may foreground the fact of the event as an interaction (the *eidos* "performance") and background all else. Here, the focus on one level or another is the result of the participant's practice, which is, in turn, dependent on his/her goals in the event, contingent situational and contextual issues, and the participant's own agency.

Exploring the theoretician's division of a domain of experience into *eidetic* form and the contingent factual details reveals further dialectics and suggests a kind of fractal burgeoning of the general and the specific. For example, the structuralist work in ethnopoetics referred to above has revealed abstract, formal features of prosody, contour, kinesics, and proxemics in various cultures, and this attempt to unearth the consistent patterns of speech and gesture in a culture can be understood as *eidetic* description. As most folklorists in the contemporary discipline will recognize, such formal performative features may themselves be more stable and characteristic of a group's tales than their Proppian narrative structures. Precisely analogous to the participant's focus on different levels of *eidos* in a folklore performance, the folklorist's analytic separation of the *eidetic* from the contingent factual details depends upon various contextual forces, the folklorist's own programmatic goals, and the folklorist's agency. I will return to this point in detail below, but for now it is important to see that, as in the process of creating *eidetic* descriptions itself, the reflective division of experiences into *eidos* and contingent factual details is limited, but not determined, by the object of those experiences.

None of this is meant to attack the act of theory building in general or Marxist, performance, structuralist, or ethnopoetic traditions in particular. It is meant to emphasize, however, that the theory builder's *eidetic* work isolates domains of experience (productive social relations, aesthetic interaction, morphological structures in narrative) and decontextualizes abstract dimensions and forms within those domains (the role of worker and boss, performance as a type of interaction, the Russian fairy tale as a morphological type). Such theoretical work is a valid and useful endeavor; however, the richness and complexity of particular situations emerge as a gestalt of *eidos* and particular factual details, and these will interact to produce new meanings that are greater than the sum of their parts.

More significant for the present argument is the possibility that the dialectics of *eidos* and particular factual details may be so complex that it necessitates a *chronic* re-examination of our initial *eidetic* descriptions. An example oriented toward performance theory will explain my meaning. In every culture in the world, there is heightened action oriented toward an other; everywhere we go, people congregate in small groups and communicate artistically. The *eidos* "folklore performance" may indeed be found in all of these situations. However, we never have pure type actors orienting themselves toward one another; we always have this particular actor and this particular small group. What is an actor? What is a medium of communication? What are the dimensions of the actor's identity? *Unique, particular situations reveal the meanings of our* eidetic *descriptions, perhaps in ways otherwise undiscoverable.* Theory gains its power through abstraction and broad applicability. But that very breadth of applicability yields the possibility of application to surprising new particular situations that may reveal and call into question our initial, tacit assumptions about the meaning of the terms of our *eidetic* descriptions. Didn't the development of print technology bring a meaning to the idea of media not hitherto predictable? Aren't electronic mailing lists, for example, new kinds of "small groups" that necessitate a re-evaluation of that notion? My questions are emphatically *not* tied to postmodernism or technological development. The "performer" in the standard definition of performance theory, for example, is conventionally assumed to be a single, biological human being. But apply this powerful concept to the situation of a "performer" trance channeling a spirit or a "performer" with multiple personalities and the concept becomes problematic. The very breadth of applicability of the theory—the root of its power—reveals tacit assumptions about the meaning of the term "performer" and calls forth a reinterpretation. Ethnography in women's folklore, occupational folklore, and African American folklore suggests that the actor is potentially a gendered being, a being enmeshed in productive relationships, a "racialized" being. But can we ever be sure that we will have isolated all of the dimensions of identity? Don't new political affiliations and historical conditions produce new dimensions of identity? The historical emergence of notions such as "race" point to the very fluidity I am trying to indicate here.

The question is ultimately one of closure. Is there an ongoing dialectic between theory and data, or does the dialectic ultimately come to an end? Taking the position that theory can encompass data, Ruth Benedict's *Patterns of Culture* ([1934] 1959) posited a great arc of human possibility from which the personality types of each culture are mere selections. Such an approach brings to mind a vast but finite library of ethnographies and the eventual description of the entire arc. This intellectual closure is plausible if we background the process of collecting data and building theory and foreground the data collected and the theory built. But if we reverse the figure/ground and bring the scholarly practices to the fore, then it is not at all clear when the complete description of human cultures might be achieved. Speaking geographically, each new ethnography that hits the shelves may be an incremental advance toward the completed library; alternatively, we may imagine that some new ethnography might suggest entirely novel domains of research. Speaking historically, each development in technology or cultural history may more fully confirm modernity as the capstone of all past culture change; however, one might also reasonably conclude that human experience is open ended and creative, that the convolutions of cultural history shows only that the future is never fully predictable from the past.[12] Can *eidos* contain all particular factual details? Do such details always escape *eidos*? Must one triumph over the other? Perhaps nontrivial abstract concepts may someday be constructed that contain all the new examples that history will have to offer. Perhaps the convolutions of particular situations have the potential to be so unique that they always impinge back on our *eidetic* descriptions and force new, theoretical exploration. One goal of this essay has been merely to suggest the importance of this question for the discipline of folklore studies as a whole. In fact, the dialectic has not yet come to closure in our intellectual history, and I see no reason to assume that it will anytime soon.

These questions are not meant to throw us back to pure collection or to damn the theoretical project. While research into particular experiences gives us new insights that may otherwise be inaccessible in pure theory building, the initial validity of past *eidetic* descriptions is not dissolved but reformulated. If theory and data are indeed locked into a chronic dialectic, this does not mean that the insights garnered by theoretical work are destined to be disproved, but rather that new data will emerge to give old theory new depth and richness. Just as twentieth-century quantum physics does not render classical Newtonian physics invalid but recontextualizes it as a useful approximation, so too does new data not invalidate current theory but instead provide it with new meanings and a more profound grounding. It is easy to misunderstand this dialectical approach to the relationship of theory and data. To caveat our theory building with "that's the way it seems at the moment" would be to dissolve the structural validity of *eidetic* description in the productivity of particular situations; to claim that any one theory is once and for all true would be to subsume the variety of data under the rubric of a single *eidetic* description. To take a genuinely dialectical approach to the two is to resist both options, continually using data to illuminate theory and theory to illuminate data.

Even thinking in the most hypothetical or speculative manner, I cannot see how the dialectic of theory and data would, at some point in the future, come to closure. As I have suggested throughout the essay, however, issues in folklore theory are best examined by treating theory as the result of theory building. Rather than merely asking if theory can entail all of the possibilities that data may produce, it may be better to treat theory as intellectual practice and ask other questions instead. How have our intellectual histories, institutional structures, programmatic goals, personal interactions with folklore, fieldwork experiences, and intellectual choices combined in the practices of academic reflection? How do we make judgments about the general and the particular, the *eidetic* and the contingent in the situated practices of reading, talking, and writing about folklore? How have our anticipations of the personal, intellectual, and larger social consequences of our theoretical practices explicitly and implicitly influenced the theory that we build? Such questions will not tell us whether the dialectic of theory and data will ever come to closure, but they will provide richer insights into both our theoretical activities and the specific people we study.

*

Folklore theory is alluring. While some of us are uninterested in the theoretical enterprise, most of us can recall the palpable sensation of excitement that we felt when the page before us uncovered "new perspectives in folklore" (Paredes and Bauman 1972) or exposed fresh insights into the relationship between "folktales and society" (Dégh [1962] 1969). But theory can also be dissatisfying as well. The interesting discontent with folklore theory is not the feeling that a particular piece of writing is intentionally obtuse, trendy, or soulless. An odd discomfort with otherwise valid theoretical apparatus arises when we feel that the theory we are reading seeks to *explain* a set of data, that the set of data is a mere instance of theory; the feeling is strongest if we sense that the theorist believes that if his/her theory is rich and comprehensive enough, we might not need the expressive culture it describes. None of these discontents pulls us toward pure collection. We all, of course, enjoy the partial sharing of experience that an evocative, descriptive ethnography provides, but this is not enough. We want the broader insights that only the analysis of particular bodies of data and larger, theoretical generalizations can give. What we are left with is a dilemma. We want broad insights, but we are made anxious when we feel that experiences of expressive culture or the relationship of expressive culture to larger social forces can somehow be contained in an abstract set of ideas.

The chronic dialectics of *eidos* and particular factual details—the positive problem of closure—is, I believe, the solution to this dilemma. We can enjoy the power of theory and still respect the particularity of data by treating the relationship between the two as a dialectic and pursuing that dialectic with vigor. We should, whenever possible, avoid merely applying theory, even our own; instead, we should challenge theory with data, using new data to shed light on old theory and new theory to reveal unsuspected aspects of old data. As Husserl suggested in a different context, we may use fantasy variations to explore the boundaries of concepts outside of empirical work, mining the rich vein of the thought experiment to unearth the buried assumptions of our scholarship. As I suggested above, we may explore the past and present contexts of our research to reveal how we have arrived at the particular place to which intellectual history has led us. More importantly, we must use that analysis not as an end in itself but as a way of returning to our data with fresh insights and fresh perspectives. In short, we must use theory to illuminate our data, and data to illuminate our theory.

As Giovanna P. Del Negro pointed out to me, such an approach treats theory building as a creative process. In this sense, theory building is not like representational painting, in which the observer views a distant object and tries to recreate it on a canvas in an act of objective description; nor is theory building like fiction, in which any literary caprice is communicated to the page. On the contrary, theory building is the analog of subtractive sculpture, in which the artist interacts with a genuine other, creatively selecting and carving, revealing both a valid possibility in the marble and the sculptor's own craft. As a piece of theoretical work, this essay has been an attempt to take theory building itself as data, to use data as the basis for new insights into theory, and to push the dialectic through one more twist of its spiral.

PART TWO

*

SELF, REFLEXIVITY, AND IDENTITY

CHAPTER THREE

Horizons of Melody and the Problem of the Self

*

Harris M. Berger

It is the late afternoon, and you are driving a car on an empty highway. The territory is familiar; bored, you watched the scenery pass by. Specks emerge on the horizon. Quickly resolving themselves into road signs, they appear small in the distance and then become larger and larger as they approach. Scanning the radio dial, you choose a frequency and at first hear static with just the faintest signal. As you drive farther, the music becomes louder and clearer, only to recede into noise a short distance later. As night approaches, you begin to move into a province that you have never visited. Music plays on several channels, largely obscured by static, but no matter how far you drive, the signal never becomes louder or clearer. A river runs parallel to the road, and mountains rise in the distance. The mountains must be far away, because they never appear to get closer. Eventually, you enter an area of rolling hills, and the road twists and turns, allowing only a limited line of sight. Signs don't emerge from the horizon now; they quickly appear around corners and rush past. After an hour, your engine abruptly cuts out, and you pull over to the shoulder.

Getting out of the car, you take stock of the situation. The rolling hills have given way to a long flat expanse, and the mountains still rise up in the distance. The sounds of the river must be reflecting off a slight depression in the road, because you hear them as immersive, seemingly coming from everywhere. In the distance, the light from a street lamp illuminates a small sign and a large rectangular shape that might be a phone booth. The cloudy sky makes the evening very dark, and aside from the road, the ground, and the distant mountains, there is nothing else to be seen. You head off toward the sign and the object.

To occupy your mind as you walk, you attend carefully to the appearance of the words on the sign. At this distance, the words are blurry and indistinct; they are too small to be read and take up only a small percentage of your visual field. With each step, though, they take up slightly more of your visual field. There is another feature of those letters that you notice. You experience them as the visual equivalent of promissory notes. Each indistinct detail seems to beckon, to be there in a way that implies that closer inspection will reveal more details.

Anxious to reach the lit area, you quicken your pace. You hear a birdsong coming from the area of the sign, but as you get nearer the sound becomes neither louder nor more detailed. The sign looms larger, but the letters become no clearer. At a distance of ten feet from the sign, the letters are simply larger indistinct shapes. You move closer. At three feet, the letters take up a fair percentage of your visual space, but they are still indistinct in the way that they were at fifty feet. They have completely lost their beckoning quality, and there is nothing more to see in them. The rectangular object fails to resolve itself into a phone booth or any other kind of object. When you have reached the distant mountains and find no smaller details—no trees, no rocks, no geographical contours of any kind, just a featureless expanse of color taking up no more of your visual space than it did at a distance—you black out.

The idea for this fantasy came to me several years ago when I began to reflect upon the notion of the horizon in phenomenology. The term has several distinct meanings in the tradition, two of which are most relevant to this discussion.[1] In one sense, the term refers to the extreme edges of the field of immediately lived experience. In another sense, the term refers to the ways in which the different facets of a single phenomenon are related to one another in experience. This second sense of the word is, perhaps, more difficult to understand. When we encounter a physical object, we experience it as possessing both facets that present themselves to us directly and hidden facets that may be there for future viewings. To illustrate this concept, Edmund Husserl, the founder of phenomenology, used the example of a die ([1931] 1960, 44; see also the useful discussion in Hammond, Howarth, and Keat 1991, 52). When I view a die, some of its faces are immediately present to me—for example, the sides with one, four, and five dots. There is more to my experience of the die, however, than the faces I immediately see; while I do not now experience the side with two dots or the side with three dots, I experience the die as having sides that are hidden from me, sides that will be there for future viewings. An accurate description of the die phenomenon takes into account this horizonal structure—the fact that it has multiple facets, that those facets are connected together, and that our focal experience of presently viewed facets is accompanied by an awareness of hidden facets that may become focal at some future time. Deceptively simple, the notion of horizon is an enormously powerful concept, and the above fantasy is meant to illustrate just how foundational horizonal structures are to lived experience. In the first phase of the fantasy, horizons operate as they normally do in everyday life—distant objects present a small and blurry appearance in visual and aural perception and on closer inspection reveal more and more details. Upon entering the unfamiliar province of the fantasy, however, phenomena begin to lose their horizonal structures. Small objects like signs and rocks take up more of our visual space when we get closer to them, but they present no richer wealth of details. Sounds are no longer localized and do not get louder or clearer as they get nearer. In the final phase of the fantasy, the mountains behave like a variation of the transportation device in the television series *Dr. Who,* failing even to take up more of our visual space as they are approached.

My goal in the first section of this chapter is to explore the notion of the horizon and illustrate its utility for the study of expressive culture. Because horizonal structures are such a basic part of perceptual experience, performers and their audiences regularly exploit them to achieve their expressive ends. This chapter argues that a complex mix of cultural resources and the agency of the participants governs the aesthetic manipulation of horizonal structures in performance. To illustrate this notion, I will present data I collected on the vocal melodies of heavy metal singer Timmy "The Ripper" Owens and show that, for metalheads, the various facets of his melodies are experienced as having a horizonal structure. Gross features of the melody are experienced focally, finer details are experienced in the near background of experience, and an endless array of ever smaller nuances are experienced with lesser and lesser awareness. Further, I will argue, this horizonal structure is crucial to the expressive functioning of Owens's music. Leaving the heavy metal case study, I will argue that there is a complex asymmetry of gross and fine details in perception and suggest some different positions that music cultures and music participants may take up in their aesthetics of the horizon.[2]

The second and third sections of the chapter explore the relevance of horizonal structures for the problem of self-experience and explore the role of the self in music. At first blush, it would seem that the self is the most intuitive and obvious element of our experience, and yet even a cursory inquiry into the notion of the self reveals endless contradictions and problems. William James long ago observed that at different moments in one's day, a wide range of phenomena (one's body, one's thoughts, one's actions) can be experienced as "self" (James [1890] 1981, 279). When we stop and reflect upon our experience, though, the self seems to be different from any given phenomenon, and the more we examine our experience, the more difficult it becomes to find the self. Building on the work of J. J. Gibson (1979), analytic philosopher José Luis Bermúdez (1998) has suggested that self-consciousness is a richly multilayered affair and that basic types of self-consciousness operate strictly in sense perception. Reading Bermúdez's work through a phenomenological lens, the second section of this chapter shows that in various perceptual modalities the self is experienced not as an individual phenomenon (a body part, thought, or action) but in the perspectival organization of phenomena in experience. The third section connects the analysis of self-experience to the problem of self in music. Music scholars have always been fascinated with the so-called "loss of self" in music, and often times this type of experience is represented as the highest state that a performer or audience member can achieve. If, however, the self is complex and multilayered, then a richer language is needed to discuss the different kinds of self-experience that may be fostered or diminished in performance, and the chapter concludes by outlining a theoretical framework for describing self-experience in music.

Horizons of Melody and the Problem of Expressivity

The starting place for this analysis is with melody. Traditionally in Western art music, composers define the pitches and rhythms of melodic lines (i.e., their gross contours) and performers are left to control the fine-grained details—circumscribed waverings of pitch in vibrato, small variations in tempo or other rhythmic elements, nuanced increases or decreases in dynamics, and most changes in timbre. Based on the division of labor suggested by this traditional production model, a truism of Western music holds that "emotion" arises from the sensitive control of these fine features and that expressive performers are those who can deploy changes in dynamic, rhythm, pitch, and timbre in a precise and meaningful way.[3] Ranging from the clearly audible to the edges of audibility, such fine-grained details often do play a key role in music. But by focusing on musical sound itself, rather than the performer's or audience member's engagement with that sound in perception, this truism tells us little about the way in which nuanced features emerge in experience. This section of the chapter uses the theme of horizons to shed light on the common wisdom about expressivity in music and explores the manipulation of horizonal structures for aesthetic ends in artistic behavior in general. Above, I mentioned that the term "horizon" operates in two distinct senses in phenomenology. We can begin our inquiry by exploring the horizonal structure of the overall experiential field and of the individual phenomena within it.

As Don Ihde has observed (1976), both visual and auditory fields are characterized by a structure of "focus," "fringe," and "horizon." Entities positioned at the focus are experienced with greater intensity and clarity; those at the fringe are grasped with lesser intensity but are, nevertheless, present in experience; and the horizon represents the edge of immediate experience. It is not merely our visual and auditory fields that possess this graded structure. When taken as a multisensory whole, our experience of the immediate situated context possesses a focal foreground and a back-grounded fringe trailing off into a horizon. Walking through a museum, for example, I foreground a particular painting and background the sounds in the room, the pressure of my clothes against my skin, and so on. Like the silhouettes and the vase in the famous Rubin's Goblet drawing, the various phenomena in the gestalt of experience define and inform one another. A bad headache, a scratchy piece of clothing, or an anxious thought may lurk on the fringe of the overall experience, only dimly apprehended but nevertheless coloring those phenomena in the focus with a negative hue. Further, the organization of experience is partially volitional. Not only may one shift one's attention from sight to sound or move the center of one's field of vision from one object to another, but also at any given moment the focus/fringe/horizon structure itself is open to various kinds of manipulation by the person. For example, Ihde notes that the "ratio" of focus to fringe is something that we can at least partially control (1976, 40). Overwhelmed by a stunning view, he suggests, we may widen the focus so that almost every sight and sound is taken in with clarity and intensity. Crushed by boredom during a tedious meeting, we shrink our focus until both thoughts and percepts are experienced as vague and indistinct. There are other dimensions of order in the horizonal structure as well. I would suggest, for example, that each sensory modality has its own attentional weightings—its range of values upon which it is inherently easier to attend—but that persons can resist these weightings and shift individual phenomena in and out of the focus. In the case of vision, because of the anatomy of the eye it is easier to focus attention on objects in the center of the visual field than it is to attend to those at the edges. However, while staring fixedly at the semicolon on my computer keyboard, I may resist the attentional weighting imposed by my anatomy and (without moving my eyes or head) focus my attention on the fuzzy appearance of the question mark printed on the key below. This example produces an experience that I tried to evoke in the fantasy at the beginning of this chapter—the experience of a blurry image situated at the center of attention.

If the edges of the present situation form the horizon of overall experience, each individual phenomenon within the scene has its own horizons as well. Further, a key element of individual percepts is that they are multidimensional and possess many qualities at once. In vision, individual phenomena may possess qualities of color, intensity, shape, and so forth; pitch, duration, dynamic, and so on are dimensions of auditory phenomena.[4] Focusing on any given phenomenon, one can at least partially control how one attends to these different dimensions. For example, while taking in the bronze man at the museum's sculpture garden, one can foreground the overall contour of the sculpture and have only a backgrounded awareness of color; inversely, one can attend to the play of green and brown in the surface and be only lightly aware of its overall outline.

Finally, attention is also organized within each perceptual dimension. There are limits of perceptibility at the extremes of each of these dimension (which I will refer to as that dimension's outer horizon), and there are also limits on our ability to discriminate fine differences within each range (which I will call the dimension's inner horizon).[5] In sound, for example, the perceived quality called pitch has an outer horizon that ranges from low to high, and psychologists tell us that the range is evoked by periodic sound waves of 20 to 20,000 hertz. Likewise, limitations exist in our ability to discriminate small differences among high or low pitches, and this limit would represent that dimension's inner horizon. For pairs of pitches below 1000 hertz, the minimum perceptible difference of frequency is approximately 1 hertz; above 1000 hertz, our ability to discriminate between pitches worsens (Hall 1980, 108). As with our experience of the overall situation, the attentional field of each sensory dimension is weighted toward certain values, but we may resist these weightings and focus attention in differing ways within that dimension's horizons. Considering the inner horizons of pitch perception, it is easier to register relatively large scale changes (between piano and forte, between the notes C1 and G1), while differences near the inner horizons of pitch or dynamic (small changes in loudness or softness, the wavering of pitch in a subtle vibrato) are more difficult to grasp, particularly in the presence of a dense aural environment with many other distracting phenomena present. Exploring the physics and psychology of these inner horizons is beyond the scope of this chapter, but operating on a strictly phenomenal level, we can define the fine details of perception as those features that exist near the edges of the inner horizon of perceptual sensitivity and gross features as those differences far from that horizon. The relationship between gross and fine features is more complex than it might initially seem, and we will explore this issue in more detail below.[6]

In sum, our experience of both the field as a whole and the individual phenomena within it is organized in a complex focus/fringe/horizon structure. While our attention within these fields is channeled in certain ways by anatomy and physiology, we may exert a fair degree of control over the shape of our experience by changing the ratio of focus to fringe, moving our attention among the phenomena in our experience, foregrounding one perceptual dimension rather than another, and shifting our focus from gross to fine details.

How we focus our attention depends upon culture as well as biology and individual agency, and in earlier work I have argued that the organization of experience is best understood as a kind of social practice (Berger 1999). Comparing the experiences of heavy metal, rock, and jazz musicians, I showed that a player's focusing of attention is informed by his/her goals in performance and that these goals in turn are informed by the aesthetic and social ideologies of the player's music culture. Among the musicians with whom I worked, no one was more concerned with the fine-grained details of musical sound than heavy metal singer Timmy Owens. Throughout our hours of interviews, Owens constantly emphasized that good singers were those who sang with feeling and that to sing with feeling meant to nuance and sculpt the melodic line, endlessly varying subtle features of timbre, pitch, dynamic, and rhythm. Most of my work with Owens centered on his role as a singer, but one of our interviews examined his experiences as a music listener, and it was these discussions that led me to think about the relationship between horizons, expressivity, and the fine-grained details of melody. Some background information on Owens and his musical experiences in performance will set the stage for this analysis.

Born in Akron, Ohio, Timmy Owens sang in school choirs throughout his youth. By his late teens he had begun singing in metal bands, and he soon established himself as a stalwart of the local scene. In the early 1990s he began fronting a popular metal outfit in Akron named Winters Bane. With four- to six-minute songs, elaborate band arrangements, and memorably "hooky" choruses, Winters Bane sought an identity more "underground" than pop metal bands like Def Leppard or Bon Jovi but more commercially viable than "underground" bands like Cannibal Corpse or

Napalm Death. The band recorded a CD for an independent German record label in 1993 and toured larger night clubs and theaters on the regional level shortly thereafter. Under the name British Steel, the band supplemented their income by performing the repertoire of seminal heavy metal band Judas Priest—sometimes playing under both names on the same night. While Owens is an original performer in his own right and has a unique and distinctive vocal style, his admiration of Priest's music and his ability to do imitations of Rob Halford, Priest's lead singer, were well known in the local scene. Halford left Priest in 1991, and the remaining members of that august band sought a replacement for him. In a Cinderella story that has since become legendary in the metal world, a video tape of British Steel made its way into the hands of Priest, and Owens was invited to audition for them in 1996. The audition was successful, and ever since Owens has performed and recorded as their lead singer. My interviews with Owens took place in 1992 and 1993.

In previous work, I have described Owens's organization of attention in depth (Berger 1999, 166–168). Here it suffices to say that, when he is singing a phrase, his own vocal line is at the center of his attention, and the sound of the instruments (drums, guitar, and bass) and the visual and aural responses of the audience occupy positions closer and closer to the horizon of his overall experience. Between phrases, the audience may move into his focus, but this is also a time when he is most likely to foreground reflective thought or his body. Owens's main experience of embodiment is a generalized feeling of vitality. While singing a phrase, this "energy level" rests in the background of his overall experience, coloring the situation with vigor or sluggishness, depending on his state that night. Between phrases, however, he will often foreground and actively monitor this energy level. Discovering that he feels especially weak, he will plan out melodic modifications and extra breaths; discovering that he feels especially strong, he will plan ways to string phrases together or add new high notes. As important as this process is, Owens sees his between-phrase routine as a means of achieving optimal performance, not an end in itself. Thus, the sound of his voice is made focal while he sings, and his attention is differentially distributed among the various dimensions and features of that sound. Fine details of timbre, dynamic, and pitch are crucial to his style, and on stage he foregrounds these and backgrounds the lyrics, intonation, and gross melodic contour.[7]

Working phrase by phrase through live and studio recordings, I engaged Owens in feedback interviews with the goal of understanding how he conceptualizes his parts and organizes attention in performance. During our first interviews, I discovered that in the composition process, Owens defines the gross melodic contours (the notes and their durations) of his lines as well as many of the nuances of timbre, dynamic, and pitch. Other fine features are left open for manipulation in performance, and it was only with subsequent interviews that I began to understand the importance of melodic details in his music. Some material from our discussion of Winters Bane's "Wages of Sin" will illustrate. "Wages" is the first piece in an elaborate song cycle about a brutal murderer whose heart is transplanted into the body of the judge that sentenced him to die. Played in four-four time, the song begins at a medium-slow tempo as a series of arpeggiated diminished chords, each lasting two measures, is played with an undistorted tone by guitarist Lou St. Paul. The chords continue, and while bassist Dennis Hayes plays alternating roots and flatted fifths on the pulses and drummer Terry Salem strikes an almost martial rhythm on the snare drum, the first lines of the song set the stage for the action: "On the hour of execution / a spiteful soul awaits his death / sobbing, he tries to tell them / that he wasn't there."

I was taken by the song the first time I heard it, and in my initial listenings I was mostly aware of the lyrics and the gross melodic contour of Owens's line; I was also aware that the timbre, dynamics, and fine pitch content of the line were constantly changing, but the nuances of these musical elements were situated in the background of my attention. My interviews with Owens, and additional listenings on my own, brought these intriguing details to the fore. Our discussions centered on a live performance of the tune that I recorded at a nightclub a few weeks before Owens and the band went to Germany to record their CD (Winters Bane [1993] 2000). Here, Owens explained which elements of his vocal lines in this song were preplanned and which were left open, as well as the amount of leeway he allowed himself in the treatment of the open elements. Discussing features unique to this particular night's performance, we explored questions of intention and meaning, and Owens critiqued the effectiveness of each detail.

A long note and a rest divide the first phrase into two parts ("on the hour" and "execution"). As an introduction to the epic, the singer explained, the first two notes of the first half of the first phrase ("on the") should be sung with an almost pitchless rasp. Owens glides into the first note from below, a device that he says draws the listener into the part, and this is a required element of the composition. The vibrato on the third word ("hour") may vary in rate and depth, and the "fall off" (a glissando to a lower, indefinite pitch) at the end of the line is optional as well. In this performance Owens sharps the note slightly before falling off, a common treatment that he says produces an eerie effect. A similar approach is applied to the last syllable of the line ("-tion" of "execution"). Here, the wide vibrato and fall off give emphasis to the key, grim lyric. In the second phrase, the staccato treatment sharply emphasizes the adjective-noun relationship of "spiteful" and "soul" and is part of the composition; the fall off on "soul" is optional, its deep plunge providing an ominous character, like a soul descending into hell. Now, well into the song, Owens adds more nasality and "edge" to the second half of the second phrase ("awaits his death"). The subtle grace notes on "awaits" are built into the part, while "his death" is accented and sung with the Grim Reaper's own rasp.

Additional listenings made the finer details stand out even more clearly in experience. In the first line, "hour" is sung with two distinct but connected syllables, and the vibrato begins immediately on the second syllable. The vibrato starts out wide and timed with the sixteenth notes and ends just before the sharpening of the pitch. After the sharpening, this higher pitch is briefly held before it "falls off" to an indefinite pitch. The dynamic is constant until the end of the fall off, at which point it begins to drop to silence; for most of the fall off the timbre is unchanged, but at the very end, it rapidly becomes raspier, entering the fry register at the final moments. In the second half of the first line ("of execution," sung in five syllables, "of" "ex" "uh" "cu" "tion"), the timbre is now clearly brighter. The first two syllables of the line build in dynamic level, reaching a small crescendo on the third syllable. The fourth syllable is placed slightly ahead of the beat, allowing it to sidestep a loud cymbal crash. Interestingly, that fourth syllable is also slightly quieter, as if the drummer was at that moment taking responsibility for keeping the music energetic, thus allowing Owens to dial back his intensity and express a measure of sadness. This syllable is also important, because it is here that the meaning of the first line becomes fully clear to the listener: "On the hour" is an incomplete phrase, and "of ex-uh" is still ambiguous; most listeners would, however, anticipate the word "execution" with the enunciation of that word's third syllable ("ex-uh-*cu*"). To my ear, the drop in dynamic, combined with the realization that Owens is singing about an execution, gives a unique poignancy to the line. Further, the first three syllables were sung with a staccato treatment, while the fourth presents a quick melismatic glide between adjacent pitches, providing a further level of contrast and detail. At its beginning, the last syllable ("-tion") rises slightly in dynamic, returning the line to its previous level of energy. As the note is held, the dynamic builds further and the vibrato returns, with that vibrato eventually decreasing in its depth (its amount of deviation from the main pitch) just before the note falls off to an indefinite pitch. The dynamic is constant throughout most of the duration of this held note, allowing the listener to clearly hear the pitch details and fading to silence only toward the end of the fall off.

We can hear other subtle changes in pitch, rhythm, timbre, and dynamic in the lines that follow: in the second line, timbral variations range in fine degrees from fullness ("a spiteful soul") to varying levels of nasality ("awaits") to unpitched, raspy declamation ("his death"); on several different held notes, playful variations of the vibrato-and-pitch-sharpening treatment; throughout, variations in the rate of the vibrato combined with timbral changes. In performance, Owens's attention to these multifaceted lines is highly organized; fine pitch details, dynamic, and timbre shift in and out of the center of his attention, while lyric and gross melodic contour lurk in the near background.

In preparing for these interviews, my initial research question centered on Owens's conception of the vocal line, but as our discussions progressed, I became interested in the way that the fine features emerged in the perceptual experiences of the performer and the listener. The issue came to the fore one afternoon when Owens and I were too tired for the exhausting work of phrase-by-phrase analysis. The interview lapsed into casual conversation; eventually Owens suggested that we spend our time listening to the recordings that had influenced him, and he put Judas Priest's *Sad Wings of Destiny* (1976) in the CD player. He explained that Halford's vocals were filled with rich details and later affirmed that one of the best things about the music was that, with each successive listening, one could discover more and more details. Owens said that he loved to "sing with feeling," and that it was the endless layering of details that gave the music its affective power. Inspired by these ideas, I listened carefully to the melodies and felt a sense of what I have since come to call *detail vertigo*—a focal awareness of gross features, a progressively dimmer awareness of finer and finer features trailing off into the background of experience, and a strong sense (evoked by this deep horizonal structure) that future listenings would reveal more and more details. With contour in the foreground and ever finer details in the background, this organization of phenomena in experience inverts the one that Owens employs in performance. By the time a song is ready for the stage, Owens is very familiar with its gross melodic contour and lyrics, and, as a result, he doesn't need to focus on them. The finest details of melody, however, approach the inner horizons of the various auditory dimensions and require the greatest attention for effective execution, and it is these that are shifted to the center stage of his attention. But on the initial hearing of a song, Owens and I (and, I would suggest, most devotees of the melodic traditions of metal) are primarily aware of the gross details and only experience the finer and finer nuances in the horizonal structure of detail vertigo.

This phenomenology of the inner horizons of melody speaks to the truisms about expressivity and detail described above. A basic move in phenomenological scholarship is to turn away from the given content of perception and to explore the emergence of that content in experience. Phenomenology does not deny the facticity of facts or the autonomy and independence of the world; however, it seeks to explore how facts, as facts, emerge in the experience of a subject. Following this basic principle, my thesis is that it is not the expressive features *themselves* that give music its power but their perspectival organization in experience into a foreground and an ever-receding background of finer and finer detail. In the performances of melodic metal bands like Winters Bane, and in a wide variety of other traditions as well, the density of details in the melodic lines presents the listener with a rich field of phenomena, allowing him/her to constitute an experience with an articulate foreground and a background of ever finer nuance. Here, the multiple levels of details comment on one another, forming a gestalt whose meanings are complex and deep. Owens repeatedly emphasized that mere quantity of detail is not sufficient to produce a compelling performance, and he often complained about singers who had a range of timbres and articulations but employed them randomly. In his music, he said, the rich details relate to one another in a coherent and meaningful fashion. For example, in the second line of the introduction, the lyrics state that "a spiteful soul awaits his death." Lasting for two and a half beats, the word "awaits" is at the heart of the line. During the first beat, sung on the syllables "a-wai," the melody moves in and out of harmonic tension, giving the line a plaintive quality and suggesting the anxiety that comes with waiting. Owens employs a nasal tone here, reinforcing the impression of pleading and worry that the note choices create. The remaining beat and a half, sung on the sustain of the final vowel of the word, is treated with a vibrato whose pitch change pulses with six cycles per beat—not, as earlier, with four cycles per beat—thus evoking the rushing anticipation that a nervous waiting creates. The dynamic swells here as well, and the timbre changes to a fuller, almost declamatory tone, giving extra energy to the already urgent vibrato. Placed against the ominous harmonic and timbral context of the rhythm section's accompaniment, this gestalt of tension, plaintiveness, and anticipatory urgency combines in a meaningful fashion with the lyrics to give the part an affective quality that can't be reduced to any one feature.

If the multidimensionality of sound is exploited to make musical meaning rich, it is the horizonal grading of those multiple details that makes it compelling for fans. Situated at the fringe of awareness, near the inner horizon of discriminability, the constantly shifting microdetails beckon our attention like a hand waving in our peripheral vision, and the sheer density of detail in the vocal line and instrumental parts ensures that multiple listenings will not exhaust the song's sonic treasures.[8]

Several related ideas about expressivity in music flow from this thesis. First, an analysis of the notion of fringe phenomena can help to demystify music's often cited ineffability. The difficulty of finding verbal descriptions of musical meanings is given an almost mystical significance in popular and academic literatures, and such writings often try to elevate music by contrasting it with prose and its allegedly limited expressive power. While it is frequently difficult to describe qualities evoked by a piece of music, the full, situated meaning of all but the most simple and pragmatic of prose utterances eludes description as well, and celebrating music's ineffability, rather than inquiring into its roots, does little more than romanticize and mystify the issues at hand. The focus/fringe/horizon structure of experience can help to shed light here. While phenomena in the focus of attention are, by definition, accessible to reflective thought, those in the fringe are present for us in a more complex and ambivalent way. Not fully absent, phenomena situated at the fringe of one's experience play a key part in one's larger experience of the music; not fully focal, fringe phenomena elude cursory reflexive awareness and may only become focal with great effort. If the meaning of a musical passage is a gestalt of features situated across the attentional space of focus and fringe, then it will, by definition, possess elements that resist easy articulation. Further, the mere cataloging of gross and fine features will only partially account for the lived meaning of a musical part. The richest descriptions of music must not merely list the present musical features and their individual meanings, they must explore the positioning of those features within the larger field of experience and the overall significance generated by the holistic gestalt of those emplaced elements.

Attending to the role of horizonal structures in musical experience can also shed light on two often neglected elements in the relationship between music and affect—the impact of situated context on the evocation of emotion, and the listener's ability to control music's emotional power. It is clear, first, that the expressive impact of musical sound is highly situational. When I am distracted by a spilled beer at a Winters Bane show, for example, the same music still plays, but I feel annoyance at my soggy jacket, not grim fascination with the judge's new heart. Likewise, if I make an effort to reconnect with the music, I may assertively shift the focus of my attention from the beer back to the band and actively engage with the music's affective potential. In these cases, what accounts for the music's expressive effect (or lack thereof) is not the music alone but the music as engaged by the listener—or, more specifically, not the melodic details alone but the detail vertigo, a structure of experience that is constituted in the listener's (situational and agentive) engagement with the sonic details in perception. Of equal importance is the fact that this perceptual engagement is informed by culture. In the melody-rich strand of the heavy metal tradition, a strand for which Judas Priest is perhaps the main exponent, singers craft nuanced melodies in order to exploit the horizonal structures of sound perception and evoke rich meanings; likewise, fans of this strand of metal prize detail vertigo and seek to manifest it in their listening. There are, however, a wide range of ways that expressive forms may be crafted by performers and experienced by audiences. For example, listeners unfamiliar with or hostile to metal's trademark vocal timbres may disengage from those features of the music, passively missing or actively ignoring precisely those details that make the music compelling for its fans. Even a moment's thought would reveal that, in minimalist expressive traditions, detail vertigo is just the opposite of what the performer seeks to evoke, and that different cultures, subcultures, or scenes may exploit the horizonal structure of perception in different ways. At first glance, it would seem that the opposite of richly nuanced expressive forms are those forms that have no fine details and solely possess gross features. However, the relationship between gross and fine features is a complex one, and we can get a richer understanding of the cultural and agentive dimensions of expressivity in music if we return once again to the notion of fine details in perception. Such an analysis will apply to performance and expressive culture broadly, including media other than sound and genres other than music.

As I suggested above, the anatomy and physiology of our bodies place limits on our perceptual sensitivity, creating for each perceptual dimension an outer horizon, which defines the range of stimuli that we can experience, and an inner horizon, which places a limit on our ability to discriminate differences within that dimension. If fine perceptual features are those that approach the limit of the inner horizon, it would seem that gross features are those that are far from the inner horizon. This formulation is unproblematic, but the difficulty lies in finding examples of expressive forms with only gross features. Take, for example, pitch in music and color in painting. In melody, the leap of a major third would be a gross feature of the musical sound; the wavering of pitch in a wide vibrato would be a middle grade feature, and a shallow vibrato would be a fine feature. In painting, the contrast of a bright red rectangle on a bright green background would serve as a gross feature; a light brown rectangle on a dark brown background would provide a middle-grade feature, and a rectangle of indigo shading into a background of deep purple would represent a fine feature. Thus, the endlessly detailed paintings of Pieter Brueghel and the songs of Timmy Owens could be considered highly nuanced expressive products—media with lots of carefully crafted features near the limits of our ability to discriminate difference. The problem with the notions of gross and fine comes when we try to think of examples of expressive forms with few or no fine details. The monochrome paintings at the famed Rothko Chapel may, for example, seem to be nothing but panels of a single undifferentiated color, but a moment's attention to them reveals fine gradations of texture and hue. Even when the most technically proficient vocalist tries to sing without vibrato, a small wavering pitch is presented to the ear. And in hearing synthesized tones or viewing swatches of color produced by machine, the act of perception itself may produce fine-grained variations, even if the physical waves of sound or light are absolutely regular. In listening, the movement of the head will bring about a tiny Doppler shift and create a pitch change in experience, while differences in the light falling on the color swatch will result in small variations in color. So how are we to understand the fine, if examples of the gross are so difficult to find?

The solution to the problem, I believe, lies in the flexible character of the horizon itself. As a physical object, almost any given expressive form (a particular song or painting) will, if examined carefully enough, reveal fine-grained details, because details at the inner horizon of any perceptual dimension are, by definition, what careful examination reveals. However, in any particular instance, the inner horizon of any perceptual parameter is defined neither by the physical details of the object of perception nor by the absolute biological limits of perceptibility but by the person's agentive and culturally informed engagement with those details as the body is deployed in perception. As listeners or viewers, we learn when to scan the horizon for fine details and when to focus on gross features. We also learn what might count as an intentional control of fine-grained features (the tiny sharpening of pitch on notes of harmonic tension in Winters Bane songs), what is mere sloppiness (the flat notes of an amateur singer), and what are the kinds of insignificant small-scale differences that linguists would call a feature in free variation—a meaningless detail that is neither an intentional nuance nor evidence of inexpert control. For each perceptual dimension, each culture possesses norms for the positioning of the inner horizon relative to the actual limits of perceptibility, the position of the focus within that horizon, and the ratio of focus to fringe. Such norms influence both the production of expressive forms, as when Owens crafts fine details with the intention that hardcore listeners will experience detail vertigo, and their reception, as when Winters Bane fans push their listening to the limit, seeking the details that Owens has placed there. Further, different cultures may seek rich detail along different sensual parameters. In the music of Timmy Owens, for example, it is ultrafine changes in timbre, dynamic, and pitch that matter the most, while the control of rhythm in phrasing is less important. In contrast, timbre, dynamic, and vibrato play an important role in the music of Frank Sinatra, but it is by the manipulation of rhythm (tempo, note value, rhythmic accent, and the fine positioning of notes in time relative to the beat) that gave this singer his expressive power. These norms for organizing attention serve as cultural resources, and like all such resources, reflective awareness of these norms and the ability to conform conduct to them is differentially distributed among the participants within a culture, subculture, or scene. Those new to the culture of an expressive genre may confuse random noise with fine detail or celebrate the precise technique of an artist only to discover later that his/her skills are considered by devotees of the style to be merely mediocre. Such norms are also open to debate, as when connoisseurs celebrate virtuosic fine-grained control, aesthetes call for tastefulness in embellishment, or populists cry for a return to basics.

These last examples also point to the fact that, for any given culture, the significance of the horizon in general and any particular inner horizon is ideologically constructed. In traditions such as Owens's strain of melodic metal or the subculture of wine tasters, control of fine features is a evidence of a desirable virtuosity, and the ability to recognize that control is a sign of the audience member's connoisseurship. But while it is obvious that the disclaiming of virtuosity and connoisseurship is a standard feature of populist expressive traditions, the interpretation of horizons is not a simple issue, and two additional examples from popular music will illustrate its ideological construction. Based on descriptions of my own experiences of these musics, the following examples are intended as hypotheses about the organization of attention in different music scenes and would require field-work for confirmation or disconfirmation.[9]

Like that of Timmy Owens, the music of rocker Bruce Springsteen is filled to overflowing with both gross and fine variations in timbre and dy-namic, and, as a first approximation, the experiences of Springsteen fans probably fit into the general model of detail vertigo outlined above—inner horizons of pitch, timbre, and dynamic are extended toward the edges of perceptibility, and an array of fringe features informs focal features to create rich meanings. Comparing these two musics, however, I suggest that a difference should be recognized between connoisseuristic detail vertigo and romantic detail vertigo. For fans of virtuosity in metal, intense listen-ing involves an active, connoisseuristic scanning of the inner horizon to il-luminate and appreciate the performer's skills. In Springsteen's music, however, expression, rather than virtuosic control, is the keynote, and his shows are understood by fans as the product of an honest man giving his emotional all in performance (Cavicchi 1998). I hypothesize that, as a result, the fine features are interpreted as a direct and unmediated expression of emotion rather than as a virtuosic display of vocal control, and that Springsteen fans do not probe the perceptual horizon in the same way fans of melodic metal do. Both metalheads and Bruce fans, I suspect, push the inner horizons near the edge of perceptibility in intensely engaged listening, but metalheads move the *focus* near the horizon to illuminate the fine details, while Bruce fans, engaging in romantic detail vertigo, center their focus closer to the gross features, thus allowing the extremely fine features to do their expressive work from the background. To the expressivist ideology of musical performance, the emotions evoked, rather than the techniques of evocation, are the point of the experience, and the connoisseuristic probing of horizons would serve no purpose. This is not to say that Springsteen is more or less reflexive than Owens in planning out his lines; it is simply to suggest that the ideology of unmediated expression informs the listeners' attention to the music and their construction of meaning.

Another example will illustrate a different set of relationships among form, perception, meaning, and ideology in music. In many ways, the music of Liz Phair typifies the rethinking of virtuosity in a style that has been very loosely labeled "alternative rock." On songs like her 1998 radio single "Polyester Bride," Phair's vocal style is extremely plain. Changes in dynamic are small, but not so minute as to suggest a virtuosic control; sustained notes possess a fast and extremely shallow vibrato that could easily be overlooked in a cursory description. Placed in the far background of experience but nevertheless present, these features serve a key function. Where detail-rich forms like Owens's vocals allow his listeners to constitute the experience of detail vertigo, Phair creates forms that, I hypothesize, allow her audience to experience what is for them a kind of (desirable) detail claustrophobia—not claustrophobia in the sense of too many objects in perception, but in the sense of boundaries close at hand. Like the landscape of the Arizona salt flats, a perfectly even sound—created by a virtuoso vocalist with "no" vibrato or a synthesizer in a piece of minimalist electronic music—draws attention toward the horizon by the very absence of fine details. This is precisely *not* what I believe is occurring in the fan's experience of Phair. On the contrary, Phair's shallow vibrato fills up the far-middle range of the inner horizon of pitch; its more or less regular rate, shallow depth, and consistent form on each repetition provide no traditionally "expressive" information to the listener. As a result, I suspect, listeners roll the inner horizon of attention away from the edge of perceptibility and situate the vibrato and dynamic details in the background, experiencing the melody as a phenomenon with a shallow horizonal structure. This experienced shallowness is a key element of the overall meaning of her singing style for her fans—a plainness that is as distinct from the aggressively virtuosic minimalism of Danish modern furniture as it is from the polished technique of "Wages of Sin," an ironic intelligence that is as far away from sarcastic off-key singing as it is from amateurish problems with intonation. Significantly, displays of virtuosic technique are present in other dimensions of the sound (the topical allusions in the lyrics, the clever chord changes in the guitar, the well-crafted production). Focal in experience and horizonally shallow, the vocals form a gestalt with the other elements of the song to constitute the overall meaning of the music for the fans.

So far, we have explored examples in which the sound produced by the musician and the perceptual practices of the listener are tailored to one another. But listeners are often confronted with music from beyond their community's repertoire, and the notion of culturally informed, actively achieved perceptual practice is relevant to these types of musical encounters as well. In my interviews with Owens, for example, he was proud to say that he had eclectic musical tastes. From the alternative band 4 Non Blondes to Elvis Presley, all the singers he enjoys have one thing in common, he said—they produce nuanced lines and "sing with feeling." Of course, vocalists from other styles both within and beyond American popular music produce highly detailed parts, and space does not allow an analysis of the complex mix of features that makes music appealing to Owens. We can observe, however, that when the listener confronts unfamiliar styles, the fit of musical sound and the listener's perceptual practices play a large role in the resultant experiences of meaning. Hearing the music of Liz Phair, for example, a metalhead used to listening for an experience of detail vertigo might respond in a range of ways—an outright denunciation of Phair's "lack of skill," a puzzled acceptance that there is no accounting for taste, a search for listening strategies appropriate to the style. In all of these cases, the listener's experience of meaning emerges as a culturally informed and agentive engagement with the music in the act of perception, and the horizonal structure of sound plays a key role in this process. By treating perception as actively achieved and socially informed, we can account for both cultural difference and the emergent and agentive processes by which cultures change and interact.

Horizons and the Problem of the Self

So far, our exploration of the detail horizon in musical experience has centered on the individual's awareness of the phenomena of the world, but an inquiry into the focus/fringe/horizon structure can also be made to speak to the problem of the self. My main goal in the remaining sections of this chapter is to explore the different ways in which the self emerges in experience and use that inquiry to shed new light on the problem of the self in music. It is a commonplace in music scholarship to observe that intense musical involvement often results in a "loss of self" for the musical participants, and such an experience is often held up as the highest possible state that a participant can reach. Drawing on the scholarship of analytic philosopher José Luis Bermúdez, I will show that there are many types of self-experience and that to speak of a loss of self is to simplify what is actually a complex, multilayered affair. Before we get to this point, however, we need to have a much clearer idea of what the self is and what self-experience might entail. I will begin by very briefly reviewing the form of the problem in modern Western philosophy and go on to develop a phenomenological account of one type of self-experience—the self that emerges from the perspectival organization of phenomena in perception. I will then situate this account within Bermúdez's larger theory of the self, explore the relationship between the self and the horizonal structure of experience, and illustrate the applicability of these ideas to the problem of the self in music.

Few problems in Western philosophy are as vexing as that of the self. What Saint Augustine said of time could as easily be said of the self: in everyday life, nothing is more intuitive and obvious than the self, but the more we reflect on the nature of the self, the more confusing it becomes.[10] For example, William James ([1890] 1981, 279) observed that an extremely wide variety of phenomena can be experienced as "self," and the line between what we experience as "me" and what we experience as "mine" is a highly fluid one. Absorbed in a physical act like washing dishes or dancing, one may experience one's acting body as self. Yet should an injury develop or bodily conduct become problematic, the nonresponsive body may suddenly be experienced as "mine"—a thing that "I" control like a steering wheel or a pen, not the "I" that is acting. Likewise, at one moment one may dwell in one's thoughts or emotions and experience them as self; the next moment, however, that same thought may be something that is merely mine, an idea I had, I emotion I felt, rather than my (!) self. Exploring the flexibility of the self, many traditions of meditation challenge their novices to observe the flow of thoughts as if from a distance, acknowledge the existence of their thoughts without being caught up in them, and actively experience those thoughts as mine, rather than as me. Sketching the canonical form of the problem in modern Western philosophy, Bermúdez cites a well-known passage from David Hume: "For my part, when I enter most intimately into what I call *myself*, I always stumble on some particular perception or other, of heat or cold, light or shade, love or hatred, pain or pleasure. I never catch myself at any time without a perception, and can never observe anything but the perception" (Hume in Bermúdez 1998, 104). In other words, the problem of the self is not just that it can take many forms; the greater difficulty is that in attending to concrete experience, we always seem to encounter individual phenomena, not the self that is experiencing them. As Bermúdez puts it, "What Hume is worried about is his introspective failure to encounter the putative owner of his sensations" (104). If the self initially seemed like a simple, unitary phenomenon, examples such as these suggest how problematic this element of experience really is.

We can make a first, small inroad into this problem by attending to the language in which it is often framed. When we use the definite article and speak of "the self," we presuppose that the self is a thing, rather than a process or an organization of things. Obviously, this is a contention to be attacked or defended, not an axiom to be assumed. More importantly, however, the use of the definite article predisposes us to think of the self as an entity distinct from one's experiences of it. While it may make sense to study billiard balls or vampire bats as entities independent of experience, this approach seems jarringly inappropriate when applied to something so (by definition) intimate to us as the self. Whether or not the self can exist independent of one's experience of it, it makes sense to begin our inquiry by examining the data at hand. Following the basic tenets of phenomenological method, some initial clarity can be brought to our thinking by conceptualizing our object of inquiry as self-experience, rather than "the self," and asking, what kinds of experiences do we mean when we say "self"? What is the nature of self-experience? And, if the definite article is appropriate, how does "the self" emerge in lived experience?

Self-experience emerges in an extraordinarily wide variety of forms, and teasing out all of the different ways in which we may be aware of ourselves is obviously beyond the scope of this chapter. In later chapters Giovanna P. Del Negro and I will explore other dimensions of this problem, and my goal here is to focus on the issue of self-experience specifically with regard to sense perception. Presenting an account of this topic, Bermúdez has observed that many modern Western philosophers deny that the self is present in the content of perception, and constructing a composite position from the ideas of different thinkers, Bermúdez refers to this stance as the "Schopenhauer/Wittgenstein view" (105). A passage from Wittgenstein's *Tractatus* is used to illustrate: "Where *in* the world is a metaphysical subject to be found? You will say that this is exactly like the case of the eye and the visual field. But really you do *not* see the eye. And nothing in the visual field allows you to infer that it is seen by an eye" (Wittgenstein in Bermúdez 1998, 105). In other words, what is revealed in the act of seeing is the external world, not the self that is experiencing that world. Certainly in vision we may see our hands or our feet, but at any given moment those body parts may be experienced as self or other. More to the point, while we may variously consider those body parts as me or mine, the hands and feet that I see are not the "the self" that is experiencing the world through vision, are not the self that is doing the seeing. But is this position true? Is it possible that we only experience ourselves as thinkers, or that the self never enters directly into perceptual experience and is only hypothesized in reflection? Clearly, there is something counterintuitive in these ideas. In everyday life, we seem to feel our embodiment, to experience ourselves in perception as well as in reflexive thought. But, as the modern philosophers point out, when we grasp any individual perceptual experience, it seems that we only find this phenomenon, this percept, not the "putative owner" who is doing the experiencing.

To compensate for the "I" allegedly missing from the content of perception, the self is often conceptualized as a little person in the head who views the images projected by the senses. This produces problems for a theory of perception as well as for a theory of the self, and the two issues are intimately related. By definition absent from experience but doing the explanatory work of the experiencing self, the hypothesized little person is referred to in philosophy as a "humunculus," and in everyday discourse, humuncular beliefs about the self are common. Consider the situation of a person with a back injury having the complicated knots in his shoelaces untied by a caregiver. If the unknotting were to take a long time and a serious conversation were to develop, it is easy to imagine that the injured person would say to the caregiver, "Come up here, I want to talk with you"—as if "I" was located "up here" in the head rather than down there in the feet where the caregiver, and his head, are located. Likewise, when we experience the body as an instrument to be controlled, we often speak of ourselves as the controller of our unresponsive body: "I couldn't make my hands play the scale," or "I wanted to run, but my legs wouldn't take me a step further." Perhaps the most vivid depiction of humuncular thinking in popular culture can be found in the movie *Men in Black*, where an autopsy reveals that what had seemed to be a person was in fact a robot, now broken, with a tiny alien sitting in the control room head, pulling levers that manipulate the limbs and watching the view screens of the eyes. By presenting these examples, I do not mean to suggest that humuncular thinking in general or the idea of a little person in the head is a universal theory of the self. The convergence of auditory and visual perspectives at a roughly similar location in the skull makes the sensation that the self is "in" the head one that most people have experienced at one time or another, I think. However, self-experience comes in a wide range of ways, and "the self in the head" is by no means the default case in "everyday life" or in any given culture. Further, as Del Negro and I suggest in chapter five, theories about self and other differ widely from one culture to the next as well.

However common or uncommon to lay folk, humuncular arguments are also present in modern Western philosophy. A strong critique of this kind of thinking can be found in Maurice Merleau-Ponty's remarks on Descartes's *Dioptric* (Merleau-Ponty [1964] 1968, 210), and James Schmidt's discussion of this passage can serve as an instructive guide here (Schmidt 1985, 97–99). The *Dioptric* is a study of vision, and Schmidt explains how one of the engravings for Descartes's text illustrates how light travels from objects in the world to the surface of the eye and how the parts of the eye present that image to the back of the retina. Beneath the diagram is the drawing of a man gazing up at the bottom of the eyeball and seeing the image projected there. Critiquing Descartes's diagram in a 1959 working note, Merleau-Ponty asks, "*who* will see the image painted on the eyes or in the brain? . . . Descartes already sees that we put a little man in man, that our objectifying view of our own body always obliges us to seek *still further inside* that *seeing man* we thought we had under our eyes"([1964] 1968, 210, also partially quoted in Schmidt 1985, 99). Such Cartesian thinking, Schmidt observes, requires us to hypothesize a second "little man" who will see the image displayed on the first little man's retina, a third little man within the second, and, of course, an infinite series of little men.[11]

Examining the underlying assumptions that produce such logical problems will be productive for our analysis of self-experience. Rather than explaining how perception brings the objects of the world into experience, humuncular arguments confect a hypothetical entity and attribute to it the functions that the argument was initially meant to explain. Thus, the humunculus comes to stand for the fact that things are experienced, but the humuncular self that does the experiencing is just an empty placeholder, an anthropomorphized black box that defers explanation endlessly. Seen in the light of our earlier discussion, humuncular thinking affirms the Schopenhauer/Wittgenstein view that the self does not appear in perception but retains the assumption that the self must be an object. Combining these ideas, the resulting stance imagines the self as a never-experienced object, as the self of the definite article. One way to overcome these difficulties and gain new perspectives on the problem of the self can be found in Husserl's methodological charge to rigorously describe, rather than explain, experience. Is self-experience an impossibility in perception? A careful return to lived experience suggests otherwise, and the idea I want to pursue is that while the self cannot be found as an object in perceptual experience, it is concretely present as the *organization* of phenomena in experience; that is, the organization of perceptual phenomena in experience constitutes for us a lived sense of self. Below, I will explore this idea in detail, but it is worth noting at the outset that even if we limit our inquiry to perception, the emergence of self-experience in the organization of phenomena can come about in a wide variety of ways. As we shall see, the perspectival organization of visual phenomena as near and far can constitute a lived sense of a here and I. Auditory perception may also involve a perspectivally consti-tuted self, and as Bermúdez argues, the registering of one's own movement by vision produces a kind of self-experience. Most significantly for the dis-cussion of the detail horizon, both our active organization of phenomena in experience (for example, when one makes an effort to attend to an indi-vidual instrument in a piece of music) and our failure to control the organ-ization of phenomena (as when a loud backfire from a car in the street dis-tracts us from the song we are trying to learn) constitute for us types of self-experience.

I first saw that the organization of phenomena could be used to over-come humuncular approaches to the problem of the self after an unusual experience I had in meditation during my first period of Ohio fieldwork. Here, I will use an analysis of this experience to support my larger argu-ments about the self; before I do, though, I want to address objections that readers might have to this unorthodox "data" by providing some back-ground information on the type of meditation I pursued and discussing the kinds of claims I am making for this experience.

Based on the suggestion of a friend and the exercises in a few introduc-tory books, I began meditating in the late 1980s to control stress and en-hance concentration. My meditative practices were very simple and were not in any way connected to spirituality, mysticism, or religion. While I suppose my practices were not incompatible with many types of theologi-cal beliefs, both then and now I have treated my own meditation in a strictly materialist manner, as a question solely of brain and body, nerves and muscles.

Some readers may feel that any evidence from meditation will necessar-ily be introspective and subjective and therefore unverifiable and useless in rational argument. Without delving too deeply into epistemological issues, I believe that there is a way in which such an experience can be legitimately employed here. First, I do not claim that my experiences are esoteric; with some practice I think it is quite possible for other people to replicate my meditation and verify my "data." Thus, while the content of my experience in July 1993 may be strictly subjective, the structure of that experience can be partially shared by others. Sitting in the living room with my friend, for example, I cannot know that the ivory color-quality that I see in the fabric of the chair before me is the same ivory color-quality that she sees. However, I can know that if we both face the same direction, she will see that the chair is to the left of the sofa. The same principle is true of the tactile experiences of breathing in meditation. While I experience my own pulmonary anatomy in meditation and you experience yours, our bodies are similar enough that we may at least try to talk about the common structure of our experiences. A different kind of comparison is the basis for the second reason why a report of these meditative experiences should be considered. In the meditation discussed below, my experience was primarily composed of tactile and proprioceptive phenomena; outside meditation, much of our experience is dominated by visual and auditory sense modalities. The following argument contrasts meditative and nonmeditative experiences in order to shed light on structural relationships that exist independent of the sense modalities involved, which operate in a similar way in both domains. Thus, even if the reader feels that reports of experiences in meditation are absolutely subjective, he/she may treat my discussion as a thought experiment useful solely to free the structural relationships of their particulars and illustrate a more general thesis. That this meditative experience did actually occur, and that my general thesis is compatible with the work of Bermúdez—whose conclusions are based on data from experimental psychology—should, I hope, lend credence to the project.

As I said above, my meditative practices were very simple. I would begin each meditation session by sitting in a chair with my eyes closed and relaxing the muscles in various parts of my body (feet, legs, torso, chest, hands, arms, back, neck, face, scalp). With my body relaxed, I would breath from my diaphragm, focus my attention on my breathing, and try to exclude from experience outside sensory information. Such techniques are common to many meditative traditions, and, as anyone who has tried such meditation knows, focusing one's attention in this way is not easy to do. I am not a particularly gifted meditator, and usually after one or two breaths my attention would shift from the expansions and contractions of my stomach muscles to bits of song, thoughts about everyday activities, images from memory, and other distracting mental phenomena. When this would happen, I would briefly note the kinds of thoughts that were distracting me and then try to return attention to my breathing. Each session would continue for about fifteen minutes, and while I was never able to fully quiet the flow of thoughts in my head, the attempt to focus attention, combined with the diaphragmatic breathing, helped me to manage stress.

One afternoon in late July 1993, I sat down to do my meditation, and, for reasons that have never been clear to me, I was surprisingly effective in focusing attention. The following passage from my journal, edited slightly for clarity, describes the experience:

In my last meditation I was intently focused on the sensation of breathing from my belly . . . As I got more involved in the meditation, I experienced my body in rich physical and affective detail—the pull of the skin over my belly and the gentle exertion outward as I inhaled, various tightnesses of my internal organs, and the slow release of muscular and skin tension as I exhaled. Getting more involved, I gently conjured mental words urging myself to ignore various distractions (the sound of people arguing outside, a phrase from a book I read earlier that day), and for a period of time, the sensations from my stomach and the distractions competed for a place in my experience. After a while, though, the distracting thoughts came less frequently, and when they did come, I experienced them with less intensity. In similar proportion, the experiences of my breathing had more and more detail—both affective (the sensation of exhalation as pleasant and gentle) and physical (the exact positions of my muscles).

At the most involved moment in the meditation, my experience was almost totally composed of the panorama of sensations in my trunk. My most vivid awareness was of the position and tension of my two abdominal muscles at a spot situated more or less below my belly button. Moving out from this focus, sensations from the abdominal muscles leading away from the belly button ("up" toward the head and "down" the feet) trailed out into the fringe of experience and constituted a horizon that was no more than a few inches in its span. Likewise, sensations of other muscles and organs proportionally distant from the tactile center of attention trailed out away from the focus in a hemispherical pattern. Occasionally present in experience, thoughts, in the forms of words or images, would emerge with the very lightest intensity. The most significant part of this meditation exercise was the self-experience that it involved. Intensely aware of the sensations of my torso and conscious of little else, I did *not* experience a "loss of self." On the contrary, I had the unusual sensation that I was located here in my torso, a short distance beneath the arc of my abdominals. The very strangeness of this sensation made it clear to me how strongly I felt myself to be located "in my skull" in primarily visual and auditory experience.

In one key sense, the words "unusual" and "strange" are inappropriate to describe this experience. Certainly, the sense of here and self in this example is unusual because of "its" location in the torso, but the form of self-experience is, I believe, the same as that found in the many nonmeditative situations of sense perception. Consider specifically the situation of a person taking in a sweeping vista from the peak of a high mountain.[12] Overwhelmed by the beauty of a stunning view, it is not hard to imagine that the person's experience might be dominated by visual phenomena and that reflexive thought in words would be largely absent. Here, trees and rocks at the mountaintop are seen as close at hand, a road appears trailing off through the middle ground of the scene, and farms and hills are present in the distance. Aural phenomena might also enter into the background of the overall experience and reinforce that sense of perspective, with the quiet rustling noises from the trail heard as nearby and the soft toot of a train whistle present in the distance. Because of the position of the eyes and the nature of binocular vision, the perspective of seeing seems to converge at a point somewhere in the middle of the skull, and the here-point produced by vision is reinforced by that of auditory perception. As a result, in this example, one would experience oneself as "up here" in the head and sensations in the torso as "down there." Even if one had a strong pain in the abdomen or foot, the compelling quality and overwhelming quantity of visual phenomena in this situation, as well as the redundancy of visual and aural perspectives, would prevent one from displacing one's sense of here away from that point in the skull.[13]

Using the language of humunculism to compare the mountain view and meditation examples, one might say that "the self" in the mountain view case is located in the head, but in the meditation case it was shifted to the torso. But is there a way of understanding these self-experiences without slipping into humuncular language? The problem dissolves, I believe, when we realize that, in these examples, it is the perspectival arrangement of phenomena (the arrangement of phenomena across lived space and graded from greater to lesser intensity) that constitutes a sense of here, and, concomitantly, a type of strictly perceptual self-experience. In other words, self-experience is indeed present in perception, not as an individual perceptual phenomenon (an object, a percept, a humunculus) but as the *arrangement* of phenomena. Stating the situation more carefully, we should acknowledge that such perspectival arrangements are only one way in which self-experience is constituted, and that other types of arrangements may produce other types of self-experience.

A comparison of the similarities and differences between the meditation and mountain view examples will make these ideas clear. In both, it is not a single, monadic phenomenon that is experienced but a perspectival arrangement of phenomena, and in both examples this arrangement constitutes the sense of here and self. By calling the arrangement perspectival, I want to emphasize two things—that the phenomena are spatial (experienced as distributed over multiple locations in lived space) and that those locations are experienced as close or far relative to a here-point. In other words, perspectival arrangement constitutes phenomena not merely as near and far from one another (i.e., as spatial) but as near and far *from me*.[14]

The concretely experienced quality of "here" inhering in the perspectival arrangement of phenomena entails a sense that I am here and is thus a type of self-experience. This sense of here is not merely a logical conclusion drawn from a description of the phenomena but a quality concretely experienced in the phenomena themselves. To experience the farms and hills as distant is to experience myself as the here-point from which the farms and hills are far. If it is, perhaps, difficult to accept this as a description of concretely experienced qualities rather than as a logical conclusion, it is because in the pragmatic rush of our daily activities, we most often foreground what phenomenologists call the *noema* (the objects of experience) and background the *noēsis* (the process by which those phenomena are brought into experience) and the sets of lived relationships among the *noema*. Relegated to the fringe of pragmatic experience and overlooked in pragmatic discourse, the *noēsis* is no less concretely lived and is in no way hypothetical. In my discussion of the humunculus problem, I will return to this point below. First, however, we can get a better understanding of how the perspectival arrangement produces a form of self-experience by exploring the differing ways in which perspective is constituted in the two examples.

In the mountain view example, the anatomy of the eye and the layout of physical space before the person make the phenomenal space perspectival, and optical and aural cues are used to constitute any given visual or auditory phenomenon as near or far. The situation is somewhat different in the meditation example. In most situations of somatic proprioception (the tactile perception of one's own body), it seems that there is nothing parallel to the cues that in seeing and hearing produce a sense of distance; in other words, proprioceptive phenomena are spatial, but, as Bermúdez suggests (152), they are not perspectival. In the particular instance of proprioception which took place in my July 1993 meditation, however, the manner in which I focused attention on the phenomena constituted the spatial array in a perspectival fashion. By making an effort to "pay attention to my breathing," the intensity of the phenomena in my experience was graded in a continuous and decreasing pattern over lived space. From a point of maximum intensity near the belly button, the pattern radiated out in a linear shape along the abdominal muscles to a fringe and a horizon; it also radiated out in a hemispherical shape through the other muscles and organs. This spatially graded arrangement of percepts constituted the arrayed phenomena as perspectival. It was not only the focusing of attention that graded the phenomena in intensity; the motion involved in diaphragmatic breathing also helped. While some proprioceptive mechanisms indicate the positions of body parts when the body is still, others operate only when we move (Bermúdez 1998, 132). It is no coincidence, I think, that the focus of the spatial field was the point of greatest motion in the act of breathing, and that the points of lesser motion were also points of lesser intensity. The motion of breathing "lit up" the muscles and organs for proprioception like a spotlight aimed at a dark stage—defining a space with a center and periphery, clearly illuminating some objects and presenting others with lesser intensity.[15]

However differently the space is constituted in the two examples, they are similar in that both involve phenomena that are perspectivally arrayed. This arrangement does not merely invest phenomena with a quality of near and far; that sense of near and far necessarily invokes a lived sense of here, which is a kind of self-experience. It is important to emphasize that in both examples, entities at the focus are *not* experienced as here; to the contrary, they are experienced as *other* and *there,* and this fact has significance for the humunculus problem. In vision, I do not usually experience myself as the entire visual array or even as the object of focus. Rather, the presence of multiple visual percepts creates a phenomenal space, and the perspectival arrangement of that space produces a sense of here that terminates at a point in the skull. In the meditation example, the spatial arrangement of my anatomy and my selective attention to the movement of that anatomy in breathing created a phenomenal space, and the graded intensity of the percepts provided the perspectival weightings that constituted the sense of here. Corresponding to this observation that phenomena at the focus are experienced as "there" is the seemingly paradoxical fact that there is no phenomenon at the location we experience as "here." But this is only paradoxical if we assume that for something to be concretely present in experiences it must be an object, and if we deny that the arrangement of phenomena is itself part of experience. Though an empty location in lived space, "here" is no less concretely experienced for being constituted by the arrangement of phenomena. Indeed, were there to be a phenomena at the here-point, we would have discovered the humuncular self! The concretely felt sense of "here" constitutes a type of self-experience, and recognizing this dispels the humunculus problem for this type of self-experience. The utility of comparing the meditation and mountain view examples is that such a comparison allows us to get beyond the concrete phenomena of the given situation and to see the structural relationships among phenomena—relationships that are just as present in experience as individual phenomena but are too easily ignored. Exchanging one dominant sense modality for another and one experienced location of "the self" for another, it becomes clear that the perspectival organization of phenomena produced the sense of here and its concomitant sense of self.

My discussion of the self is consistent with broad trends in phenomenology and allied intellectual traditions in the twentieth century. From Edmund Husserl ([1929] 1964, [1931] 1960) to Maurice Merleau-Ponty ([1945] 1981, [1964] 1968) and beyond, from William James ([1912] 1967a, [1890] 1981) to a wide variety of other thinkers, many writers have sought to critique those philosophical systems that view the essence of the person as something outside of the world or that define their study objects as entities that are by definition independent of experience. Following these approaches, I have tried to understand "the self" not as a thing lurking behind experience or a distinct type of metaphysical entity but as a concrete element of experience that emerges from the person's engagement with the world. While the majority of my writings have been informed by phenomenology, analytic philosopher José Luis Bermúdez is the thinker whose research bears most directly on this chapter, and it will be worthwhile to explore his work here.

In *The Paradox of Self-Consciousness* (1998), Bermúdez seeks to unravel a worrisome circularity in contemporary ideas about the self. Stated in a somewhat simplified fashion, the problem Bermúdez sees is as follows: it is commonly believed in analytic philosophy that language and thought are strictly interdependent, and that to have the ability to think thoughts of a given type is to have the ability to use the linguistic means through which those thoughts are expressed (13). Applying this concept to the problem of the self yields the proposition that to be self-conscious is to attain "mastery" over the first person singular.[16] The problem with the conventional view of the self, Bermúdez argues, is that if thought and language are strictly interdependent, it is difficult to understand how self-consciousness could emerge during the process of child development. The child can only learn to master the first person singular if he/she has a concept of self, but he/she can only develop a concept of self if he/she has already mastered the first person singular. Bermúdez labels this paradox "capacity circularity" (18), and his solution to the problem is to suggest that there are multiple forms of self-consciousness.[17] Non-linguistic forms of self-consciousness are present from the very earliest stages of development, and they are the foundation from which self-consciousness in language emerges later. Such forms stay with a person throughout his/her life and can be found in the experiences of both infants and adults. The middle chapters of the book cite experimental work done with non-language-bearing creatures (children and non-human animals) to argue that strictly perceptual, nonlinguistic forms of self-consciousness do exist and to illustrate how they come together to enable self-consciousness in language. I formed the core idea for the present chapter (that the perspectival organization of phenomena constitutes one form of the self in experience) in the period before I encountered Bermúdez's work. While Bermúdez's research goes into far greater depth than my own and approaches these issues from a different intellectual tradition, our ideas can be seen, I think, as different but compatible perspectives on the same underlying human phenomena. We can get a much richer understanding of the self by examining Bermúdez's arguments in more detail.

Bermúdez's analysis of self-consciousness in vision is grounded in the work of psychologist J. J. Gibson. In *The Ecological Approach to Visual Perception* (1979), Gibson argues that vision does not merely provide information about the visual world, it also provides information about the self, and the latter is necessary for us to make sense of the former (Bermúdez 1998, 110). Self information is not deduced in reflexive thought or dependent upon the use of language but is directly present for the individual in perceptual "invariants" in visual experience. Two examples of such invariants are "looming" and "optic flow." Bermúdez explains:

Consider the relatively straightforward example of moving toward a wall and looking ahead of one to the point of impact. As one approaches the wall, the array of illuminated surfaces will obviously change. But there is a certain order to the change. The part of the wall at which one is looking remains stationary, although, of course, the magnification of the solid visual angle will accelerate dramatically as the wall is approached (the phenomena of *looming*). But around the stationary part of the wall there are textured surfaces radiating outward in what Gibson terms patterns of *optic flow*. (109, italics in the original)

As the person moves through space, the looming of approaching objects and the regular pattern of optic flow provide the person with information about his/her movement.[18] One need not reason or argue in language that one is a body moving through space; the invariant structure of the visual field provides information about both the wall that one approaches and the body that approaches it. In phenomenological language, one could say that in looming and optic flow, the organization of phenomena in experience constitutes a sense of self that emerges independently of reflexive thought in words. These elements of perception are genuine forms of self-consciousness. Gibson emphasizes that vision is not just a question of the eye and the brain, but of the eye and the brain attached to a head that is part of a body that is situated in an environment (1979, 1). When it occurs, movement through the environment must therefore be considered part of the act of visual perception. In motion, we experience the "putative owner" of our experience—not just individual perceptual phenomena, but the self that is perceiving those phenomena—in optic flow and looming.

Shifting away from visual perception, Bermúdez then presents a sophisticated argument that shows that somatic proprioception is a form of perception and that this sense modality does indeed involve self-consciousness. Building on Gibson and striking Merleau-Pontian themes, he argues that tactile perception, like visual perception, is simultaneously exteroceptive, providing information about the external world, and proprioceptive, providing information about the body (139). Feeling an object with one's hand, for example, one perceives the shape of the object by conforming one's hand to it, and one's awareness of the shape of the object is coterminus with one's awareness of the shape of one's hand. Such "narrow" self-consciousness in somatic proprioception (consciousness of the position of one's anatomy at a given moment) is accompanied by what Bermúdez calls "broad" proprioceptive self-consciousness—one's awareness of one's body as a spatially bounded entity distinct from other objects in the world and unique in that it "is responsive to one's will" (150). Bermúdez argues that to flesh out the notion of broad proprioceptive self-consciousness, we must have a clear vision of how the body is experienced proprioceptively, and he presents a detailed description of the bodily space of propriocieved locations (154–161).

Self-consciousness in vision and somatic proprioception are important phenomena, but there is still a gap between these forms of self-consciousness and self-consciousness in language. Intervening between them is what Bermúdez calls the "nonconceptual point of view" (168), and the next sections of his book explore this notion. At a most basic level, to possess a nonconceptual point of view is to be aware that there is a distinction between one's experiences and the objects to which those experiences point. This does not merely entail the simple distinction between what is self and what is not-self found in somatic proprioception (168–169). In order for a creature to have a nonconceptual point of view, he/she must have a "temporally extended" awareness—what in phenomenology would be called a living present (Husserl [1929] 1964, Ihde 1976). For such a creature, experience does not occur in an infinitely thin moment but continuously extends to include retentions of events in the recent past and anticipations of events in the near future. Without a temporally extended awareness, Bermúdez argues, there is no way that a creature can distinguish between his/her experiences and the objects to which those experiences point. With such an awareness, though, the creature's momentary experience of one facet of an object may be conjoined with an awareness that that object has other facets that have been revealed in the past and may be revealed in the future, and thus the creature may experience phenomena as having autonomy from his/her immediate awareness of them (168–169).[19]

Temporality clearly goes hand-in-glove with spatiality, and to have a nonconceptual point of view is to be aware that one's body is located in a spatial world, a world of places and things that has a permanence and reality beyond one's momentary experience. This awareness is the groundwork upon which basic navigational abilities are built, and Bermúdez cites a variety of experiments with infant humans, dogs, and rats to show that non-language-bearing creatures possess such a point of view. One experiment studied the navigational abilities of Alsatian dogs. Here, the dogs were led to three locations on a field that were distant enough from one another that at any one location, the other two locations were not visible. The three locations formed a triangle, and the first and third of these contained food (215). The dogs were then released from the first location and allowed to get the food. Researchers observed the paths that the dogs took and found that, rather than merely retracing the route that had been shown to them, 96 percent of the dogs went directly from the first point to the third point. The inference Bermúdez draws from this data is that to take the more direct route, the dogs must be aware of space as distinct from their experiences of their paths through it; this in turn implies a point of view and its related forms of self-consciousness. Because dogs are non-language-bearing creatures, Bermúdez argues, such a viewpoint must be independent of language (i.e., it must be a *nonconceptual* point of view), and similar experiments with prelinguistic infant humans are presented to bolster these conclusions.

One final idea in Bermúdez bears upon this chapter, and it comes from the section of Bermúdez's discussion that lays the foundation for his analysis of psychological self-awareness. Tying together the various threads of his argument, Bermúdez argues that, across its many forms, self-consciousness always comes about in a "contrastive" manner (237). "I have a distinguishing self-awareness of myself as ø [i.e., any given feature]," Bermúdez argues, "to the extent that I can distinguish myself from other things that are ø" (238). For example, one's proprioceptive awareness of oneself as a body extended in space emerges through a contrastive awareness that there are other objects extended in space (237); likewise, one's awareness of oneself as a moving body emerges through a contrastive awareness of the world as a space independent of one's experience and through which one can move. Building on these ideas, Bermúdez suggests that psychological self-consciousness in the prelinguistic social interactions of infants comes about in a "contrast space" of self and other. It is well beyond the scope of this chapter to summarize Bermúdez's ideas on this topic here, but the central points are now in place: self-consciousness exists in many forms. While it can take the form of reflexive thought in language, self-consciousness is also present in perceptual experience as a function of the individual's bodily engagement with the world. Perceptual or nonperceptual, self-consciousness emerges in a contrastive fashion.

These ideas have important consequences for the analysis of the organization of attention and for inquiry into self-experience in music studies. In the first section of the chapter, I explored some of the ways in which a person can shift the focus of his/her attention among the various phenomena in experience and along the continuum of gross and fine details of a given perceptual parameter. Allowing the phenomena of the world to enter experience in a meaningful fashion, such organization is a basic feature of perception. But if, as Bermúdez suggests, there is a reciprocity between perception of the world and self-perception, then, I argue, we should also expect that the organization of attention involves a type of self-experience. This is exactly what I want to show here. When we actively shift the focus of attention (for example, from the vocals to the drums, or from gross melodic contour to fine melodic detail), we become aware of ourselves as *organizers* of attention. The first point to consider here is that the act of shifting or maintaining perceptual focus might entail a type of self-experience at all. Following Bermúdez's line of thinking in his discussion of the nonconceptual point of view—a line of thinking inspired by Strawson and, ultimately, Kant (Bermúdez 1998, 165–168)—we can observe that actively organizing attention involves an awareness that there is a distinction between a given phenomenon and our momentary experience of it, and that this in turn entails an awareness of oneself as an experiencer. For a creature to actively shift a phenomenon from the fringe of attention to the focus presupposes that that creature is aware that there is more to that phenomenon in the fringe than its immediate blurry appearance, and that if brought into the focus of attention, that same phenomenon would be present for the creature, only now appearing in sharp detail. Such an awareness of phenomena as distinct entities independent of my immediate experience implies an awareness of myself as the experiencer of the phenomena.

These ideas are valid as an argument about the logical implications of particular types of actions, but to understand how this form of "the self" concretely emerges in experience, to illuminate the structure of this type of self-experience, we must shift over to the mode of phenomenological description. At first blush, one might be tempted to say that as entities change position in the attentional space of foreground and background, one experiences oneself as the force that causes that movement. Such a formulation, however, misinterprets the phenomena. To say that one experiences oneself as the force that causes the movement imagines the self as some kind of invisible hand, picking up phenomena and shifting their position in a field of fringe, focus, and horizon. An explanatory device, this "invisible hand" accounts for self-experience in the focusing of attention in the same highly problematic manner that the humunculus does in accounting for spatial self-experience. Employing either concept, we rightly recognize that a type of self-experience is present in a certain perceptual process. However, assuming that the self must be a thing but finding no self-phenomenon there, we wrongly posit the self as an entity outside of experience that accounts for the process in question. As in our analysis of the humunculus problem, we can get beyond reifying misreadings by seeing that self-experience is present in the lived arrangement of phenomena. In the active focusing of attention, "the self" is not a moving hand that lurks behind experience; to the contrary, we concretely experience our self as the *movement* of the phenomena. When we foreground the vibrato and background the melodic contour, "the self" is present in experience as the shifting of the phenomena in the focus/fringe/horizon field. Even when there is no motion of phenomena between focus and fringe, the fact of graded intensity constitutes a form of self-experience. When a phenomenon stands out in the focus and others lurk in the fringe, I experience myself as their arrangement, as the fact that phenomena are not just present but present in an organized fashion. Though the terminology may be somewhat misleading, I will, for ease of expression, refer to the type of self-experience that comes from the focusing attention as the "attentional self."

The most elaborated discussions of perceptual self-experience in this chapter have relied on the notion of space, and exploring the differing uses of the term "space" here can bring the larger argument into sharp focus. In the first section of the chapter, I used spatial metaphors to describe the organization of attention in musical experience—detail vertigo, the perspectival arrangement of the phenomena of melodic details into a foregrounded focus and a backgrounded fringe. Obviously, the shifting of the focus of attention from gross to fine features is not a movement through "space" in a literal sense of that word. When I hear a stationary guitarist play a melody, I experience the gross melodic interval of a major third and the fine wavering of pitch in vibrato as situated at the same location in lived physical space—the place where the guitarist is standing. However, the literally perspectival organization of phenomena in the lived physical space of the meditation and mountain view examples and the metaphorically "perspectival" organization of phenomena in the attentional "space" of the musical examples are analogous in one key respect: both the literal and metaphoric spaces "contain" phenomena that are greater than our momentary experience of them. In the mountain view example, I see the farmhouse as located at a distant point in space. It appears as dim and lacking in detail, but part of my experience is an awareness that the fuzziness is a function of the farmhouse's location in lived space and is not an inherent feature of the farmhouse itself. In other words, I am aware that the farmhouse is greater than my momentary experience of it. Likewise, in the examples of focusing attention in music, the sound of one element (the fine features of Owens's vibrato, a quiet instrumental part lurking in the musical mix) is located at a distant point in the attentional space of focus, fringe, and horizon. The sound appears dim and lacking in detail, but part of my experience is an awareness that the fuzziness is a function of the sound's location in attentional space and is not an inherent feature of the sound itself. In other words, I am aware that the sound is greater than my momentary experience of it.[20] Literal or metaphoric, space operates in these examples as a container in which multiple phenomena emerge with greater or lesser intensity and in which multidimensional phenomena may exhibit different facets over time. Finally, the graded form of these spaces creates a literal and metaphoric perspective and the concomitant senses of self discussed in detail above.

Three related ideas about the relationship between different modes of self-experience will flesh out this section of the chapter. First, reflexive thought in language (thought in words that refers to the person who is thinking them) is an important type of self-experience that we have discussed little so far. While Bermúdez has shown that self-consciousness may occur in perception alone, it is important to remember that in any given context, language-bearing creatures also have the option of generating self-consciousness through linguistic thought. (For ease of expression, I will refer to this type of self-experience as the "self of reflexive thought.") During music events, the co-occurrence of the self of reflexive thought and the attentional self or other forms of perceptual self-experience is common. For example, beckoned by some softly played guitar part in a dense musical mix—a guitar part invitingly situated at the fringe of experience—I may stop and think, "What was that guitar line? I need to pay closer attention." Here, the presence of the first person singular makes the thought in language a type of self-experience. By the same token, of course, I may fail to think these thoughts entirely and simply focus my attention on the guitar.

Second, in situations where the arrangement of phenomena produces a type of self-experience (i.e., in the spatial self-experience of the meditation and mountain view exercises or the attentional self-experience of the musical examples), the person may foreground the phenomena per se and background the fact of their arrangement, or that person may structure his/her experience in the opposite way, foregrounding the arrangement and back-grounding the phenomena. This dimension of phenomenal organization is important, because it determines the intensity with which the self-experience emerges. The distinction here is a subtle one, and the point will be made clearer with an analogy from visual art. In viewing a Renaissance landscape, I may foreground the quality of the colors used and background the way in which they are arranged on the canvas, or I may foreground the composition as a whole, thus feeling more strongly the intensely spatialized perspective, and background the hues and pigments. In an analogous man-ner, I may in any given experience of arranged phenomena focus strongly on a single phenomenon and background its relationship to other, weakly present phenomena (i.e., background the arrangement of the phenomena). Alternatively, I may focus on a given phenomenon but this time more strongly attend to the relationships among the various phenomena in the field. In either situation, both the phenomena and their arrangement are present in experience (to imagine the absence of one or the other would be like imagining a coin with only one side!), and the relative amount of atten-tion given to one or the other determines the intensity of the self-experience. Foregrounding the phenomena and backgrounding their ar-rangement yields only a dim self-experience, while the reverse yields a strongly present sense of self.

A third point worth noting is that we often experience the organization of phenomena as imposed upon us by the world, rather than as something that we actively control. Interestingly, this imposed organization can also constitute a sense of self. Trying to hear the quiet guitar line in a busy musi-cal mix, I may be distracted and feel my focus irresistibly drawn to the louder vocal and drum parts. In a related vein, it is not unusual for one lis-tening to Baroque polyphony to actively surrender control of the focus and allow the motion of the melodies to draw his/her attention back and forth among the parts. As in the examples we discussed before, the mere fact of perspective constitutes a type of self-experience, and the difference between the active focusing of attention and the focusing of attention imposed by the world is in the agentive or, to modify slightly a term from linguistics, er-gative qualities with which that experience is invested.[21] Lifting a light tray from the kitchen table, my experience of my moving arms will be invested with a quality of ease and responsiveness to will. The addition of a heavy serving dish to the same tray would invest that same lifting gesture with a quality of resistance, and should a 250-pound weight be suddenly dropped on the tray, the lived quality of external compulsion would be present in the experience of my arms and the succeeding dropping motion. Likewise, the movement of phenomena in attentional space may be invested with analogous ergative qualities of ease, effort, or external compulsion. Though freighted with different qualities, all of these cases, however, involve a type of self-experience.[22]

Taken together, these last three points suggests a few of the many different ways in which the self can emerge in experience. In experiences dominated by emphatically perspectival sights or sounds (when taking in a sweeping mountain view or listening to recordings with an exaggerated stereo field), spatial self-experience may emerge strongly. In those situations where attention is very actively managed, or, conversely, where distraction or an active letting go of attention allow the world to push and pull the focus from one phenomenon to the next, the attentional form of self-experience may also come to the fore. When we are less focused on the arrangement of phenomena and more on the phenomena themselves, these forms of self-experience do not disappear entirely but are merely backgrounded. And any of these types of self-experience may, with greater or lesser intensity, be accompanied by the self of reflexive thought. As I have suggested throughout, the organization of attention is best understood as a type of social practice—conduct that is both actively achieved and profoundly informed by situated and larger scale social contexts. Because so much of self-experience is constituted through the organization of attention, the various processes we have explored above must also be thought of as types of social practice. While this chapter has identified some key dynamics in the experience of the self, I do not claim to have cataloged all of the types of self-experience that a person may undergo. On the contrary, my goal has been to suggest that self-experience involves a diverse set of phenomena and that self-experiences are deeply embedded in most forms of perception and action. These ideas can help us to achieve more nuanced perspectives on the role of the self in music and the problem of the musician's or listener's "loss of self" in performance.

Horizon, Music, and Self

In music studies, the loss of self is often discussed in conjunction with the topic of intense musical involvement, and a well-known tool for analyzing this nexus is Mihaly Csikszentmihalyi's notion of "flow." We can best frame our discussion of music and self by briefly exploring his work.

In its broad outlines, *Beyond Boredom and Anxiety* ([1975] 2000), one of Csikszentmihalyi's first fully developed articulations of his theory, argues that flow is the state of consciousness achieved in those situations where the activities required of a person correspond to his/her ability to respond. Neither overwhelmed by calls for action that are too difficult or numerous nor bored by possibilities for action that are too easy or limiting, the person in flow becomes "involved" in the task that immediately confronts him/her. A wide range of activities can lead to flow, and most offer the participant unambiguous goals (which serve to structure his/her conduct) and strong and direct feedback from the environment (which make that conduct involving and meaningful). Highly pleasurable, "flow states" range in intensity from the shallow flow of trivial tasks like doodling or daydreaming (141) to the "deep flow" of more engaging endeavors, and *Beyond Boredom and Anxiety* devotes chapters to the achievement of flow in situations as diverse as chess playing, rock climbing, performing surgery, and dancing to rock music. A range of outcomes can be associated with flow, including the partaking in a task for its own sake, "the merging of action and awareness," and the "loss of self construct."

Discussing this last point, Csikszentmihalyi is careful to emphasize that flow states do not involve unconsciousness, a disassociation from the body, or a complete loss of self.[23] On the contrary, one often has a heightened awareness of one's body and one's actions in flow. What disappears in flow, Csikszentmihalyi argues, is "the self *construct,* the intermediary which one learns to interpose between stimulus and response" (43, emphasis in the original). Citing Freud and Mead, Csikszentmihalyi explains that this "self construct" exists to reconcile one's needs and abilities with the requirements put upon one by the physical and social situation that he/she confronts. While quotes from informants provide evocative descriptions of the loss of the self construct in flow, here Csikszentmihalyi defines the notion of the self construct in terms of the psychological functions that it serves, rather than its lived structure in the experience. Because of this, it is not easy to reconcile Csikszentmihalyi's terminology on this point with my own phenomenological language.[24] Without delving deeply into the phenomenology of psychological functions, it is a reasonable approximation to interpret Csikszentmihalyi as saying that in flow, one ceases to be aware of the sedimented image that one has of oneself as a person. Similar ideas are developed in Csikszentmihalyi's later work. In "The Flow Experience and Its Significance for Human Psychology" (1988), Csikszentmihalyi argues that, as one gets involved in flow activity, one's reflexive awareness of oneself "disappears" (33) and one loses one's "self-consciousness" (34; see also Csikszentmihalyi 1990, 64). Csikszentmihalyi is not explicit about noetic modes through which "self construct" or "self-consciousness" are experienced, but I think that it is plausible to say that, minimally, they would be experienced in the form of reflexive thought in words.[25] Reading these ideas through the theoretical lens I have developed above, Csikszentmihalyi's self construct or self-consciousness is not unlike Bermúdez's psychological self-consciousness and thus is one of the many types of self-experience.

The relevance of Csikszentmihalyi's work to music has not gone unrecognized (see, for example, Herndon and MacLeod 1980, 92–95; Sugarman 1997; Sawin 2002), and while the term "flow" is not always explicitly employed in music studies, the concept has been widely absorbed into the discourses of the social sciences and the humanities. In analyzing intense involvement in music events, though, music scholars have not always been as careful as Csikszentmihalyi to distinguish between the loss of the self construct and a complete absence of all forms of self-experience. In academic as well as popular writing, the "loss of self" in music events is often represented as a blanket phenomenon in which the participant's involvement with sound removes all forms of self-experience. It is here, in helping us to correct these overly broad ideas about the loss of self, that the previous section's discussion of the different forms of self-experience has its utility. Above, I have tried to show the wide range of ways in which "the self" may emerge in the experiences of performers and listeners. Future research should attend to the specific types of self-experience that are heightened or diminished in the performance events of a culture, subculture, or scene and the ways in which those experiences are given meaning and value.

Consider first self-experience in reflexive thought. Reinterpreting in phenomenological terms Csikszentmihalyi's view about the self and involving activity, and applying those ideas specifically to music, we can agree that very often when performers and listeners are deeply engaged in musical activity, they will experience a diminishing of the self of reflexive thought; indeed, in many music cultures, achieving this type of involvement is the goal of the performance. A recent illustration of this type of situation can be found in *Music of Death and New Creation* (1999), Michael Bakan's highly personal account of learning a style of drumming in Bali. There, the author explains that he achieved a breakthrough in his musical skills during a recording session in which he allowed himself to "let go" and stopped trying to control his performance—in other words, when he let his music making commence without actively managing it with reflexive thought. Bakan's description of his breakthrough performance bears many of the marks of deep flow, including an explicit reference to the loss of self (327), and Bakan represents this unique experience as a "transformative moment" (323).

Accounts such as this are indeed compelling. However, there is good reason to believe that reflexive thought and intense musical engagement are not necessarily incompatible, as data from my research with musicians in northeast Ohio illustrate (Berger 1999, 119–173). As I suggested above, the work centered on the organization of attention by performers from four scenes in the area—a heavy metal scene, a commercial hard rock scene, the predominantly European American jazz scene in Akron, and the largely African American jazz scene of Cleveland's east side. All of the musicians whom I interviewed spoke glowingly of those "magic moments" on stage when music making activities proceed in an effortlessly fashion. But while musicians from three of the scenes said that the ideal performance did not involve reflexive thought in words, players from the Cleveland jazz scene had a different view. For them, the best shows involved effortless bodily performance on their instrument accompanied by effortless reflexive thought about the improvisation that was transpiring, effortless planning of improvised parts to be played, and an effortless enactment of those plans. If players in the first three scenes saw reflexive thought as an activity ultimately separate from music making—as a problem-solving tool omitted in those ideal situations where performance is proceeding smoothly— Cleveland's jazzers saw reflexive thought as an integral part of musical activity, as something to which effortless action must obtain. (See chapter four for a fuller discussion of these data.) What these data suggest is not merely that flow and reflexive thought in words may be compatible, but, more importantly, that the elimination of the self of reflexive thought is *not* universally considered to be the highest goal of music making. Reflexive thought is merely one form of self-experience that may be heightened or diminished in the performance events of a given music culture, and this form may be treated as desirable or undesirable.

A second form of self-experience that can be heightened or diminished in performance is what I have called above the "attentional self," and such experiences may emerge either from the organization of attention along a single perceptual dimension or from the organization of attention to the overall situation. As I have illustrated above, the performer's deployment of fine musical details near the horizon of pitch, rhythm, or timbre discrimination, combined with the listener's active, connoisseuristic probing of the fringe in perception, can serve to evoke the attentional self. Of course, even when the performer makes no effort to evoke detail vertigo, audience members bent on critical listening may probe the horizons of any given sensual parameter and heighten the attentional self. The example of a listener trying to hear a quiet guitar part buried in a dense musical mix and the Baroque polyphony example illustrate the emergence of the attentional self in the overall focusing of attention. Both the assertive management of attention (in focusing on an instrument or an element of musical form) and the act of giving one's focus over to the music generate the attentional self, although in these differing contexts that self will emerge freighted with different ergative qualities. Inversely, where attention is centered on the phenomena themselves and not their arrangement in the attentional space, or where the focus shifts so smoothly that one feels as though it is neither actively managed nor assertively pulled about by the phenomena of the world, the attentional self will be backgrounded, but not absented, in experience. A third form of self-experience in performance is the perspectival self of visual or auditory perception. Obviously, those cultures in which music making or listening is typically achieved with closed eyes will eliminate the self of visual perspective. But where music is accompanied by markedly perspectival visual displays (i.e., in the box of an immense opera house or, perhaps more strongly, in listening to music while driving or roller skating), the self of visual perspective may be fostered. As many writers have observed (Ihde 1976, Tagg 1990, van Leeuwen 1999), sound may be differentially deployed in space to heighten the sense of spatial perspective or to dissolve that perspective in an immersive aural field, and these two poles will correspond with a heightening or diminishing of the corresponding forms of self-experience. Finally, somatic proprioception may be increased or decreased by the various types of motion or motionlessness that participants employ in music events of their cultures (dancing, head banging, foot tapping, sitting still), and with these forms emerge accompanying types of self-experience that are beyond the scope of this chapter to analyze.

We can better see how the analysis of self-experience may play out in music scholarship by examining an exchange between Philip Tagg (1994) and Dave Hesmondhalgh (1995) in the "Middle Eight" section of the journal *Popular Music*. In the first piece of the exchange, Tagg argues that rave music may represent a new spirit of anti-individualism in the West. That argument is based on his interpretation of the musical sound and performance events in rave, with special attention focused on a dimension of musical form referred to as ensemble texture—the relationships among the musical elements in a composition, such as melodies, accompanying parts, and so forth. Building on his earlier work (1990), Tagg observes that Western music in the last several hundred years has tended toward ensemble textures made up of a dominant melodic figure and a supporting ground of harmonic and rhythmic accompaniment.[26] By uncovering the significance that a music culture gives to the various elements of the texture and analyzing the formal relationships among those elements, Tagg argues, one may interpret the overall meaning of a given piece or genre and see how that "music encodes patterns of socialization" (217). This approach is primarily applied to rave, a form of electronic dance music with an attendant music scene and type of performance event. To highlight rave's uniqueness, he contrasts rave with heavy metal. Metal, Tagg argues, is a case study in figure/ground textures; with its gruff vocal melodies projected above a noise-rich accompaniment, heavy metal music, Tagg suggests, provides an aural image of a lone individual (represented by the melody) living in a loud, harsh technological world (represented by the accompaniment) and "beat[ing] it on its own terms" (218). In contrast, the ensemble texture of rave music—specifically the subgenres variously referred to as "'techno-rave,' 'techno-house,' 'alternative dance,' or 'progressive dance'" (215)—does not involve a melodic figure and a ground of accompaniment. Instead, there are many, equally important parts, and these, working in combination with other features of the music and the event, make the rave experience a "collective" and "immersive" one. Tagg's semiotic analysis of these two styles serves as part of a larger critique of the "rockology" scholarship of the early 1990s, which argued for music's direct and unmediated impact on the body.

Responding to Tagg in a succeeding "Middle Eight" article, Dave Hesmondhalgh supports Tagg's critique of rockology but disagrees with his interpretation of rave. The idea that rave performances involve a uniquely collective and immersive experience is one key point of contention. Pursuing the issue, Hesmondhalgh asks if heavy metal audiences do not also undergo an ecstatic, collective immersion in performance. By the same token, he asks, might not the raver's dance involve a kind of self-absorbed individualism in which the raver is lost in his/her own entranced world of sound and motion (263)? We should avoid "taking rave discourse at face value" (263), argues Hesmondhalgh, and instead recognize the elements of individualism that are sometimes denied by the scene's explicit ideological statements.

Tagg's and Hesmondhalgh's work can help to illuminate contemporary approaches to the self in music, but before discussing these articles, it is important to note the context in which they appeared. The "Middle Eight" section of *Popular Music* is reserved for short, polemical pieces whose goal, according to the editor's note that preceded Tagg's article, is "inviting controversy and debate" (209). Tagg is careful to caveat the strong positions he takes in this piece by reminding the reader of the polemical nature of the "Middle Eight" venue and framing his ideas about rave as hypotheses to be tested by future research, not as final conclusions. Keeping this in mind, my criticism here is aimed at the approach to questions of self in music that this piece represents, rather than Tagg's piece in specific or his scholarship in general.

To my reading, the crux of the issue is that Tagg's argument posits different types of phenomena in the two subcultures and, as a result, goes on to compare incommensurate things. The discussion of heavy metal makes an argument about the meaning content of the musical sound, while the discussion of rave makes an argument about the overall structure of the raver's experience in the performance event. In other words, the former makes an argument about representations of self and other encoded in musical form, while the latter makes an argument about the full lived experiences of self in performance. Tagg's analysis of heavy metal argues that listeners interpret the melody and accompaniment as icons of the individual and society, and, taken together, these elements encode a larger meaning that the listeners decipher. In the analysis of rave, Tagg seems to suggest that the ensemble texture combines with other elements of the musical form and social context to result in an overall experience for the participants that is immersive and collective. Thus, if I interpret Tagg's phraseology correctly, rave involves not just a set of meanings but the experience of a loss of self in performance. Tagg does not use the term "loss of self" in the article, but, to my reading, the text strongly suggests this idea. Here is a representative passage: "[R]ave is something you immerse yourself into together with other people. There is no guitar hero or rock star or corresponding musical-structural figures to identify with, you just [as a rave participant told Tagg] 'shake your bum off' from inside the music. You are just one of many other individuals who constitute the ground—musical and social—on which you stand" (219).[27] Whether or not Tagg is correct in the details of his interpretation of the scene, it seems to me that he is making an argument about the type of self-experience the ravers undergo, not the meanings that the music encodes for them. It is possible that the self-less experience that they purportedly sustain may, at some later moment, be interpreted by them as the point or meaning of the event. However, this type of "meaning" (the overall significance of the performance deduced after the fact from the quality of one's lived experience) is at least structurally different from the representational meaning posited for heavy metal, and the distinction between these types of meanings is, I believe, one that must be recognized.

The difference between Tagg's analysis of metal and his analysis of rave is parallel to the difference between his ideas about figure/ground in metal and my ideas about the detail horizon. In Tagg's argument, melody and accompaniment represent individual and society; acting as signs, they encode a meaning content that listeners presumably interpret. In my argument, the densely packed details can serve a representative function, commenting on the meaning of the lyrics or other elements of the sound. However, this representative function has nothing to do with the types of self-experience present for the listener. With regard to self-experience, the melodic details do *not* serve a representative function and do not point at meanings; instead, I suggest, they set up a perspectival array in the attentional space of focus, fringe, and horizon that listeners may, or may not, use to constitute a form of self-experience in the culturally specific act of listening. It is possible that Tagg intends to argue only that rave music depicts the loss of self in community and does not involve a loss of self-experience; to my reading, the line between the two is blurry in the text, and beyond the context of these "Middle Eight" pieces, this seems to me a key distinction to make. It is important to note that my argument is not a return to the notion of meanings inherent in musical sound. The heightened attentional self that metalheads may experience in listening is not represented by the music, but neither is it an inherent feature of the sound directly operating on the body. On the contrary, it is the outcome of the listener's culturally specific style of engaging with the sound in the practice of perception.

What the analysis of self-experience in this chapter suggests is a different way into the issues that concern Tagg and Hesmondhalgh, and I would like to close by proposing a set of methodological principles for studying self-experience in music. First, we must be certain to keep separate the different levels of analysis in music research and carefully distinguish between, on the one hand, representations of self and other in the lyrics or musical form and, on the other, lived qualities of self-experience present for the participant in the performance event. Second, as I have suggested above, we must avoid blanket pronouncements about the "loss of self" in music and attend to the many ways in which self-experience may be constituted in the performance event. In the particular case of rave, for example, I can imagine a loss of the self of reflexive thought and a heightening of the self of somatic proprioception. In my own very limited knowledge of electronic dance music, I know that some pieces offer very clearly situated spatial effects while others involve a highly immersive sound field; from the previous discussion, it is clear that these different sound fields may foster or diminish the self-experiences of aural perspective, respectively. Third, we must avoid the tendency to romanticize the loss of self and assume that all music participants seek the ecstatic abandonment of reflexive thought in performance. Such a state may be valued as the most exalted condition an event participant can achieve; however, it may be taken as just one of many goals for performance, or it may be actively avoided as a mindless, or even shameful, loss of self-control. And as John Blacking recognized long ago, we must recall that whatever psychological states music may invoke for its participants, those states are made meaningful in culturally specific ways ([1969] 1995, 34–35). In those scenes or cultures that seek in performance the loss of the self of reflexive thought, the meanings given to such a loss by accompanying linguistic or musical discourses can vary widely. Such a state may be interpreted through a sacred lens as a gift from heaven or through a secular lens as the achievement of a party-hearty spirit. Further, and most importantly, recent work on gender and music by feminist ethnographers such as Jane C. Sugarman (1997) and Patricia E. Sawin (2002) has shown that, in any given culture, both access to flow states and the meanings that are associated with those states are informed by power relations specific to that culture.[28] A rich description of the self-experiences of the performance events of a music culture, subculture, or scene must account for all of the different types of self-experiences that are fostered in performance, the meanings with which they are freighted, and the explicit discourses of self and other that accompany them.

Finally and most importantly, we must keep in mind that the types of self-experience achieved in performance are the outcome of social practices. Self-experience is not imposed on the participant by the musical sound or any element of the event; to the contrary, it emerges from the participant's active, culturally informed engagement with that sound and with that event in perception. Embarking on practice-based research requires us to pay attention to the ways that self-experience is differentially achieved by the various types of participants in the event (performer versus audience, subculturalist versus mundane, critic versus lay listener; participants of varying ethnicities, ages, genders, classes, and so forth) and the differing ways in which the same participants structure experience in the varying event types of their social worlds (rehearsal, performance, recording; the club, the house of worship, the recital hall). Further, an analysis of self-experience that is truly practice based must acknowledge that, on any given occasion, participants are not always able to carry out their intentions (of getting lost in the music, of listening in a critical and reflective manner), and that the organization of experience is a skill that participants develop over time. This ensemble of practices and lived qualities of self-experience—differentially distributed across the participants in a performance event or scene; culturally specific and actively achieved—is the broad empirical domain to which any analysis of "the self" in music must be addressed. Data about "the loss of self in music" have often been invoked to serve the ends of political arguments, and one goal of this chapter has been to clarify the domain of data indicated by that phrase so that fieldwork can proceed in an adequately theorized manner and so that stronger arguments about music and politics can be built. By attending to the specific types of self-experience concretely present for music participants in any given context, we make our work more solidly empirical in its grounding and protect ourselves from the errors of over-reading that are so tempting when dealing with a philosophically resonant concept such as the self. Most of the dynamics and cases that I have examined here are musical ones, but these ideas are, I believe, applicable to dance, verbal art, and other forms of performance as well. Exploring the ways in which "the self" emerges in the lived experience of events, we can begin to gain purchase on one of the most complex and compelling issues in music and performance studies more generally.

CHAPTER FOUR

The Role of Reflexivity in the Aesthetics of Performance

Verbal Art, Public Display, and Popular Music

*

Harris M. Berger and Giovanna P. Del Negro

Three pursuers learn that a fugitive boarded a train for Philadelphia.
To the first pursuer, it's obvious that the fugitive has gone to Philadelphia.
To the second pursuer it's obvious that he left the train in Newark and has
gone somewhere else. To the third pursuer, who knows how clever
the fugitive is, it's obvious that he didn't leave the train at Newark,
but stayed on it and went to Philadelphia. Subtlety chases the
obvious up a never-ending spiral and never quite catches it.

—Rex Stout, *The Silent Speaker*

Could we be much closer if we tried?
We could stay at home and stare into each other's eyes
Maybe we could last an hour
Maybe then we'd see right through
Always something breaking us in two . . .

—Joe Jackson, "Always Something Breaking Us in Two"

Expressive culture is a peculiar thing. Often, when someone tells a story, models their new clothing, or plays music, the listeners, viewers, or audience members have an aesthetic response.[1] Such responses are instantaneous and can be endlessly nuanced and disarmingly potent. Evoking these responses may be the participant's goal in performance, or that evocation may itself be a means toward larger social, religious, or political ends. Yet despite all their power, or perhaps because of it, aesthetic responses are notoriously difficult to describe and analyze. Richard Bauman's classic work, *Verbal Art as Performance* (1977), made a profound contribution to research on aesthetics by helping to ground the study of expressive culture in situated activity and by identifying the unique social dynamics of performance. Building on ideas suggested by Bauman's landmark text, the guiding notion of this paper is that the aesthetics of performance are tightly bound up with the issue of reflexivity—the performer's awareness of herself as a participant in an interaction, his/her signaling of this awareness to others, and the reciprocal phenomena experienced by the audience.

We suggest in the first part of this essay that the question of reflexive awareness is part of the larger problem of the organization of attention in performance events. That is, how one attends to oneself or to the other in performance is part of the larger question of how one arranges all of the diverse elements of one's experience (one's body, thoughts, percepts, memories, and experiences of the other participants) during the event. Using ideas from Edmund Husserl's phenomenology and the writings of contemporary performance theorists, we will examine these issues and discuss the relationship between reflexivity and metacommunication. Data from Berger's fieldwork on the metal, rock, and jazz scenes of northeast Ohio will illustrate that the organization of attention and reflexivity is both actively achieved by the participants and deeply informed by culture and larger social forces. Having explored the dynamics of the organization of attention, we will return again to Husserl and suggest that reflexivity is neither an optional accompaniment to performance nor the domain of highly ironic, fey, or experimental art. On the contrary, the issue of reflexivity is crucial for *all* forms of expressive culture, and even the absence of reflexive thought or explicit metacommunication may contribute to a participant's experience of the meaning of a performance. Examples from Del Negro's fieldwork on the central Italian *passeggiata* (ritual promenade) will show that cultures possess complex and contested ideas about appropriate and inappropriate forms of reflexivity in performance, and that these ideas are fundamental to the overall aesthetics of the performance event.[2] Developing intellectual tools for examining the organization of attention and the reflexive dimension of performance, we hope to gain insights into the ways in which expressive communication achieves its aesthetic effects.

The Notion of Reflexivity, Verbal Art as Performance, *and the Study of Reflexive Language*

One of the main difficulties with the notion of reflexivity is the confusingly wide range of ways in which the term is used. Barbara Babcock has observed that, in its most abstract sense, the term "reflexivity" refers to any kind of doubling back or self-reference (1980, 2), and both she (1980, 1987) and Bauman (1989) have identified three distinct but related contexts in which the term is used. First, it appears in the analysis of language and sign systems. Here, reflexivity refers to the capacity of a language or sign system to refer to itself, and a wealth of terminology has emerged to differentiate various types of reflexive language and language use, including "metacommunication" (communication about communication, Bateson 1972), "metalanguage" (language specifically about language, Bateson 1972), "metanarration" (talk about the act or content of narration in a narrating event, Babcock 1977), "metapragmatics" (talk about language use and the social and communicative functions of language, Silverstein 1976, 48; 1993), and "metafolklore" (folklore about folklore, Dundes 1975). Second, the term has been used in the context of ideas like attention, consciousness, subjectivity, and interaction. Here, reflexivity refers to the capacity of the person not merely to have an experience but to be aware of the fact that he/she is having an experience and to be aware that he/she might be the focus of another's experience. Reflexivity in this sense has interested scholars in a wide variety of areas, including philosophers of the phenomenological tradition (Schutz [1932] 1967; Merleau-Ponty [1945] 1981; Sartre [1943] 1956; Husserl [1931] 1960) and social psychologists (Mead [1934] 1967). We shall use the term "reflexive consciousness" to refer to this type of second (and higher) order awareness. Third, scholars in the tradition of symbolic anthropology (Turner 1969; Geertz 1973) have used the term "reflexivity" to refer to the capacity of participants in rituals or display events to creatively employ stocks of shared cultural knowledge to explore, negotiate, comment on, or transform the culture itself. Beyond these three senses of the word, the term "reflexivity" is also used by scholars concerned with the effect of the scholar's situatedness in history and culture on the practice of fieldwork and ethnographic writing (see, for example, Schutz [1932] 1967, 220; Stone and Stone 1981; Schechner 1985, 55–65; Clifford and Marcus 1986; Feld [1982] 1990; Lawless 1992; Briggs 1993a; Lucy 1993; Solomon 1994; Berger 1999). Such methodological reflexivity is, we believe, a special case of Babcock's second sense of the term, and, in this paper, we will primarily concern ourselves with reflexivity in sign systems and reflexive consciousness.

Many of the key themes in current research on reflexivity and expressive culture were introduced or suggested in Bauman's *Verbal Art as Performance,* and, while some of these ideas are familiar, it will be worthwhile to explore this ground carefully once again.[3] Synthesizing many of the threads of the then-emergent critique of text-based folklore studies, *Verbal Art* laid out the basic structure of the performance event and set the program for future inquiry in this area. There, Bauman's only explicit discussion of reflexivity occurs in his foundational analysis of "keying" or "framing." Bauman explains that one of the many techniques that may be used to mark a stretch of behavior as a performance is explicit disclaimers and denials of performance (1977, 21–22). Remarks such as "I am not really much of a storyteller, but . . ." are often formulaic and serve to indicate that the utterances that follow are not meant to be taken literally but instead as artistic behavior. Explicitly referring to both the speaker and the speech, such remarks are clear examples of reflexive language.

More relevant to the subsequent scholarship and our present concerns is the *implicit* reflexivity suggested in *Verbal Art* and developed more fully in Bauman's later work (1989). Early on in the text, Bauman defines performance as a special type of interaction in which the performer assumes "responsibility to an audience for a display of communicative competence" (Bauman 1977, 11). Following earlier scholars, he goes on to explain that performance is always framed—introduced by metacommunication that establishes the behavior as a performance. While the act of framing may be brief, backgrounded, or taken for granted by the participants in a performance event, framing informs all of the behavior that follows and constitutes that behavior as performance. Such a perspective places implicit reflexive language and reflexive consciousness at the center of performance theory in two ways. First, as behavior specially framed for public scrutiny, performance draws attention to the fact that the performer is a participant in an interaction and the focus of the audience's attention. Second, the act of establishing the performative frame refers to the communicative practice itself and thus, at least implicitly, to the performer. More important, these features of performance blur the boundary between reflexive language and reflexive consciousness. Framing, like all metacommunication, *invokes* the reflexive consciousness of the participants. Whereas the performer may be unaware of himself/herself as an actor at the moment before the framing takes place, the act of framing, by definition, marks the performer as a performer, marks the audience members as audience members, and calls attention to the fact of interaction. In his 1989 *Encyclopedia of Communications* entry on performance, Bauman makes the connections among the types of reflexivity more explicit. Not only does the formal framing of the behavior invoke reflexive consciousness, he suggests, but the heightened attention to the performer's communicative competence foregrounds the expressive resources of the culture, which in turn makes performance the ideal instrument of reflexive commentary on that culture. These insights are important to our present concerns because they suggest that implicit reflexive language is a constitutive and unavoidable feature of performance (see the discussion of Bauman in Lucy 1993, 21).

Since Bauman's text first appeared, this vision of reflexivity has informed research on folklore and other forms of expressive culture in two ways. First, performance theorists have long sought to demystify the rhetorical power of verbal art by laying bare the mechanics of performance, and the explicit or implicit analysis of reflexive language has played a crucial role here. Building on the work of Alan Dundes (1975), Barbara Babcock's 1977 article on metanarration (reprinted as a supplementary chapter in the book form of *Verbal Art*) set the stage for much of this research. There, Babcock called on scholars to seek the power of folk narrative in the social interactions of the narrative performance, rather than in the narrative text alone. Case studies by scholars of folklore such as Briggs (1993b), Butler (1992), Allen (1991), Moore (1993), Parmentier (1993), and Bauman himself (1986) have illustrated how performers use metacommunicative techniques such as framing in, framing out, indexical reference to tradition or the situated context, direct and indirect speech, code switching, and various types of metapragmatic commentary to claim the floor, garner the authority to perform, assess their interlocutor's level of cultural knowledge, draw the audience into their performance, and establish the legitimacy of their narrative. Richard J. Parmentier's careful study of a political speech in Belau, Micronesia, is a case in point. He presents an ethnopoetic transcription of a particularly powerful example of political oratory and shows how the speaker creatively employs metapragmatic comments about the speech, carefully framed reported speech, stock phrases, and embedded narratives to make the audience interpret a recent historical event in ways the narrator finds politically advantageous. Like all of this literature, Parmentier shows that it is reflexive language that frames discourse as performance and links the discourse to situated and larger social contexts.

Reflexive language has also been important in the analysis of what is sometimes referred to as "subject positioning." In performance theory, case studies such as those by Kratz (1990), Allen (1991), and Solomon (1994) do not merely show that performers use reflexive language to comment upon the identity of the participants in the event; such authors also illustrate how reflexive language actually "positions" the participants, implicitly locating the performers or audience members in the social world of the event and the larger society.[4] Corrine Kratz's careful analysis of girls' initiation rituals among the Okiek of Kenya illustrates this line of inquiry. In the rituals, the girls and their close relatives trade off lines of sung verse in a long performance that precedes a harrowing clitoridectomy. Kratz shows how the girls are placed in the center of the performance event and situated in the larger community by the relatives' use of call and response patterning, emotionally resonant kinship terms, and carefully orchestrated meta-pragmatic exhortations to complete the ritual. Such positioning devices, Kratz argues, account for the ritual's persuasive power.[5]

The great advantage of contemporary analyses of reflexivity is that they allow us to look at a key set of mechanisms by which performance is achieved; building on this work, we want to suggest three new directions for research. One difficulty we find with much of the contemporary performance studies research on reflexivity comes in its privileging of reflexive *language*.[6] As we have seen, the reflexive capacity of language is responsible for establishing the performance frame and achieving many of the performance's expressive effects. But this reflexive capacity is not unique to language; as Barbara Babcock (1980) suggests, all sign systems have the potential for self-reference. As a result, key performance functions can be accomplished and the participants can be positioned through nonlinguistic sign systems or through the interaction of linguistic and nonlinguistic dimensions of the expressive act. For years, folkloristic ethnographers and folklife scholars (for example, Glassie 1982; Toelken 1979; Yoder 1976) have argued that we must attend to nonverbal lore and the integration of various expressive genres in the performance event. While performance theorists have examined nonverbal performance (Fine 1984; Schechner 1985; Stoeltje 1988; Kapchan 1994; Sugarman 1997), most performance-based analyses have focused on language, and research can only benefit by more richly exploring the nonverbal elements of performance.

A second opportunity for new perspectives flows from a different concern of post-1960s folklore scholarship—the creative nature of interpretation. Since the 1970s, performance scholars such as Kirshenblatt-Gimblett (1975), Briggs (1993b), Parmentier (1993), and Solomon (1994) have illustrated how the subjectivity of authors and performers is not determined by the linguistic resources of their language but how authors and performers creatively employ those resources to serve their larger ideological needs. What has been given less attention is the audience's practices of interpretation.[7] Thomas Solomon's study of insult exchanges in Bolivian song duels (1994) comes close to the issue of interpretation by illustrating how the singer's improvised insults interpret and criticize the disparaging innuendo suggested by his/her (for the sake of simplicity, let us say, her) opponent's previous remarks (in this connection, see also Briggs 1993b); however, a more direct focus on audience members (as suggested by Solomon's postscript) can help us to appreciate the importance of the audience in the reception of reflexive language. No performance or text is so explicit, clear, or forceful that audience members do not play some role in the constitution of their experience of its meaning. While reflexive language can play a positioning function, audience members may embrace, misinterpret, or creatively resist the positioning promoted by the performer (Sawin 2002, 44). Further, the actions of performers are situated within the larger environment of the event, and audience members must actively organize their attention to that event, shifting focus among sense perceptions, thoughts, feelings, bodily sensations, and the various elements of the performance event. As Berger has suggested (1997, 1999), the organization of phenomena in experience plays a key role in expressive culture, and here we hope to show the importance of these interpretive dimensions of reflexivity for performance. In our view, reflexive signs alone do not determine one's reflexive awareness of oneself as a participant in an interaction; such reflexive consciousness comes about through a complex interplay between the performer's creative deployment of expressive resources (including reflexive signs) in performance conduct and the audience member's practices of interpretation. None of this, of course, is to argue for a return to the transcendent subject that is merely described by communication and exists independent of history or society. On the contrary, examining the dialectics of performance and interpretation can only help to reveal how lived experience is situated in history and society.[8]

Finally, and most important to the overall aims of this paper, we hope to suggest new ways in which reflexivity is important for the aesthetics of performance. Performance theorists have tended to see reflexive language primarily as a device for connecting text to situated context (Butler 1992), indexing tradition (Foley 1992), or negotiating the performers' roles (Briggs 1993b). Other authors have suggested that the exchange of reflexive signs themselves may be the focus of aesthetic evaluation (Stone 1982, 97–121; 1988; Silverstein 1993, 52, 54). While these indexical mechanics and aesthetics are important, our main goal here is to show that the *reflexive metacommentary by which a performer signals her awareness of herself as a participant in an interaction—and by which she signals her awareness of the audience's attention to her—colors and informs all of the "primary" communication in the performance and plays a crucial role in the overall aesthetics of the event.* Further, each culture, subculture, or participant has an aesthetic ideology of reflexivity—a specific set of ideas about the kinds of reflexive stances that are appropriate and desirable in a given type of performance event.

Our perspective has affinities with Roman Jakobson's Prague school semiotics. In his "Closing Statement" in *Style in Language* (1960), Jakobson argued that the communicative act is comprised of six distinct dimensions (or functions), one of which is metacommunication; all six dimensions occur at once, and while the relative importance of any one dimension may vary from situation to situation, the full meaning of any utterance is a gestalt (synthetic whole) of these various dimensions.[9] Like the framing devices that Bauman identifies, implicit or explicit commentary on the performer's or audience's attention to themselves and to each other is one kind of information that is transmitted along Jakobson's metacommunicative dimension. Because the various dimensions of the communicative act make up an indivisible whole, such signaling of reflexive consciousness informs the overall aesthetic and rhetorical effects of the communication.

The dialectics of metacommunication and reflexive consciousness are endlessly rich and complex. Metacommunicative signals of reflexive consciousness may be foregrounded or backgrounded in the ongoing process of interaction; they may be intentionally or unintentionally exchanged and may depict the participant's reflexive consciousness with varying amounts of honesty or deceit. And, as we suggested above, while reflexive signs may invoke reflexive consciousness, such signs are also actively interpreted, and the interpretation of these signs plays a key role in determining the meaning that is finally experienced. To gain a richer understanding of this situation, we must see that reflexive consciousness is not merely plentiful or even vital but is in fact a *dimension* of experiences of interaction; foundational to all forms of interaction, the issue of reflexivity plays a role in the experienced meaning of performance, even in the absence of explicit metacommunication or reflexive consciousness. Bauman (1989) and Caton (1993) have both observed that one pathway to understanding reflexive consciousness can be secured through the writings of George Herbert Mead and the Chicago school of social psychology. While Mead's writings are indeed important, phenomenological work on the subject and intersubjectivity can provide a different route to these insights.

The Body, the Subject, and Intersubjectivity in Husserl's Fifth Cartesian Meditation

Taken as an object of serious consideration, the idea of experiencing an other is paradoxical and enigmatic. Our experiences seem, by definition, to be our own and to be personal. How can it be, and what does it mean to say, that I experience an other subject? This problem is a more general statement of what, in Martha B. Kendall's felicitous expression, is the primary paradox of language and of dialogue: "How can your words be in my head?" (personal communication, 1988). Such a paradox is both a central problematic and a sustaining phenomenon in the study of performance, folklore, and expressive culture in general. To understand one phenomeno-logical approach to this problem, a small amount of background is in order. Responding to difficulties in idealist philosophy, Edmund Husserl sought to overcome the sharp and worrisome distinction that past philoso-phers have drawn between experience and reality. To do so, he said, we must place an *epoché* (set of brackets) around any claims that a particular ex-perience is subjective or objective and investigate the data of experience in an unprejudiced manner. When we return to experience in this way, Hus-serl suggests, we make a startling discovery: nothing has changed. Strictly as lived experience, the desk before me, for example, is a genuine other, an autonomous entity in no way subject to my whims. As a result, we never need to remove the phenomenological brackets. The world—as autono-mous and subject to rational inquiry as we know it to be—is there in and for experience. This is not to say, of course, that I cannot misdescribe my experience or that one momentary experience of the world exhausts all of its complexity and possibilities. When we examine the world in experience, it is given to us in direct evidence that the world possesses endless contin-gent details. That there is a world, however, and that that world is there for experience, is given with certainty.

It would first seem that such a philosophy, grounded radically in one's own experience, could never come to terms with the existence of others, let alone provide insights into the reflexive awareness of one's self as a partner in an interaction. This serious concern—that phenomenology might be a kind of solipsism—is central to Husserl's *Cartesian Meditations* ([1931] 1960) and is explored at length in the well-known Fifth Meditation (89–150). Later existential phenomenologists took exception with elements of Husserl's discussion, and we will not take the time to recapitulate his dense and technical argument here.[10] While largely abandoned by Jean-Paul Sar-tre ([1943] 1956), elements of Husserl's argument were carried over by Maurice Merleau-Ponty ([1945] 1981). Interpreting Husserl in the existen-tial spirit of Merleau-Ponty, we will review ideas from Husserl's discussion of the body and space relevant to the problem of reflexivity.[11]

Seeking a direct and unprejudiced inquiry based strictly on the givens of experience, Husserl says that if we are going to address the problem of the other, we must create a second *epoché;* within it, all one can admit are expe-riences that are one's alone. When one applies this *epoché*—what Husserl calls the reduction to the "sphere of own-ness"—one discovers that one's body is uniquely experienced as one's self. Explicit in his rejection of Carte-sian mind/body dichotomies, Husserl observes that one experiences one-self not solely as a consciousness that constitutes experience but as an "em-pirical ego"; this "empirical ego" is referred to by Husserl in other places as an "animate organism" and is experienced as a "psycho-physical unity" (Hammond, Howarth, and Keat 1991, 213)—a body whose actions and responses are one's own. After elaborating upon what it means to experience one's self as a body in the world, Husserl goes on to explain that it is through our embodied nature that we understand the existence of others. When I see the body of another person, I have what Husserl calls an "analogical apperception"—an experience of that other body not merely as an object but as another *subject, another entity who has experience.* Apperception occurs in all instances in which someone recognizes a thing as one of a type, and, confusingly, it does *not* consist of reasoning by analogy, nor is it even a "thinking act" ([1931] 1960, 111). Husserl illustrates this with the situation of a child learning about scissors; once the concept of "scissors" is assimilated, each later act of experiencing an object as scissors happens in a prereflective manner. The child grasps the basic sense of the concept of scissors (which we can roughly describe as a thing that uses opposable motion to cut), and, confronted with kitchen shears or any other double-bladed cutter, the child constitutes them in experience as scissors. Apperception occurs in any experience of things as examples of a type, but the apperception of other subjects is unique. The type "subject" emerges from the most primordial level of our experience—the sphere of own-ness. While I recognize the individuality of my own subjectivity and the individuality of you as a subject, as subjects, your body and mine are inherently "paired" in experience. One implication of this idea is that the concept "subject" establishes the apperception of both "self" and "other," that the subject is not radically my own but inherently social.[12] As a result, our awareness of others as subjects and ourselves as a subject in a social world is at the very foundation of experience.[13]

Just as Husserl's account of the subject emerged from an examination of experiences of the body, Husserl's account of social interaction emerges from a discussion of the experience of space. Early in the Fifth Meditation, Husserl explains that we experience the world as inherently intersubjective. When I (Berger) look at a physical object, I directly experience the surfaces that face me; I don't, of course, experience the details of its back (the color and texture of the back of this desk, for example), but I am aware that the back is there and would be available for future viewing. For example, when I look at this table, I directly experience its brown color and the grained texture of its wooden front. I do not directly experience the details of the back of the desk, but, as I look at the front, I experience the fact that it has a back that could be the object of my future experiences. While I can't know the color, texture, or any other contingent details of the back of the desk without moving my body, the fact that it has a back is part of my experience as I look at its front. In Husserl's terminology, the back of the desk is "presentiated" to me. Two important ideas stem from this analysis. First of all, the fact that the physical world admits other perspectives is important because it shows that the physical world is an intersubjective world. Built into my experience of the physical world is an awareness that it possesses surfaces and features that are beyond my immediate grasp but may become the focus of future experiences—for myself at some other point in time or for others situated at a different location in the same space. Second, the notion of presentiation applies not only to the other facets of physical objects but to the experiences of others. In the same way that my experience of the front face of the desk presentiates the existence of the back of the desk, so does the body of the other presentiate a realm of particular experiences to which I do not have direct access but that I know with certainty is there.[14]

Taken together, the analysis of the body and of space shows that experience is, at its base, social, and the complex dialectics of self and other that stem from this fact form the basis of our phenomenology of intersubjectivity and performance. While I cannot know all of the details of the other's experience, I do know that she is a subject in a world of subjects, and I have the potential to partially share some of her particular experiences. While there is a world of contingent facts about the other that I may not know, I *do* know that she is a subject in the world, that she experiences the world from a particular perspective in space, and that those experiences are never complete. In sum, I cannot know all the details of the other's experience, but I can know the most abstract structure of her subjectivity, and I have the potential to partially share her particular experiences. Though Husserl's insistence on the centrality of the subject in philosophy may sound like an older, problematic form of idealism, his grounding of subjectivity in the body in the Fifth Meditation, and Merleau-Ponty's more elaborated body phenomenology ([1945] 1981), both serve to situate the subject in the physical and social world.

Moving from Husserl's philosophy to more social-scientific concepts, we can observe that with the awareness that the other is a subject comes the awareness that any of the other's actions may be signs. Those signs become part of the dialectic of intersubjectivity, facilitating or obfuscating the partial sharing of specific experience in the complex ways with which scholars of expressive culture are so familiar. While two people can never completely share an experience, making connections between your specific experiences and mine—in Alfred Schutz's celebrated terminology, "partial sharing" ([1932] 1967)—is possible. Schutz's massive *Phenomenology of the Social World* presents a systematic attempt to account for the dynamics of partial sharing. Brilliant yet in some ways problematic, his analysis goes beyond the needs of the present essay. Here we need only observe that between your experience and mine develop concrete conjunctures and disjunctures, reciprocities and linkages, similarities and differences.

Mediating between these general phenomenological ideas about the nature of the subject and the various ways in which a particular subject may experience herself at any given moment are the factors of "attention" (the arrangement of phenomena in experience) and reflexivity.[15] In everyday experience, the subject is confronted with a world dense with phenomena. Numerous individual experiences vie for her attention, and the physical context that surrounds her exists as a kind of potential experience. Emotions, thoughts, sights, smells, tastes, and so forth bombard the subject, and, at each moment, she organizes this motley of phenomena into a dynamic structure of foreground and background (Berger 1997, 1999). For example, as I (Berger) work on this paragraph, my thoughts are foregrounded while my typing hands and the sensation of hunger in my stomach are backgrounded. These varied phenomena form a gestalt, mutually informing one another in the same way that figure and ground do in painting. While only an expert meditator can manipulate the shape of experience willy nilly, all subjects have some control over the organization of attention. As I type, for example, I constantly focus my attention, now foregrounding my typing hand as I feel for a pen in my desk drawer, now focusing on the ideas for the upcoming sentence, now actively backgrounding the distraction of my hungry stomach.

Our ability to organize the phenomena of experience is crucial for the constitution of reflexive consciousness in its various forms, and here we can begin to tie together the various threads of the discussion so far. George Herbert Mead ([1934] 1967) observed that in situations of effortless activity, experiences move from one to the next with little or no reflexive thought; when we confront a difficulty, we stop to think, and this series of linguistic thoughts constitutes a reflexive "me" distinct from the acting "I." Connecting the contemporary analysis of language to Mead's classic model, Steve C. Caton (1993) has maintained that Mead's "me" is tied to forms of reflexive language such as shifters, performatives, and reported speech. The "me" thus formed is a constant accompaniment to our social-psychological life, and it is suggested in Caton's text that greater or lesser amounts of explicitness in reflexive language map to a more or less foregrounded self in experience. Interpreting these ideas in the terminology of our chapter three, one might say that reflexive thought in language (thought that involves the first person pronoun) is one of the many possible forms of self-experience (specifically, what that chapter calls the "self of reflexive thought"), and it is indeed true that the employment of reflexive language does operate in this way. But as we saw in chapter three, self-experience is tied to other types of experience as well; some forms of self-experience emerge from perceptual processes, and the organization of attention plays a key role in the particular form that any given instance of self-experience may take. While all persons have the ability to actively organize the elements of their experience, performers (verbal artists, musicians, *passeggiata* participants) are particularly adept at these skills.[16] As we will illustrate, good musicians know how to control the "talking voice inside the head," quieting reflexive thought and losing themselves in the procession of musical sounds or invoking that reflexive voice to solve problems on stage. Finally, while the performer's use of reflexive language in performance may inform the constitution of the audience's reflexive consciousness, nonverbal communication and the audience's active interpretation also play key roles.

All of this leads us to the threshold of our analysis of the foundational role of reflexivity in the aesthetics of performance. Husserl's Fifth Meditation shows that when it is physically present to me, the phenomenon of the body of the other is directly experienced as a subject—an entity that has experience. This idea can easily be misunderstood, and at the risk of belaboring this point, we will specify exactly what this formulation does and does not imply. To say that I experience the body of the other as a subject is *not* to say that I can perfectly understand the other's experiences. It is certainly the case that in any given situation I may fail to even partially share any of the other's individual experiences. We *do* wish to say that when I experience the body of the other, I experience that body as an entity that has experience and that I may partially share those experiences. Further, to say that I experience the body of the other as a subject is not to say that, when I see her, I must form a reflexive thought in words (such as "That is an experiencing subject"), nor is it even to say that such an idea must be logically implicit in the content of such thoughts. We do wish to say that when I see the body of the other, I "see it as" a subject in the same way that, when confronted with a double-bladed cutter, I may "see it as" scissors—independent of whether or not I accompany such "seeing as" with reflexive thought.

The relevance of these ideas for interaction in general, and for the aesthetics of performance in particular, is substantial. First, it is clear that the type of phenomenon called "subject" is an inherently reflexive phenomenon. To see a body as a subject is to see that body as an entity that can have experience, that can potentially experience me, and so forth. Those situations in which I perceive present others as subjects are referred to as social interactions, and to be involved in social interaction is thus to be in an inherently reflexive situation. The adumbration of this statement directly parallels our earlier discussion. To say that interaction is an inherently reflexive situation is not to say that each participant must actively engage in reflexive thought or explicit metacommunication at each (or any) given moment of the interaction. It is only to say that for any interaction between two or more participants (A, B, and so forth), A's understanding of the meaning of B's actions will always be informed by A's grasping of B as a subject; likewise, A will be aware that the meaning of her own actions for B will be informed by B's grasping of her (A) as a subject. Just as values along each of Jakobson's six metacommunicative dimensions inform the overall meaning of any given communication, the overall meaning of one's actions (for oneself or another) is informed by the inherently reflexive nature of the type "subject."

Performance is a subcategory of interaction and is thus inherently reflexive. Again, the adumbration of this idea parallels our previous discussion. Here, we are not saying that all participants must engage in reflexive thought or explicit metacommunication for their performances to be meaningful; it is clear that in any given event, any performer may or may not enact specific, contingent acts of reflexivity. What we do wish to say is that to be a participant in a performance is to see the other as an entity who has experience, and all of one's conduct will be read in terms of this basic understanding—whether or not it is acknowledged in a specific act of explicit metacommunication or echoed in a given instance of reflexive consciousness. It is clear that in performance, any kind of overt reflexive signaling of one's attention to the interaction will play a part in the overall meaning of one's conduct for the other participants. But it should also be emphasized that, because one is seen as a subject, even one's failure to metacommunicatively signal one's awareness as a participant in an interaction will have significance for the other's interpretation of one's conduct.

For this reason, we say that reflexivity is a *dimension* of interaction in general and performance in particular. When, for example, an audience cheers a virtuosic lick in the middle of a rock guitarist's solo, that guitarist may scream out her thanks to the crowd, subtly nod her head to acknowledge the applause, repeat a chordal vamp to take up time until the crowd noise settles down, or stare into space and completely fail to acknowledge the audience's metacommunicative signaling of their enjoyment of the music. Such responses will play a part in the audience's interpretation of the guitarist's conduct. The guitarist is free, of course, to engage in any kind of metacommunication that she so chooses; what she cannot do is escape the reflexive dimension of interaction, as even the total failure to acknowledge the audience will be read as part of the meaning of her conduct.

When plotting points in a two-dimensional space (X,Y), a zero value along one of the axes (0,4 or 7,0) does not mean that that point has no value along that dimension; the zero value is simply one location in the space. Like the X and Y axes of two-dimensional space, reflexivity is a dimension of experiences of interaction, and because of this even the absence of meta-communication on the part of a performer may have significance for an audience's interpretation of the meaning of an event. In Bauman's important 1989 article, reflexivity is seen as significant for performance on a variety of levels (the formal, the social-psychological, and the cultural). Building on his work, we hope to have used Husserl to show how and why the issue of reflexivity is not merely important for but actually necessary to performance, independent of any contingent enactment of reflexivity in thought or action in any given event.

Even briefly considering the example of a musician ignoring an audience's applause, it is obvious that the significance given to particular forms of reflexivity depends heavily on the cultural context of the performance and the interpretive practices of the participants. Such cultural dynamics are crucial to understanding the role of reflexivity in performance, and we shall take them up in detail below. But before we examine how reflexive attention is deployed in performance, it will be helpful to explore how attention in general is managed and the diverse elements of experience are organized by audience members and performers. Like reflexivity, the organization of phenomena in the participant's experience is profoundly influenced by culture. In fact, this organization is a type of social practice, an element of the social world that is both informed by situated and large-scale contexts and actively achieved. We will use the term "organization of phenomena" to refer to the culturally specific ways in which the participant of a performance event arranges the various elements in her experience. We will use the terms "organization of attention in an event" to refer to the typical patterns of partial sharing among the participants in a performance event and "ideology of attention" to refer to ideas about partial sharing that participants employ there. Some examples from Berger's research (1997, 1999) will illustrate these concepts.

The Social Organization of Attention in Metal, Rock, and Jazz

In his fieldwork, Berger has explored the onstage experiences of four groups of musicians in northeast Ohio: Cleveland's African-American jazz musicians, largely in their thirties, whose styles are related to the post-bop jazz of players such as McCoy Tyner or Chick Corea; Akron's European

American jazz musicians, largely in their forties and fifties, whose styles are related to the post-bop jazz of George Shearing or the Modern Jazz Quartet; Cleveland's commercial hard rockers, largely in their twenties, whose styles are related to those of bands like Def Leppard or Poison; and Akron's underground heavy metal musicians, also largely in their twenties, whose styles range from those of well-known metal bands like Pantera to those of death metal bands like Morbid Angel who have a more circumscribed audience. For ease of expression, we will use the capitalized term "Rock" to refer collectively to the commercial rock and metal scenes and "Jazz" to refer collectively to the two jazz scenes; this usage will refer specifically to these two pairs of scenes in northeast Ohio and is not intended to indicate rock or jazz in general.

As a phenomenological ethnographer, Berger's goal is to richly share the experiences of his research participants and understand the social processes by which those experiences are structured. One stage of his inquiry focuses on how the participants arrange the various elements in their experience. In performance, the musician is presented with an enormously wide range of phenomena — the sound of her instrument, the sounds of the other players, the audience, and her own bodily sensations, thoughts, feelings, fantasies, and so forth. If the performance is to be successful, these phenomena cannot merely emerge in experience but must be organized; that organization is profoundly informed by the situated context of performance and the musician's immediate musical goals and larger social projects — in short, the practical world of her music scene.

In discussions about the organization of phenomena in experience with the musicians, a wealth of information has emerged, and here we will only focus on those data immediately relevant to our larger concerns. As Mead observed ([1934] 1967; see also Schutz 1976, 64), the organization of experience is practical, and, comparing across all of the musicians, certain commonalities were clear. For example, all of the musicians said that, in an ideal performance, the sound of the music inhabited the foreground of their experience. In most performances, however, problems arise, and when they do, other phenomena vie for the center of attention. For example, all of the musicians said that, ideally, the body should lurk in the background of experience; only when the player is physically incapable of performing a desired part does the body become foregrounded. Across the scenes, those players that push the envelope of their bodily capacity are the ones most likely to be aware of their bodies in performance. For example, the heavy metal drummers explained that long passages of sixteenth notes on the bass drums can be a tough workout for the legs; when playing a particularly demanding passage toward the end of a performance, the drummer's feet and calves may get tired, and these aching limbs inevitably steal into the center of the player's experience. Similarly, the Jazz pianists explained that they are constantly pushing the limits of their physical technique; if their fingers feel weak or stiff, they become focally aware of their hands and are forced to adjust their improvisations to compensate.

While some problems in performance are common to all the musicians, many are specific to each scene, as are the techniques of organizing attention that the musicians employ to correct them. With the cheap amplification found at Rock bars, for example, the Rockers often had a hard time hearing the other musicians in the band. The drummer's playing, however, is almost always audible onstage, and the non-drummer Rock musicians focus on the drums to coordinate their performance with that of the inaudible band members. Following the drummer's tempo and using her parts to guide them through the song's form, the Rockers used their drummer as an implicit conductor and would frequently supplement this conducting by conjuring in imagination the musical lines that were absent in perception. While audibility was a far less frequent concern for the Jazz musicians, occasionally the achievement of basic coordination with the other musicians became an issue. Ideally, all of the members of the band agree on the chord changes and have synchronized their tempi; in such a situation, each player's attention is free to flit effortlessly among the elements of the band's sound, now foregrounding one instrument, now the next. Occasionally, however, the chord changes, tempo, or voice leading do become problematic, and when this happens, the Jazz musician must actively manage her experience. For example, Jazz bassists and drummers feel a special responsibility for maintaining a constant and swinging tempo; if they detect a problem, bassists and drummers will "lock in" on one another, mating the sound of their own instrument with that of their partner and holding the two at the center of their attentions to correct the rhythmic difficulty. Such a technique of organizing attention was basic to Jazz but is used only sporadically in Rock. In sum, while each music scene has its own set of typical problems and techniques of attention, the fact of attending to the problematic is true of all scenes.

Some features of the organization of attention, however, cannot be captured under such a universal rubric. For example, the Akron jazzers, the commercial hard rockers, and the metalheads all explained that their onstage experience was ideally composed of a moving stream of sounds and that they would actively engage in reflexive thought in language only if a problem presented itself in the performance. Any kind of thinking that didn't solve a problem on the stage was treated as a distraction, and players from these three scenes made an effort to quiet such thoughts or move them to the margins of their experiences. For example, should the bass player in an Akron jazz combo relentlessly rush the tempo on a particular song, the other members of the band would commonly accompany their perceptual experiences of the event with reflexive thoughts, weighing the options of whether to follow the bass player to her new tempo or to stick with the original pace of the tune. Likewise, should a rock or metal guitarist extend his solo beyond its usual limits, the other players might try to decide if they should move back to the verse or continue through another round of the solo's chord changes. In either case, the procession of perceptual phenomena is accompanied by a procession of reflexive thoughts that often takes the shadowy form of abbreviated mental words and ideas, a form familiar to each of us from our mundane experience. The main point here is that for the Rock and Akron jazz musicians, such thought is strictly a means to an end.

As mentioned in chapter three, this attitude does not hold true for the Cleveland jazzers. Like the players from the other scenes, these musicians actively engage in reflexive thought if there is a problem on the stage. Unlike the players from the other scenes, however, the Cleveland jazzers would also engage in reflexive thought even when there are no immediate problems. On an ideal night, these players would often accompany the effortless procession of perception and performance with an effortless procession of reflexive thought in words; such thoughts may map out the overall form of a solo or plan chord substitutions, rhythmic superimpositions, instrumental techniques, or other devices. The players said that while they enjoy getting lost in the music, and while the emergence of thoughts should never occur at the expense of attention to the sound, effortless, creative reflexive thought can make for a great performance and is a pleasure in itself. Such reflexive practices (the constitution of what we called in chapter three the "self of reflexive thought") are deeply influenced by the larger goals for music making that are found in the Cleveland jazz scene, goals that are an anathema to the more romantic ideologies of the Rockers and Akron jazzers. Whether pro- or anti-reflexive, musicians from all scenes agreed that the organization of phenomena in experience has an active component. While Cleveland jazzers enjoy both reflexive and non-reflexive performances, they can exert a level of control over their reflexivity, quieting the procession of thoughts if they want a more direct performance and conjuring that procession if they fancy a more cerebral approach; similarly, the anti-reflexive Akron jazzers and Rockers spoke of actively silencing the reflexive voice and losing themselves in the stream of musical sound.

These data bear powerfully on the complex interplay of contextual forces and agency in the achievement of performance, and it will be worth our while to briefly explore this issue. Since at least the mid-twentieth century, one prominent strand of discourse about jazz has sought to depict that tradition as an elite music that constantly strives to break older stylistic boundaries and explore new formal structures. Such an attitude is informed in complex ways by both the Western European classical traditions and the dynamics of race in America. The Cleveland jazzers' prizing of reflexive thought in performance is of a piece with this larger art music ideology. But while the musicians' attitudes are informed by these larger social and ideological contexts, they are not determined by them, and the practices of reflexivity are not accomplished by them. In fact, the musicians' agency in the constitution of the performance is manifested in several different ways and on several different time scales.

On the time scale of an individual performance, the Cleveland jazzers actively choose whether or not to lose themselves in the ongoing musical sound or to accompany their performance with reflexive thought. When they do engage in this form of reflexivity in performance, those thoughts can never become the sole focus of experience; on the contrary, attention to reflexive thought must be carefully and actively balanced against attention to the musical sound if the player is to achieve an effective performance. On the time scale of their overall musical careers, the Cleveland jazzers work hard to hone and develop their improvisatory skills. Endlessly rehearsing scales, arpeggios, rhythmic approaches, stock phrases, and other devices, these musicians seek to have so profoundly assimilated the raw materials of improvisation that they may a-reflexively spin out improvised parts or engage in reflexive thought without having their planning disrupt the act of performance.[17] Finally, while the jazzers' attitudes toward reflexivity are deeply informed by larger social contexts, they are not the static product of an underlying art music ideology. Paul Berliner (1994) has shown that, over time, jazz musicians not only develop and expand their technical facilities but continuously examine and re-examine their attitudes toward improvisation; across the spans of their careers, such players frequently reassess their goals in music making and their attitudes toward the role of reflexive thought in improvisation. Of course, the Cleveland jazzers are not the only musicians that possess these forms of agency. For example, among the staunchly anti-reflexive Akron jazzers, the quelling of the thinking voice is not a passive affair. On many nights, the Akron jazzers have to work to quiet reflexive thought, and some players spoke of the process of learning to focus solely on the body and the sound as a lifelong project akin to meditation. In sum, we can see that for all performers, the organization of attention arises through a complex interplay of larger social contexts and differently deployed forms of agency.[18]

All of this leads us to the issue of the player's attention to the listeners and the larger patterns of partial sharing that take place between the performers and the audience members; it is here that the distinction between Rock and Jazz is most acute. In interviews, the Rockers were adamant about the importance of attending to the crowd. Their goal in performance, they said, was to *compel* the audience's attention, to draw them away from the distractions of the bar, the pool table, or their everyday concerns and command the focus of every eye and ear. An evening of commercial hard rock, for example, is more of an elaborate stage show than a simple concert. Set in the cavernous spaces of Cleveland's major nightclubs, such shows involve elaborate props, dazzling lights, and, on occasion, live pyrotechnic displays. Mostly in their teens and twenties, audiences of several hundred members gather at these performances to court and flirt, enjoy the show, and rub shoulders with musicians they believe are poised for stardom. Part Chippendale dancer, part Burlesque clown, the commercial hard rockers deploy flashy costumes, catchy melodies, pounding rhythms, richly distorted guitar timbres, and goofy or macho stage antics in an ongoing attempt to draw the audience into the show. Interactive techniques play a key role as well, and the commercial hard rockers described how eye contact, facial gestures, singalong sections, and various kinds of stage banter invite audience response and pull the listeners into the performance. Not merely attentive to the crowd, these musicians are also aware of the crowd's attention to them, and they constantly monitor the crowd's response level to get a fix on how their antics are emerging in the experience of the listeners. While the metalheads employ different imagery in their stage personas, they too attend to the crowd and seek to draw them into the performance. *Compulsion,* achieved with various amounts of success by different performers on different nights, is the ideology of attention in the commercial hard rock and metal scenes. Such an ideology is shared by Rock listeners as well, and most Rock fans go to shows seeking to be swept away by the music.

The organization of attention between audience and performer in Rock events displays a dynamic typical of feedback loops. On a good night, the musicians and the audience members attend to one another in a powerful fashion, and their mutual attention and interactive exchanges spur each other to ever more intense partial sharing and enjoyment. Conversely, Rock performers that fail to attend to and interact with the crowd receive a distracted or apathetic response, which in turn may demoralize the musicians and further limit their engagement with the music and the crowd. The dynamics of attention in Rock performances exist in the space defined by these poles of complete engagement and complete disengagement, and, across the span of a performance, the level of mutual attention constantly varies. It is important to keep in mind here that the audience member's active interpretation plays a key role in these dynamics. While the best Rock band may be able to compel the attention of even highly hostile and distracted audiences, listeners also have the ability to decide whether or not to attend to the music. Even if the band makes every effort to engage the crowd, a display of disattention by particular crowd members sometimes can serve as a self-fulfilling prophecy, dissuading other crowd members from engaging with a failing band. In fact, the crowd's reflexive monitoring of their own engagement is the primary yardstick by which listeners and critics rate Rock bands. While some fans and critics judge bands by specific musical techniques, performances are primarily deemed successful or unsuccessful on the basis of whether the band was able to compel the audience's attention, irresistibly pulling them into the music and giving them their money's worth.

In contrast, the ideology of attention for nightclub Jazz is one of *invitation*. Discussing audience-performer issues, the Jazzers said that they enjoy an attentive crowd, but the patrons of the clubs where they play rarely come to listen to the band. Most players said that, because of this, the musician must focus on the music, creating sounds that invite the patron's attention. If the crowd listens to the music, good; if crowd ignores the performance, the Jazzers said, the player must simply accept their disattention. While a few of the Akron musicians were careful to quote the composed melody during improvisation and use other techniques to make their playing accessible to the listeners, all of the Jazzers agreed that actively drawing the crowd into the music was difficult and undesirable. Some said that jazz improvisation is so demanding that they can't play at their best if they have to focus on the audience and try to make them listen; others said that if the crowd wouldn't make the effort to listen, why expend effort trying to draw them in? Led by this ideology of invitation, the Jazzers explained that, on an ideal night, musical sound is situated in the foreground of the experience, and an attentive audience rests in the defining background; lurking just outside the center of attention, an appreciative crowd shades the focal sounds with excitement in the same way that a dull headache rests on the margins of a bad day, shading all of the foregrounded experiences with a quality of annoyance. On most nights, however, the players are aware that few people are listening, and the chatter of the drinkers and the bustle from the bar are distractions that must be ignored.

The nightclub audience's ideology of attention cogs into that of the Jazz musicians. Although some Ohio jazz fans go to nightclubs with the express intent of listening to the music, most of the patrons of the nightclubs where Berger's research took place attend to the musicians only sporadically. For most of the night, the music lurks in the background of their experience and sets a mood. The ideologies of the Jazzers and their audiences produce an organization of attention in the event that has greatly differing dynamics from that found in Rock. While attentive crowds can inspire the players, many great Jazz performances have occurred in empty bars or while an oblivious crowd drinks and chats. Even if the audience is attentive, they only serve as a defining background to the players' experience, and the direct interactions between the stage and audience that characterize rock performances (eye contact, singalong sections, cheering) are largely absent in the Jazz performances of northeast Ohio. On most nights, the partial sharing of experience is intense among the musicians on the bandstand and among each individual group of chatting patrons; the crowd as a whole serves as a background in the performers' experiences, while the band and the other patrons in the bar serve as a background for each individual group of chatting drinkers. Like the organization of phenomena in experience, the larger patterns of attention and partial sharing in an event emerge as a dialectic of social context and agency, informed by the practical contingencies of the performance, larger cultural beliefs about the uses of music, and the participants' own creative agency.[19]

The Reflexive Dimension of Experiences of Interaction and the Aesthetics of Reflexivity

The issues examined in the last section are significant for performance theory and the larger interests of this essay because they show that the organization of experience is neither capriciously individual nor peripheral to expressive behavior; on the contrary, the effective organization of experience is a necessary condition of interaction in general and performance in particular. Within this area, the participant's reflexive attention to herself and her metacommunicative signaling of that attention forms a specific set of subproblems. Participants in a performance do not merely arrange the elements of their experience and attend or disattend to the others in the event. On the contrary, the participant may be aware of herself as the focus of another's attention, and that participant may partially share how her actions are emerging in the experience of the others; as a phenomenon, awareness of this type may be foregrounded or backgrounded in experience and metacommunicatively signaled in a variety of ways. Such reflexive consciousness and metacommunicative signaling play key roles in the aesthetics of performance, and we can gain insights into this process by returning briefly to the Ohio data. As they monitor the audience's attention, for example, the Rockers do not merely share with the crowd the meanings of the words and the emotions portrayed by the music; the players are also partially aware of the intensity and affective tenor with which the crowd is listening to them (for example, distracted appreciation or riveted disgust). We will use the term "reflexive dimension of experiences of interaction" to refer to a performer's or audience member's awareness of herself as a participant in an interaction, her awareness of the other's attention toward her, and any additional higher-order reflexive awareness that is present in her experience.

The dialectics of this reflexive consciousness and the participant's metacommunicative signaling of that consciousness are rich and complex. Such signaling may be intentional (as when a rocker actively makes eye contact with a front-row audience member to try to engage her attention) or unintentional (as when the same musician may inadvertently yawn during the hundredth performance of the same song); obvious in the process of interaction (as when a derisive musician turns his back to a listening crowd), subtly stated (as when a jazz drummer plays a bossa nova flavored phrase to acknowledge the attention of a Latin music fan in the club), or implicit (as when a piano player drops his dynamic level during a bass solo); an honest representation of the participant's attention (as when an entranced audience member stares with rapt concentration at the performers) or a dishonest representation (as when a tired rocker suppresses a yawn to obscure her boredom).

However they relate to a performer's actual awareness, metacommunicative signals of the performer's reflexive consciousness play a key role in the audience's experience of the meaning of the performance, informing all of the other elements of the communication in a holistic fashion reminiscent of that described by Jakobson in his analysis of language functions (1960, see above). Rock guitar players explained, for example, that creating a good performance isn't just a question of playing the right songs or having a good light show; to entertain the crowd, they said, the musician must display the fact that she is having a good time, engaging with the music and attending to the crowd. Such metacommunicative expressions of reflexive awareness form a gestalt with the other elements of the performance, infusing them with affect and meaning. In rock guitar technique, subtleties of vibrato, pick attack, and string bending are taken as signs of the performer's engagement, and their presence in a guitar solo infuses that solo with a quality of energy and vitality. Audiences interpret weak vibrato, dull attack, and inaccurate bends as signs of the guitarist's distraction, and such metacommunicative signaling informs the listener's overall experience of the solo, making dull a performance of even the most stunning composed melody. Further, even those soloists who are able to provide nuanced vibrati, strong attacks, and accurate bends in a distracted state accompany their solos with facial expressions, gestures, stage antics, and other metacommunicative signals that indicate their engagement with the music. Such signaling is the mark of a professional. Jeff Johnston, a stalwart of the Cleveland rock scene, explained to Berger that the musician is paid to excite the crowd; to do her job, the rock musician must display intense engagement, regardless of whether or not she enjoys the music or can even hear her instrument above the sound of the other performers. No matter the quality of the composition or the techniques used, a bored and distracted stage demeanor colors the audience's interpretation and ruins the aesthetic and rhetorical effect of the performance.

While performance is experienced as a gestalt of metacommunicative signs and the other expressions in the event, audiences may constitute such gestalts in a variety of ways. Alternative rock listeners, for example, relentlessly criticize commercial hard rock musicians for their facial expressions, bodily gestures, and instrumental techniques. While the commercial hard rockers feel that such metacommunicative signaling displays deep involvement with the music, the alternative fans believe that such exaggerated signaling produces an obnoxious self-consciousness rather than an intense involvement with the music. Further, while metacommunicative signals play a positioning role, the mere existence of these signs does not guarantee subject positioning; such signals are actively employed by the performers and actively interpreted by the audience. In the rock data, for example, the high decibel levels, pyrotechnics, bodily gestures, flashy costumes, and displays of virtuosity are all intended to serve a positioning function—to literally transform the variously drinking, flirting, and chatting bar patrons into a music audience. But this transformation is not guaranteed by the fact of performance. While the best rock bands on their best nights may be able to almost fully compel the crowd's attention, the ability to do this only comes about through great effort and must be achieved anew in each performance. Further, as we have shown, bar patrons actively interpret rock performances—ignoring the band if they are involved in a serious conversation, foregrounding mistakes and backgrounding positive features of the performance if they choose to be difficult, or actively silencing the critical voice and losing themselves in the music if they wish to support the band.

Finally, such signaling and interpretation may be highly multilayered. For example, the angst-ridden singer/songwriter who stares into a rapt crowd with an expressionless visage signals "I know you are listening, but I am singing these songs for myself and do not care about your attention"; such multilayered metacommunication colors the confessional narratives and meandering melodies in the foreground of the crowd's experience and is crucial to the overall aesthetic effect of the performance. Like the "never-ending spiral" to which Rex Stout alludes in the first epigraph of this essay, reflexive signals and reflexive interpretations have a nearly infinite potential for layering and self-reference.

The examples used so far might suggest that reflexive signaling is only important in popular culture or in situations where the performer's style and persona are foregrounded, but this is not the case. Reflexivity is crucial for all types of performance. Metacommunicative signaling may be embedded in the "text" (as in the vibrato and pick attack of the guitar solo), presented in accompanying communication (such as facial gesture, kinesics, or proxemics), or both.[20] At certain moments in the history of Western art music, for example, audience members and performers were expected to attend to the musical sound and disattend to gesture, kinesics, costume, and so forth. Though signals of the performer's reflexive consciousness were primarily embedded in the musical sound (timbre, embellishment, dynamic, tempo, etc.), such signaling was still plentiful. Further, adjectives used to describe the performer's reflexive awareness were (and are) omnipresent in the vocabulary of the classical music critic. It is common, for example, in that discourse to refer to a pianist's dynamics or a singer's timbre as "self-conscious," "intimate," or "precious." And while muted gestures and facial expressions may be taken for granted in performance and highly backgrounded in the audience's experience, they are still important for the participants' experiences of the event.

The importance of reflexivity for all types of performance leads us back to our phenomenology of intersubjectivity and the central point of this discussion: it is certainly true that at any given moment, any participant in an interaction may or may not engage in metacommunication or reflexive thought. However, the entities that constitute interaction (the paired subjects self and other) are inherently reflexive entities, and interaction is thus an inherently reflexive situation. As a result, reflexivity is a dimension of interaction, and even the failure to engage in reflexivity necessarily will have significance for the participant's experience of the meaning of the event.

That reflexivity is a dimension of interaction flows from the very nature of subjectivity. Husserl's examination of the body showed us that the concept of the subject is necessary for our awareness of both self and other, that self and other are two examples of this larger, more basic notion. Husserl's discussion of space demonstrates that, because of the richness of perception, our experience of objects in the immediate physical environment directly implies the possibility of other subjectivities—our own future subjectivity and the subjectivity of others—and this richness secures the very possibility of intersubjectivity and social interaction. As we suggested above, the notion of interaction implies that the participants have a mutual orientation toward each other's experience. As a result, when two people (A and B) interact, A's participation in the interaction implies her awareness of herself as a subject and her awareness of B as another subject attending to her. In other words, the very definition of interaction entails that each subject at least has the *potential* to be aware of how she is emerging in the other's experience. Because the awareness of the other's experience is the necessary condition for interaction to occur at all, reflexivity is a dimension of all experiences of interaction. While the act of engaging in a particular instance of explicit metacommunication or reflexive consciousness is a contingent feature of any participant's conduct in a given interaction, the reflexive structure of interaction is a necessary and constitutive feature of all interaction. The overall meaning of that participant's conduct (for herself and for others) will partially depend on the content of that reflexive dimension. Any metacommunication or reflexive consciousness will constitute such a "content," and even the total failure to be aware of oneself as a participant in an interaction or the total refusal to engage in metacommunicative signaling of one's awareness of the other will count as such a content and play a role in the meaning. Thus, the bore who blathers on, even when her interlocutor is clearly dozing, has not transcended the reflexive dimension but simply found an unfortunate place in its continuum. Likewise, the rocker who fails to display her engagement with the music and her awareness of the audience has not escaped the reflexive continuum, because her very absence of reflexivity informs the audience's experience of the event.

These ideas impact research into performance in several ways. Like much theoretical work on expressive culture, this discussion has sought to provide ethnographers with the intellectual tools necessary for achieving richer insights into the experiences of their research participants. We hope that ethnographers of performance, understanding reflexivity in the manner we have suggested here, will attend to the subtle and pervasive ways that reflexive consciousness and metacommunicative signaling inform performance. None of this is to suggest that performance is merely about the participants' attention to one another. Performance has contents beyond mere reflexive signaling. (In fact, the hallmark of preciously hyperreflexive art is that it, like the insular relationship described by Joe Jackson in the second epigraph of this essay, seems to be about nothing more than endless self-reference.) The point of our discussion of Husserl has been to show that one's awareness of oneself as a partner in an interaction and one's orientation toward the other's experience are constitutive of interaction; as a result, reflexivity is a key issue for all performances, even the most text-centered or unselfconscious, and it is crucial for the overall aesthetics of performance. But while reflexivity is a universal feature of performance, attitudes toward reflexivity in performance vary greatly. In the last section of this chapter, we wish to show that each culture, subculture, and event participant has an aesthetic of reflexivity, a set of ideas that dictate the desiderata of reflexive consciousness and its metacommunicative signaling in performance. The ideologies of attention we have described above (compulsion for the Rockers, invitation for the Jazzers) contribute to the aesthetics of reflexivity in those scenes. Such ideas do not merely describe the norms for how attention is typically shared in those social worlds, they also set an aesthetic standard for that sharing. But rather than continuing to explore the Rock and Jazz examples, we will shift our focus and discuss Del Negro's research on the central Italian *passeggiata* (ritual promenade; see also Del Negro 1999, 2004 and Del Negro and Berger 2001). By exploring such different examples (regional American popular music performances, a traditional European display event), we hope to emphasize that an aesthetics of reflexivity is a structural feature of performance, independent of the culture area involved or the expressive genres employed.

The Aesthetics of Reflexivity in the Ritual Promenade of Central Italy

Del Negro's research focuses on Sasso, a rapidly industrializing town of three thousand people on Italy's Adriatic coast.[21] In the local view, Sasso has been seen as a cosmopolitan village with close affinities to the nearby coastal centers. The townsfolk affectionately call it *la piccola Parigi dell' Abruzzo* (the little Paris of the Abruzzo) and point to its attractive *piazza* (downtown area) and well-known *passeggiata* (ritual promenade) as a sign of the town's *civiltà* (civility). More than a source of local identity, the *passeggiata* serves as the main occasion for public sociability and expressivity in the town. Set in the lively, cinematic atmosphere of the *piazza,* the *passeggiata* involves an array of "greetings, glances, gestures, and costumes" (Silverman 1975, 67) that intertwine to create a richly textured canvas of meanings. The main activity of the event is strolling, and on summer evenings and weekend afternoons a cross section of the population descends into the *piazza* to pace their *vasche* (laps or circuits) up and down *Vittorio Emanuele,* the town's main *corso* (street). While the term *passeggiata* literally means "promenade" and specifically refers to the period of *piazza* strolling between 5:30 and 8:00 p.m., Sassani often use it as a broad concept to refer to any kind of leisure or play. The weekday *passeggiata* announces the end of the workday and serves as a moment of shared public culture before the private family meal. A condensed version of the *passeggiata* occurs after church on Sunday, during which families, kin groups, and factions of the local political elites walk together, often strolling arm in arm, and dominate *il corso*.

The ideology of attention in the *passeggiata* is one of spatially organized, interactive scrutiny, and a variety of beliefs and practices inform the typical patterns of organizing phenomena in experience that the participants employ. While Sassani view the entire event as a performance, townsfolk can frame their actions as more or less performative by their choice of clothing and the location of their strolling on the street. Maximally performative participants dress to the nines and stroll down the center of the street, while those who desire less public attention walk along the side of *il corso*. Participants who choose to watch the proceedings are largely segregated by gender, with the men viewing the event from the sidewalk bars and the older women and widows observing from terraces and stoops. Dress and comportment are carefully monitored, and while those observing from the bars and porches are not considered to be promenading, to even appear in the *piazza* between 5:30 and 8:00 is to submit oneself to a sophisticated aesthetic of public performance. In interviews, Sassani explained that the good stroller has upright posture and a forward-oriented gaze, while glances to the side are considered to be bad form, especially for young women. As a result of these various beliefs, the focus of the stroller's attention constantly shifts from person to person in the oncoming stream of promenading townsfolk. Like the sound of a car radio in the experience of a sightseeing driver, thoughts about the other strollers' performances and the conversation of one's immediate strolling companions rest in the near background of the stroller's experience. In the more distant background, but no less important, are those Sassani walking on the side of the street or sitting on the porches and in the bars. Their presence in the *piazza* and careful attention to the event inform the experiences of those in the center of the street, coloring those experiences with energy and transforming the simple act of walking into a performance. In a complementary fashion, the observers focus on the ongoing parade of strollers, now admiring Paolo's new jacket, now noting Maria's flirtatious glance. The commentary of one's immediate companions rests just off the center of attention, while a background awareness of the performance as a performance constitutes the very possibility of the event.

The organization of attention in the event that stems from these ideas and practices is rich and complex. As in the Rock events, the partial sharing among the participants displays the dynamics of a feedback loop. On the best nights in the *piazza,* the gaiety and grace of each participant's display is reflected back to her in the admiring gazes of the other strollers, amplifying their enjoyment and making the event come alive. On slow nights, the paucity of other strollers to see and to be seen by limits the performative potential of even the most elegant Sassani. Unlike the participants in the Rock events, however, most of the *passeggiata* participants are both performers and audience members, with the greatest attention focused on the participants in the center of the street. As a result, partial sharing is focal and bidirectional among the numerous strollers walking along the center of *il corso.* Partial sharing between the street crowd and the sidewalk crowd is also interactive, with the strollers in the center and the observers on the margins of both the physical and the phenomenal space.

In a highly interactive event such as this, seeing and being seen are chronic, ongoing activities; indeed, they are the very point of the event. The manner in which the stroller looks at the others signals her attention to them, and acknowledging the attention of others is not merely part of the interactive mechanics of the event. On the contrary, the style with which these practices of observation and signaling are achieved is one of the primary aesthetic criteria by which performance is judged. In the experience of the other participants, the stroller's metacommunicative signaling of her reflexive consciousness forms a gestalt with her clothing, coif, and gait and informs the overall aesthetic effect she generates. To gain insight into this process, Del Negro videotaped the event and conducted feedback interviews about those tapes with the townsfolk. In the interviews, the concept of *disinvoltura* emerged as one of the main aesthetic standards by which performance is judged; in fact, *disinvoltura* is, at least in part, an aesthetic of reflexivity. Directly translated, the term means poise or ease of manners, and during the event, the criteria of *disinvoltura* is most strictly applied to the maximally performative participants—those strolling in the center of the street or wearing especially fine clothing. To achieve *disinvoltura,* the performer must acknowledge that she is performing and that others are paying attention to the performance, without drawing undue attention to either fact.

The concept is best illustrated by negative example. In the feedback interviews, a woman whom we will call the haughty walker was sharply criticized by all of the interviewees. As she paraded down the center of the street in a skirt, sweater, blazer, and pumps, her proud, mechanical gait marked her walking as a very self-conscious performance. At the same time, however, she conspicuously failed to make eye contact or greet passersby, a fact that the interviewees interpreted as active and ostentatious disattention. As a result, her walk issued contradictory messages—"I am performing, pay attention" and "I don't see you, I am alone on *il corso*." What this stroller actually intended we do not know for certain. What is clear, however, is that the other *passeggiata* participants interpreted her performance in this way, and that they experienced such metacommunicative dissonance as rudeness, the opposite of *disinvoltura*. While this stroller exhibited neither disheveled hair, clashing accessories, nor an unsightly slouch, her metacommunicative signaling of her awareness of herself as a performer colored her overall performance and produced a display that drew the ire of all of Del Negro's respondents.

A second example will illustrate a different set of relationships between reflexive consciousness, the metacommunicative signaling of that consciousness, and the aesthetics of performance. On another piece of tape, a women in her twenties whom we will call the distracted walker promenades down the center of the street in a fine quality beige tailored suit. As she walks along, however, she constantly glances left and right in a bored fashion, as if searching for a person in the crowd. Though her dress is impeccable, she completely fails to achieve *disinvoltura*. If one simply looks at the distracted walker, her clothes and location in the street frame her behavior as a performance and call out for other participants' attention; however, her unconcealed distraction tells the audience that they are not appearing in her experience. She could eliminate this *faux pas* in one of two ways. If she strolled on the side of the street or the sidewalk, she would no longer attract the critical attention of others and would be free to search for her friend. In so doing, she would not achieve *disinvoltura*—this term is usually reserved for those in full performance mode—but neither would she *fare una brutta figura* (cut a poor figure) and draw the opprobrium of the crowd. If she wishes to stay in the center of the street, she must keep her head forward, gracefully acknowledge the attention her performance prompts, and glance about for her friend with greater subtlety. But calling out for the attention of all and sundry *and* clearly disattending to the event, this stroller cannot achieve *disinvoltura*, no matter how fine her tailored suit or how well-coiffured her hair. Independent of her distraction, or even because of it, this woman's dress would almost certainly be considered stylish by onlookers at a jazz nightclub in Akron, Ohio. But in an event dominated by an aesthetic of *disinvoltura*, such a performance was widely seen as a fiasco.[22] With respect to our earlier theoretical analysis, it is worth noting that it is exactly this stroller's *failure* to achieve a reflexive awareness of herself as a participant—the absence of reflexivity—that transforms the performance into a fiasco. The reflexive dimension of performance cannot be transcended.

The aesthetics of reflexivity suggested by these examples is deeply informed by larger ideas about gender in central Italian society, and the politics of the *passeggiata* is fraught with power relations and contradictions. As Deborah Kapchan has argued (1994; see also Del Negro and Berger 2001), it is not uncommon in world cultures for posture to be given a moral value. The Sassani proscription against glancing to the side, for example, is taught to girls from a young age and explained in terms of the biblical injunction to *fare la strada diritta* (walk the straight path). Unconcealed sideward glances are interpreted as sexually suggestive, as if the woman in question were looking for sexual partners, while those women who promenade with a straight posture and literally "walk the straight path" are seen as chaste and proper.[23] While women's performances are regulated by an almost panoptic public scrutiny, some female participants actively contradict the conventions of the event, and others use those conventions to explore and even resist prevailing ideas about gender and local identity. For example, a few young women—dressed in short skirts and low-cut tops and glancing about flirtatiously—openly disregard the norms of *passeggiata* performance and are routinely criticized for their displays. In a rather different vein, a number of middle-aged, professional women actively co-opt the local value of cosmopolitanism to garner for themselves an image of power and respectability. Attired in markedly conservative designer clothing, these women use fashion to reference both the urbane sophistication so highly valued in the town and their own status as bourgeois professionals; in so doing, they earn themselves a measure of respect outside of the traditional roles of debutante, wife, or mother. While their demeanor and comportment conform to a fairly standard version of Sassani *disinvoltura,* their display of respectability is so potent that they are free to comment on the displays of other performers with an openness that would be unacceptable for most *passeggiata* participants. Our final example goes beyond these relatively straightforward dynamics and illustrates how one local *passeggiata* participant creatively manipulates local ideas about gender, cosmopolitanism, comportment, and reflexivity to achieve a subtle, multilayered performance that is interpreted in a variety of different ways by local observers.

A popular woman in her early twenties, Rosa Di Roma is well known throughout the town for her unconventional clothing and style. While she sometimes wears short skirts, her *passeggiata* performances are not especially sexualized, and she is best known in the *piazza* for her heavy, thick-soled Jean-Paul Gauthier shoes and the sharp contrast of her naturally pale complexion with her raven-dyed hair and black, Cher-inspired eyeliner. A conventional top, jacket, and haircut round out her look. Such elements of style make a statement in themselves; while the shoes, eyeliner, and hair color reference the contemporary and assertive fashions of Rome or Milan, her unexceptional clothing downplays the significance of style, suggesting a cooler attitude to the event and the high value the town places upon it. But the clothing never appears in the *passeggiata* by itself, and the meta-communicative signals that accompany the performance color and transform the larger aesthetic effect generated by Rosa's strolling. An infrequent participant in the *passeggiata,* Rosa does not achieve *disinvoltura* in the conventional sense. While she fails to acknowledge the passersby in the traditional manner, she is not oblivious to her surroundings, as the distracted walker is. Instead, her gaze registers the fact that others are watching but communicates neither anxious concern for the others' reactions nor haughty disdain for their attention. Her reactions to the others' performances are equally bland, betraying neither pleasure nor disgust. In sum, Rosa is indifferent to the attentions and the performances of others.

The interpretations of this multifaceted display vary. Many traditional Sassani see Rosa as a clown. While designer clothes are popular on the *passeggiata,* Chanel suits and tailored outfits are the styles that appeal to the more conservative townsfolk. Though her heavy shoes and retro-sixties eyeliner may reference the fashionable styles of Italy's major cities, Rosa's detractors see her bored demeanor and unpresupposing top and skirt as a criticism of Sasso's cosmopolitan pretensions and restrictive sexual mores. More importantly, these participants see little distinction between Rosa's indifference and the haughty walker's failure to acknowledge others; both are affected displays, they feel, and both fail to achieve *disinvoltura.* Others in the town, however, take a different view. While these residents see her shoes, eyeliner, and hair as a stylish, daring statement, such objects would be meaningless without the proper comportment and the metacommunicative signals such comportment provides. Locating Rosa's indifferent gaze in the context of her only occasional participation in the event and her common top and skirt, Rosa's supporters interpret her indifferent glance at face value—as a genuine indication of indifference. From this perspective, Rosa is experienced as her own person, a cosmopolitan figure who enjoys style (the shoes, eyeliner, and so forth), but is neither mired in the time-consuming rituals of shopping and pre-*passeggiata* primping and preening nor impressed by the displays of the other townsfolk. If Rosa completely ignored the presence of others or wore aggressively cheap or disheveled clothing, she would almost certainly lose these supporters and be interpreted as nothing more than an obnoxious *poseur.* But her combination of stylish and common clothing and the (perceived) effortlessness of her indifference serve as metacommunicative signals of a genuinely partial engagement with the event; such signals inform the overall aesthetic effect of her performance, producing a sense of stylishness that resists the more restrictive options of Chanel-suit respectability and come-hither sexuality. Such fine points of performance are, of course, open to interpretation, and it was for this reason that Rosa was frequently the topic of debate in the Sassani *passeggiata*.

In all of these displays, we see clear examples of Bauman's notion of performance—heightened, aesthetic action oriented toward an other (1989). Implicit in Bauman's definition is the fact that performance is not merely the creation of text or the transmission of signs; performance is grounded upon an underlying awareness that both one's self and the other are subjects, that both the self and other have the potential to experience the world and share their experiences with others. Mediating between this grounding potential, this fact of being subjects, and the particular experiences of performers and audiences are the contingencies of each individual situation and endless layers of sedimented social practice and belief. Ideologies of attention and reflexivity inform the participants' practices of organizing their experiences, partially sharing those experiences with others, and signaling their awareness of themselves as actors and objects of attention. The aesthetic effects that emerge in this complex space are never simply the outcome of the referential meaning of the words, the sensual appeal of the sound, or the abstract structural relations of the parts, though such factors may indeed play a key role. For performance to occur at all, the participants must have an awareness of one another as experiencing subjects, and this fact constitutes the reflexive dimension of experiences of interaction, a continuum where even the absence of self-awareness is merely a kind of self-awareness. Such reflexive consciousness and its metacommunicative signaling interacts with the other elements of the performance to produce a complex whole, a gestalt in which each element informs the other and contributes to the overall aesthetic and rhetorical effect of the performance.

It is important to note that metacommunicative signals of the performer's reflexive consciousness are transmitted through both transitory and durable media. While gaze and comportment may indicate a participant's immediate attention to others, expensive clothing and carefully applied make-up show that the participant has thought about the event beforehand and is committed to the act of display. In the distracted walker example, the very care that went into her choice of clothing serves as a signal of her concern for the attention of others, and it is the tension between her highly performative outfit and her highly distracted demeanor that produces the overall aesthetic effect. The various media of *passeggiata* performance range in their durability, from the physique (which is achieved through ongoing effort and remains relatively stable during a performance event), to the wardrobe (also achieved through ongoing effort and only fully displayed across several performances), to the clothes and make-up donned for a particular occasion, to the ever-changing details of comportment, demeanor, and gaze. In fact, it is the interplay of metacommunicative signs of varying degrees of durability that constitutes the overall aesthetic effect of the performance.

The potential of durable media to indicate the participant's reflexive consciousness makes the ideas in this essay applicable to the study of recorded music, foodways, literary studies, material culture, and other performances that do not take place through face-to-face interactions. The overproduced recording, the novel dense with allusion, and the carved box covered with too much decoration all signal their creator's precious, reflexive attention to herself as one creating an object for the heightened aesthetic attention of others. The rich dialectics we have explored throughout (the interplay of reflexive consciousness and its metacommunicative signaling, the dialogue of text and interpretation) apply in more mediated communication as well, but the nature of the media and the attendant generic and practical constraints bring about different dynamics of reflexivity. Take the example (partially inspired by the film *Big Night*) of an Italian food critic dining in an Italian American restaurant. Here, the pasta sauce lightly flavored with garlic and served especially for the critic not only signals the chef's awareness that the patron is a connoisseur; such flavoring also signals the chef's awareness that Italians feel that Italian Americans stereotype the Italian board as nothing more than a platform for garlic and olive oil. As in face-to-face interactions, interpretation plays a key role in the participants' aesthetic responses. Thus, the critic's experience of the sauce may be positively informed by the chef's implicit reflexive awareness, metacommunicatively signaled by the muted garlic; alternatively, the critic may also interpret the paucity of garlic as a self-conscious and ostentatious reference to Italian tastes. Further, the interaction of the chef and the patron is influenced by the dynamics of the media. Unlike the face-to-face interactions of the *passeggiata* or the Rock and Jazz performances, the more slowly mediated interaction of the kitchen-bound chef and the dining critic allows feedback to occur only between courses or when the restaurant review appears in print. But like the face-to-face interactions, highly mediated interactions still involve partial sharing, reflexive consciousness, metacommunicative signaling, and a mutual orientation of the subjects to each other's experiences. It is beyond the scope of this essay to explore how the dynamics of media and genre impact on the aesthetics of reflexivity, but it is our hope that these concepts will be useful in the interpretation of all manners of folklore and expressive culture.

Our main point has been to suggest that reflexivity is not some optional addition to over-sophisticated and highly ironic performances, but that, on the contrary, it is built into the very structure of intersubjectivity and is essential to the aesthetics of performance. Do you like Barbra Streisand's music? The question, we argue, does not turn solely on your evaluation of her vocal quality, choice of repertoire, or arrangements. To us—and, we suspect, to most people—Streisand's performances are supremely self aware; each note is accompanied by a reminder that she knows you are watching, that she wants you to share her emotions, and that she believes that her performance deserves the greatest attention. If you find this reflexivity to be the justifiable honesty of a great artist or a refreshing feminist self-confidence, then you probably like her music. But if you prefer singers who generate the impression of intimacy, who engage in Bauman's denial of performance, you will probably find Streisand to be stagy and affected. We hope other scholars find the concepts we have introduced to be useful and believe that scholarly attention to the reflexive dimension of experience can substantially enrich our understanding of the aesthetics of performance. Our larger goal has been to further the central program of Bauman's performance theory—the grounding of the study of expressive culture in practice and lived experience.

CHAPTER FIVE

Identity Reconsidered, the World Doubled

*

Giovanna P. Del Negro and Harris M. Berger

The notion of identity is an extremely powerful and pervasive concept in contemporary folklore studies. Anything can be interpreted in terms of identity, and, explicitly or implicitly, the concept is foundational to much of the work in our field. But for all the popularity and importance of this concept, it remains strangely undertheorized. While various scholars have shed light on the dynamics of identity in particular domains, relatively few works in our field have sought a general theory of identity. Ideally, such a theory would explain what is similar about the diverse ways in which the word is used and could account for its apparent malleability and ubiquity in scholarly discourse. We suggest that new insights can be gained if we treat the problem of identity as a problem in interpretation, and the goal of this essay is to explore how the notion of identity operates in both the creative artistry of folklore and the creative theory building of folklore studies. Our goal in all of this is neither to champion a given model of identity nor to advocate for or oppose more identity-oriented research; instead, we seek to understand better what it means to say that folklore is an expression of identity, and to develop a set of intellectual tools that will help make this pervasive concept more useful for those who employ it.

Our perspective proceeds from a communication model of folklore. For the sake of argument, we take as fundamental the situation of an actor or group of actors creating an item of folklore or engaged in a performance and another actor or group of actors receiving that folklore. Further, we assume that, in creating the folklore, the performer has an experience of meaning and that, in reception, the audience also has some experience of meaning. What we wish to suggest is that the term "identity" refers to an interpretive framework and a set of interpretive practices, a particular way of making sense of social conduct and expressive culture. Both performers and audiences can interpret folklore in terms of identity, and scholars are emphatically included in the category of audiences. To interpret folklore in terms of identity means to take the meaning of the lore and to inject it into "society," a space of social individuals and social groups. We place the word "society" in quotes here because the kind of society into which that meaning is thrust depends on the implicit or explicit social theory of the actor interpreting the lore. Such a society can be understood by the participants as a network of relationships or a group of essentially unique individuals; "society" can be construed on the micro-scale of families, neighborhoods, or traditional communities or on the larger scales of regional, ethnic, national, or transnational groups. Visions of identity can be institutionalized and restrictive or situational and expressive, and the multidimensional character of identity is a basic difficulty in all forms of social interpretation. Identity interpretations may be made in an intentional fashion by the performer or "read in" by the audience, and the problem of intention and over-reading is a central concern of this essay.[1]

Below we will explore the various facets of this problem in detail. The central point, however, is that all talk about identity involves an interpretive act in which one set of meanings (themselves already the product of interpretation) is projected into the interpreter's vision of the social world. This basic structure accounts for identity's ubiquity in both scholarly and non-scholarly discourse, as well as its slippery and mercurial nature. Talk about identity is ubiquitous because *all* practices can be interpreted in terms of identity. While the validity of any given interpretation is an empirical question, the idea that all conduct has the potential to be the legitimate object of an identity interpretation has a solid grounding in social research. Beginning with the earliest days of ethnography, researchers have never tired of revealing how even the most prosaic activities (or the most seemingly natural or commonsensical beliefs) are tied to a social history and a cultural context. Just as theatrical directors of the method school know that each word and gesture may reveal the character's past experiences, folklorists, anthropologists, sociologists, and all scholars who study social life know that anything that a person says or does may be a product of his/her cultural tradition and may therefore be interpreted in terms of identity. The broad scope of this concept has made identity the common theoretic property of folklorists of every stripe and scholars from most of the other branches of the humanities and social sciences. Just as the objects of an identity interpretation are nearly infinite, so too are the images of the society with which they may be connected, and this flexibility explains why the notion of identity is so elusive and difficult to examine. Inserting an other's practices into a social space of unique and self-willing individuals, for example, Enlightenment individualists will interpret identity in quite a different fashion from communitarian socialists or postmodernists. Tied to a concept as flexible as society, the notion of identity is as multiform as quicksilver and just as difficult to pin down.

If identity is best understood as an interpretive framework, then a logical place to begin our analysis is with a group of interpreters who use the concept frequently and with great skill—folklorists. Our goal here is not to present a comprehensive intellectual history of the notion of identity but to place this concept in its social context and suggest some of the many ways in which it has been used in our discipline and related fields. Having suggested a scheme for making sense of this complex theoretical heritage, we will then shift our attention to the performance event itself and explore the dynamics of identity interpretation in face-to-face interaction.

Cross-Cultural and Historical Perspectives on the Notion of Identity

As Philip Gleason (1983) has observed, the term "identity" comes from the Latin root *idem*, meaning "the same," and has been in use since the sixteenth century. The *Oxford English Dictionary* defines identity as "the sameness of a person or thing at all times or in all circumstances . . . individuality or personality. *Personal identity* (in *Psychology*), the condition or fact of remaining the same person throughout the various phases of existence." While this definition effectively describes the notion of the person in modern Western philosophy, it is by no means universal. In his article "Is 'Identity' a Useful Cross-Cultural Concept?" (1994), Richard Handler maintains that there are significant differences in the ways the person is conceived in different societies. Comparing ethnographic examples from native North America, Bali, and India, Handler problematizes the assumption that an individual's identity is sharply bounded from others, unique to each person, and stable across time. For example, drawing on the work of A. Irving Hallowell (1976), Handler suggests that the traditional Ojibwa category of the person includes beings that modern Western philosophy would normally exclude—supernatural entities, inanimate objects, and the dead. Hallowell explains that, for example, "the kinship term 'grandfather' is not only applied to human persons, but to spiritual beings who are persons of a category other than human" (359). Not merely individuals from beyond the grave, the dead are believed to express themselves through the actions of the living, and the boundary between the identity of the individual and that of his/her ancestors is considered to be porous. Resisting the classificatory scheme foisted upon them by their colonizers, the Ojibwa never fully assimilated the strict opposition of the animate and inanimate worlds and continue to believe in the anthropomorphic attributes of nature. The relationship that Ojibwas have with what Hallowell calls "other-than-human persons" is clearly distilled in an anecdote in which an Ojibwa man recalls how an elder interpreted the sound of thunder as the voice of a Thunder Bird and responded to it in the same way a European American would to another person in conversation (Hallowell 1976, 372). Here, identities are expressed in both human and nonhuman action, and human actions do not maintain a one-to-one correspondence with human identities.

If Ojibwa belief questions Western philosophical assumptions about the boundedness of identity, Balinese conceptions challenge the criteria of uniqueness. Clifford Geertz recounts that in traditional Balinese society, infants are assigned specific social roles at birth. Here, identity is a culturally sanctioned, predetermined, generic representation of an idealized type rather than a "unique creation of private fate" (Geertz 1983, 63). At birth all Balinese receive a birth order name, of which there are four—firstborn, secondborn, and so on. Significantly, a family's first child may be named "secondborn," as the rankings are not meant to identify individuals but rather are a part of a four stage cycle of procreation. Thus, while an individual's body may die, their identity type continues to exist. In this context, specific persons are less unique individuals than they are expressions or incarnations of permanent character types. If traditional Balinese perspectives depict identity as proscriptive and unchanging, Indian visions see it as constantly in flux, the byproduct of one's daily commerce with others. McKim Marriott's "Hindu Transactions: Diversity Without Dualism" (1976) suggests that, in Hindu belief, identity is not the wholly integrated and unchanging essence postulated by modern Western philosophy. On the contrary, it is seen to be made up of different component parts that are absorbed into the person through his/her interaction with others; the result is a "dividual" (rather than individual) self. While people assimilate aspects of the other's identity, "they must also give out from themselves particles of their own coded substance" in return; giving back what is taken, the interaction "reproduces in others something of the nature of the person in whom they have originated" (Marriot 1976, 111). Here, the human being is infinitely variable and unstable—a combination of particles and elements that are continuously shared in social intercourse. In reviewing these examples, our goal has been to suggest some of the various ways in which identity can be conceptualized. Of course, no matter how rich or accurate the ethnographic research on these groups may be, it would be an error of essentialism to reduce the diverse everyday experiences of an entire population to one underlying world view or philosophical system, and we do not mean to imply that all Ojibwa, Balinese, or Hindu Indians have the same vision of identity. By the same token, we do not wish to suggest that individuality and agency are strictly Western notions. What we do want to say is that identity can be imagined in a wide variety of ways, and it would be an equal error of essentialism to ignore the ethnographic record and assume that the notion of identity found in modern Western philosophy is universal and unproblematic.

If Handler suggests that the Western philosophical notion of identity is culturally specific, Stuart Hall (1996) and Philip Gleason (1983) illustrate that it is historically emergent as well. According to Hall, the idea of the fully rational human being with a stable and continuous inner core developed in the Enlightenment. Before that time, the individual was thought to be one link in the great chain of being. Humanity was situated in an unchanging continuum that ran from the inanimate world through animals and humans to the panoply of heaven, and within this great chain, the individual's social status and identity were divinely ordained and immutable.[2] The notion of the individual as an autonomous and self-willing agent, Hall suggests, came in the eighteenth century after the rising sway of Descartes's rational cogitative subject and the Enlightenment principles of equality, democracy, and private property. While empiricism and liberal economic theory entrenched these perspectives, it was not until the development of sociology in the nineteenth century that identity was seen as an intersubjective process. In this view, individuals are formed "through membership of and participation in wider social relationships" (Hall 1996, 605), and the concepts of role and group became paramount.

If nineteenth-century sociologists challenged the individualism found in Enlightenment theories of identity, it was psychologist Erik Erikson who synthesized these divergent perspectives and helped the term become a basic part of twentieth-century intellectual discourse. Trained as a psychologist and formed by his harrowing experiences in Nazi Germany, Erikson's work showed how individual identity, in Philip Gleason's apt phrase, stems from "participating in society, internalizing its cultural norms, acquiring different statuses, and playing different roles" (1983, 914). Taking a developmental approach, Erikson constructed a multistage model of identity formation and showed how cultural contradictions in a society might lead the emerging individual to what Erikson called an "identity crisis." As Gleason observes, the Eriksonian focus on identity was given a further boost by the rise of national character studies in the United States. In works like *Coming of Age in Samoa* (Mead 1928) and *Patterns of Culture* (Benedict [1934] 1959) anthropologists from the culture and personality school tried to show how particular societies fostered particular character traits. As America rose to prominence on the world stage, its military and political leaders turned to anthropologists to gain insights into the unfamiliar others they were forced to confront. World War II–era studies like Ruth Benedict's *The Chrysanthemum and the Sword* (1946) tried to offer American readers a glimpse of the Japanese soul, and, on the homefront, Erikson himself was enlisted to work on the Committee for National Morale (Gleason 1983). Throughout all of this, the notion of identity received greater and greater exposure in both academic and popular writing.

Identity has not only been important for philosophy and the social sciences, it has also played a key role in folklore studies, and Elliott Oring (1994) has shown that even before the word "identity" was used in the field, the underlying concept was a basic part of the folklorist's theoretical toolkit. Tracing out the intellectual history of this idea in folklore, Oring argues that foundational thinkers like Johann Gottfried von Herder or Elias Lönnrot saw folklore as an "artifact" of identity, a lasting remnant of past, more authentic cultures. Performance scholars from the 1960s and 1970s, he suggests, viewed folklore as an enactment and public statement of cultural identity, while contemporary folklorists of the mass media or tourist industry theorize expressive culture as the "artifice" of identity—an actively constructed image of group character. For Oring, the latter category includes both nontraditional expressive culture created for commercial ends (i.e., Richard Dorson's notion of "fakelore") and the reflexive recreation of the past in historical re-enactments and museums. We agree with Oring that, while the term "identity" has received some theoretical scrutiny in our field, it is often used in an uncritical fashion and requires greater attention. Addressing this issue, we suggest that identity is best understood as an interpretive framework—a set of ideas that scholars and folklore participants use to make sense of expressive culture—and a brief review of selected examples of folklore theory will illustrate this concept. Our goal here is not to retell the history that Oring recounts so richly but to suggest that the notion of identity imposes certain interpretive dynamics whenever it is employed, and to illustrate some of the different ways in which these dynamics play themselves out. Three themes guide our examination: identity in lore; identity as differential, situational, and contested; and legal and political definitions of identity.

As Oring rightly suggests, the idea that a nation's identity resides in its lore is present in the founding work of our discipline. Herder ([1764–67] 1992), for example, believed that the poetry and song of the German peasantry were an expression of the German soul and a window onto that soul for outsiders and strayed German urbanites. Similarly, the antiquarians and salvage folklorists of the nineteenth century viewed the protection of quickly disappearing rural folkways as basic to the preservation of national cultural identities. In the case of England, for example, William Thoms ([1846] 1964) saw the rapid changes that the nineteenth century brought to traditional peasant customs as nothing less than an all-out attack upon Anglo-Saxon culture, and he argued that folklore preservation was the only way to defend that culture against the onslaught from the city and the factory. This defensive posture was part of a larger resistance to modernity. Articulating the basic assumptions of nineteenth-century folklore, sociologist Ferdinand Tönnies ([1887] 1963) held that modernity undermined homogeneous, convivial *gemeinschaft* communities and fostered large-scale, legalistic *gessellschaft* social relations. For the nationalist antiquarians and folklorists of the day, folklore was rooted in *gemeinschaft,* and modernity could do nothing but tear at the seams of cultural identity.

These ideas found elaboration in the American folklore research of the twentieth century, and Richard Dorson's scholarship exemplifies these developments. In many ways, Dorson kept the faith with earlier approaches to identity, folklore, and culture. As a product of the American Civilization program at Harvard, Dorson (1959) saw folklore as an entry point into American character, and his attacks on "fakelore" condemned modernity in its midcentury theoretical guise: mass culture.[3] But unlike traditional nationalists, he studied small-scale expressive culture wherever he found it and believed that folklore could flourish in industrialized settings. Spurning a homogenizing view of American culture, Dorson's studies of Michigan's Upper Peninsula (1952) celebrated regional and ethnic diversity, while his *Land of the Millrats* (1981) repudiated antiquarian visions and explored the folklore of the city. Throughout these significant intellectual expansions, folklore was consistently viewed as an expression of identity, and the author of *Bloodstoppers & Bearwalkers* was not alone in this perspective. Folklorists from George Korson (1943) to Svatava Pirkova-Jakobson (1956) saw occupational, ethnic, or regional identities in the expressive culture of the various groups they studied. In a 1966 work, Tristram P. Coffin and Hennig Cohen recognized the rising prominence of these forms of identity and seven years later argued that occupational groups were rapidly becoming the primary source of folklore in the United States. Developing their notion of the "semifolk," Coffin and Cohen's *Folklore from the Working Folk of America* (1973) suggested that the demise of the small-scale community and the rise of the mass media allowed individuals to affiliate with a variety of crosscutting and overlapping occupational groups, each with its own character and lore. Here, "occupation" was construed in an extremely broad sense, including "'being a child,' 'being a student,' 'being a housewife,' . . . 'being a hobo' and 'being a drug addict.'" (xxxiv). A variant of Durkheim's observations about the growth of associations in modern societies, the notion of the semifolk challenged the idea that national character must always be a superordinate category, subsuming other dimensions of identity within it. As Richard Bauman (1983) has suggested, it is unclear whether traditional communities had ever been as totalizing as folklorists had believed; what is certain is that folklorists began to conceptualize the folk group, and thus identity, in ever more fragmented ways. The broadest theoretical statement of this disciplinary reorientation came in 1965 with Alan Dundes's widely cited definition of the folk group as "any group of people whatsoever who share at least one common factor" (1965, 2). Implicit in Dundes's construction is the idea that shared expressive culture and shared identity are coterminous.

In crystallizing contemporary trends, Dundes articulated the widely held assumption that group identity depends on intragroup processes and social harmony. As Regina Bendix points out, it was the very power of this synthesis that paved the way for Richard Bauman's now classic work on between-group folklore and conflict (Bendix 1997, 198). Bauman's ideas were not completely without precedent. In a 1959 article, William Hugh Jansen ([1959] 1965) explored what he called "The Esoteric-Exoteric Factor in Folklore." Here, a brief but suggestive discussion of a mixed-race audience viewing the 1957 World Series is used to show that folklore takes on different meanings when it is presented to outsiders rather than insiders. While this example suggests a growing sensitivity toward the situated negotiation of identity, the article largely conceptualizes expressive culture as an intragroup phenomenon, and Jansen charges folklorists with the task of discovering how the members of folk groups use lore to construct images of themselves and others. In contrast, Bauman's "Differential Identity and the Social Base of Folklore" (1972) argues that expressive culture often emerges across, rather than within, group boundaries. Focusing on social interaction, Bauman conceptualizes identity as something that actors construct in performance, rather than as an essence passively expressed in texts. Like Jansen, Bauman is concerned with understanding how insiders view outsiders and how those insiders imagine that they themselves are viewed by outsiders. Building on the symbolic interactionist, however, Bauman suggests that identity is inherently situational and relational.[4] One's sense of one's own identity is constructed in interaction with the other and at least partially defined in relation to one's image of that other. The various examples that Bauman provides—the story-swapping event of Tahltan and

Tlingit traders in the Pacific Northwest, the gentile comedian who references the esoteric humor of Jews, the ironic tall tales told by frontiersmen to city folk—all clearly reveal that identity can stem from cultural difference as well as in-group sharedness.

Bauman was not alone in his concern with identity and interaction, and contemporary scholars from a variety of fields could agree with Richard Handler that "social groups are symbolic processes that emerge and dissolve in particular contexts of action" (1991, 30). In the years that followed the publication of "Differential Identity," a wide range of case studies explored these issues. For example, in her excellent examination of the situational use of ethnic labels in Malaysian society, Judith A. Nagata (1974) shows how identity is constructed in the emergent communicative processes of everyday face-to-face interaction. Nagata's ethnographically grounded research astutely describes the complex ways in which Malays, Indians, Arabs, and Chinese manipulate their identities for political expediency and upward mobility in the context of Malaysian ethnicity laws. Here, group membership is depicted as flexible and strategic. Social actors draw on group stereotypes and espouse varying ethnic allegiances to make differing statements about their characters—hardworking or lazy, business-minded or lacking in entrepreneurial skills. In an attempt to benefit from the economic incentives that are by law afforded exclusively to the dominant group, Arabs and Indians will often define themselves as Malay. Even the identity cards that legally classify people according to their respective ethnicities do not prevent individuals from invoking membership in groups to which they do not formally belong in order to enhance their social positions or foreground special skills or attributes. While ethnic shifting is widely acceptable, it is not equally tolerated by all groups at all times; the common bond of Islam affords Arabs and Indians the occasional opportunity to claim Malaysian identity, but ethnic Chinese find it more difficult to make this ethnic shift. This last point draws attention to the fact that situated negotiations of identity always occur within larger social contexts, often contexts of power and domination. As a technology of social control, identity cards serve a gatekeeping function, and the vision of identity upon which they are premised is restrictive and limiting. While Nagata does illustrate how Malaysian residents creatively manipulate identity in situated contexts, it is important to keep in mind that such manipulations are not a game playfully enjoined for pleasure or caprice but a set of tactical and political responses to a very real set of social strictures.

Related dynamics are also illustrated in the work of Deirdre Evans-Pritchard (1989). In her analysis of the Portal Case, Evans-Pritchard provides a compelling account of how a dispute among local craft workers in the Sante Fe, New Mexico, of the late 1970s became the battleground upon which the concept of Indian identity was debated. In an attempt to protect and support Native American arts, the Museum of New Mexico lobbied the city government to pass an ordinance preventing non-Indians from selling their wares in Santa Fe's Portal Plaza, a public space frequented by tourists. Further, museum officials encouraged the sale of handmade objects and urged Native merchants to wear traditional costumes while selling their wares. Not surprisingly, Hispanic and Anglo artists felt unfairly excluded by the native-only policy. Entangling themselves in municipal legislation, museum officials declared themselves arbiters of Native American identity and arts and endorsed a vision of Indian traditions that ignored the Anglo-Hispanic influence on Native material culture. In many ways, the Portal Case represented a cultural institution's attempt to draw sharp, fixed boundaries between cultural identities that have developed in a dialectical and historically emergent fashion. Both Nagata and Evans-Pritchard explore the legislation of identity and situated responses to it. If Nagata's research emphasizes the tactical manipulation of identity by situated actors in everyday life, Evans-Pritchard's highlights the ways in which institutions and legal systems may impose restrictive and discrete definitions of identity. The effects of the legislation have been paradoxical. Indian arts still have a large audience, but, by the museum's definition, the tradition is in decline. Evans-Pritchard suggests that the museum holds much of the blame—partially because the city laws count a dwindling number of artists as Indian and partially because the official cultural policies impede Native artists from drawing on outside influences or using new techniques.[5]

The interplay between identity, folklore, and political power is nowhere more apparent than in nationalist discourse, and the case of Quebec illustrates these dynamics. Up until the 1960s in Quebec, the primarily urban English speaking minority dominated the Francophone majority. Language and ethnicity were seen as interchangeable, and the *de facto* restrictions on the use of the French language discriminated specifically against Quebeckers of French ancestry. Not surprisingly, French language folklore was seen by most Anglophones as an anachronistic survival of Quebec's preindustrial past. During the 1970s, the separatist *Parti Québécois* came to power. Language laws were passed to foster the use of the French language, and the new ministry of culture strongly encouraged the expression of *notre patrimione* (our [Québécois] heritage) in French-language folksong, poetry, and literature (see Handler 1988). The 1980s, however, saw waves of immigration from former French colonies, and issues of language and ethnicity became decoupled. In response, the ministry of culture and the provincial media began to espouse a discourse centered around the terms *Allophone* (someone who speaks neither French nor English), *néo-Québécois* (literally "new Quebecker," an immigrant), and *Québécois de vieilles souches* (Quebecker of old stock), thus differentiating, and privileging, Francophone Quebeckers of French ancestry from French-speaking immigrants. In the wake of the defeat of 1995's separatist referendum, the *Parti Québécois* was forced to acknowledge the importance of the ethnic vote and began to treat identity as a function of *citoyenneté* (citizenship, place of birth) rather than ancestry or language.

If the Quebec case illustrates a shifting relationship between folklore and identity in nationalist discourse, the research on state control of expressive culture in Bulgaria shows how identity can emerge from the framing, rather than the content, of folklore. Chronicling the politics of culture in the socialist period, Carol Silverman (1989) describes how the Bulgarian government sharply curtailed the performance of Gypsy folklore. Gypsy and other ethnic musics were routinely excluded from state folk festivals, and ethnic instruments were outlawed, as was the performance of certain genres of Gypsy-identified music. With the fall of the Soviet Union, the legislation of expressive culture changed, and Gypsies and other ethnic performers were now encouraged to participate in the state-run festivals. As Amy Shuman (1993) observes, the new situation represented only a marginal tolerance for the expression of ethnic identity. The performances of Gypsies and other ethnic groups at the festivals were carefully framed by the state organizers as an expression of pan-Bulgarian unity, and Gypsy musicians were still prevented from performing the Gypsy-identified genres outside the festival context. Discussing Silverman's work, Shuman suggests that the point of the festivals "was to neutralize cultural difference, to remove the music from the context in which being a gypsy marks a political difference and put it in a context in which cultural difference can be used to demonstrate human similarity" (358). Regulating the framing of expressive culture rather than its content, the Bulgarian policies illustrate the centrality of interpretation in the politics of identity.

The Problem of Identity in Folklore Studies: Identity as Interpretive Framework

At the beginning of this essay we said that identity is a kind of interpretive framework. To interpret folklore in terms of identity means to take the meaning of folklore and project it into the interpreter's vision of the social world. While this idea may seem relatively intuitive, our brief discussion has shown that society can be imagined in an extraordinarily wide variety of ways. Furthermore, different scholars and participants may interpret the same performance or item of folklore with respect to different images of the social world. To make sense of this problematic theoretical area, we propose a three-parameter model for categorizing scholarly interpretations of identity in folklore. The x axis of our model specifies the scale of social life that the identity interpretation posits (from small- to large-scale social affiliations) and the type of social group to which it refers. The y axis ranges from relational to affirmative visions of identity. The z axis ranges from institutionalized and regulating ideas of identity to situated or expressive representations of identity. Any given identity interpretation will be defined along all three parameters, and an illustration of the model is provided in Figure 1. The rendering of this model in visual and spatial terms should not be taken too literally, because the relationship between the poles of each axis is not one of simple opposition but of dialectical interaction.

While the "scale or type" parameter is the easiest of the three to understand, it is in no way free from complications. Interpretations that depict folklore as an expression of the author's individual character focus on the smallest social scale, while those that explore the identities of families, neighborhoods, towns, regions, ethnic groups, or nations focus on larger

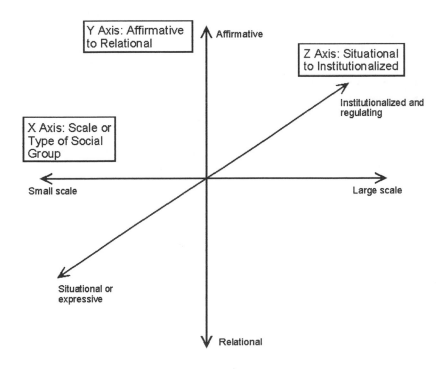

Figure 1. Typology of Identity Interpretations in Folklore Studies

and larger scales. Of course, not all social groups fit neatly along the axis of scale. Gender, sexual orientation, generation, or class find no obvious place along a smooth continuum of large to small, and in many cases it is best to think of this parameter as the type of social group posited by the identity interpretation in question. Below, we will discuss the problem of identity interpretations that reference more than one dimension of identity.

The y parameter is richly dialectical and describes how the social category of the x axis is defined. On the one pole, affirmative visions of identity define the individual through a list of attributes or qualities. Focused on the scale of national identity, Richard Dorson's *Bloodstoppers & Bearwalkers* represented Canadians as being "colorful" and expressive (1952, 71). Similarly affirmative, Giovanna Del Negro saw Graziella Di Corpo's trickster tales as the expression of a personal identity that foregrounded the qualities of familial devotion and wily creativity (Del Negro 1997). On the other pole, relational interpretations see identity as defined in a negative or oppositional manner. By negative, we do not mean that relational identity is necessarily contestatory or insulting, but rather that identity is defined by systematic contrast with other identities. When Bauman suggests that the Jews and Tlingit construct their identity interpretations through a system of implied contrasts with other groups, he offers up examples of relational identity. Focused on the larger scale of culture areas, Edward Said makes a similarly oppositional argument about the mirror image constructions of the Orient and the Occident (1979). It is worth noting here that purely affirmative or relational visions of identity are rare occurrences. Most affirmative representations of identity are at least partially constructed through an implied contrast with others, and all but the most strictly oppositional constructions of identity imply some positive qualities to be contrasted.

The z parameter ranges from institutionalized and regulating representations of identity to those that are situational or expressive. Institutionalized and regulating identity occurs when a representation of individual or group identity is codified in law, policy, or dogma and used to dictate behavior. Situated or expressive identity refers to the identity interpretations that are achieved in social interaction and includes almost all of the interpretations of identity in expressive culture as well; such situated interpretations always occur in larger social contexts and may respond to, collaborate with, or subvert institutionalized visions of identity. The relationship between the two poles of this axis requires careful attention. We can begin by observing that all ideas about identity are created in situated practices of interpretation, but only a small number of these ideas become codified in law or regulation. When Judith Nagata describes the ethnic legislation of Malaysia or Deirdre Evans-Pritchard explains the rules about the selling of native jewelry in New Mexico, both authors are discussing institutionalized identity. Nagata's description of the "on the ground" manipulation of ethnicity laws by Malaysian citizens, however, shifts the focus from institutionalized visions of identity to situational ones. It is important to note that we use the term "institutionalized" rather than "institutional" identity here, because ideas about identity achieve the strange, quasi-autonomous status of law or policy only when they have been negotiated through political processes and actively established as institutional by legislators, bureaucrats, or other administrative agents. Taking institutionalized identity in this restricted sense, ethnographic studies of the construction of identity in courts and legislative bodies are examples of situational identity, and institutionalized identity only exists when ideas about identity are reified in regulation and experienced by actors as anonymous social forces.[6] Institutionalized and regulating identity interpretations primarily exist on the large-scale end of the x axis, but if sufficiently reified and regulating, the rules of a family (the Smith children must go to bed at eight) or a dyadic relationship (neither spouse in the Jones-Doe marriage may go to sleep angry) may involve institutionalized identity as well. Institutionalized and regulating identity usually ranges across the y axis by defining groups in strict systemic opposition to one another (the Anglophones, Francophones, and Allophones of Quebec) and assigning different affirmative qualities, as well as rights and privileges, to each. Situational and expressive identity may invoke any scale or type of social group and may be configured in either affirmative or relational ways.

In defining the opposite pole of the continuum, the term "situational," rather than "micro-level," "personal," or "interactive," was carefully chosen as well. By using this word, we wish to emphasize the fact that all acts of interpreting identity, either in expressive behavior or other types of social interaction, are *located within* larger social contexts, are constrained and enabled by those contexts, and can only be understood in those contexts. For example, the ethnic shiftings of Indians and Chinese in Malaysia are indeed active achievements of identity interpretation. It would, however, be an error of romanticization to forget that, no matter how creative and resistant such acts may be, they are situated within the context of a highly restrictive state power, motivated by needs that arise from the context of that power, and performed with the risk of sanctions and reprisals. Likewise, however creative the visions of identity found in an example of expressive behavior, the creativity of that behavior always emerges from a social history, a social context, and a set of given cultural resources. From visions of Polish ethnic identity in American polka music (Keil, Keil, and Blau 1992) to the images of women's working-class identity in the bodily adornments

of Latina gang members (Mendoza-Denton 1996) and beyond, all interpretations of identity in expressive culture are situated within a social
world, and it is within that context that much of their meaning lies. Thus,
while rappers like Queen Latifah and Salt-n-Pepa interpret African American women's identity as self-reliant and proactive, this interpretation does
not emerge from thin air. As Tricia Rose suggests (1997), such a vision
comes about as a creative response to a social context of racism and misog-
yny and a cultural context (both within and beyond the world of hip hop)
that often depicts black women in the stereotypical images of compliant
sexual objects or lazy welfare cheats.

The poles of institutionalized versus situational identity effectively account for a key dimension in the scholarly perspectives we have examined,
but it is worth noting that these ideas point to deeper questions about the
nature or origin of identity. Both scholars and non-scholars theorize about
the nature of identity, and to make sense of this diverse array of ideas we
will use the terms "agentive" and "given." These terms should not be con-
fused with the notions of "ascribed identity" and "achieved identity" commonly found in sociology. There, "ascribed" and "achieved" are used to categorize the social roles or types of identities found in a given society. An
ascribed identity is one that a society views as fixed, while an achieved identity is one that a society allows the individual to acquire. (In the United
States, for example, race and gender are usually thought of as ascribed,
while elements of identity like occupation or political affiliation are
achieved.) Our notions of agentive and given identities operate at a logical
level different from this one. Unlike ascribed and achieved, which categorize specific identities, agentive and given categorize implicit or explicit *theories* about the very notion of identity—theories about what identity is and
how it works. By extension, agentive and given also sort the theorists who
hold such ideas.

At one end of the agentive/given axis, we find those who interpret identity as the achievement of the social actor. Included here are both traditional literary scholars who see the authorial composition of the text as the
active construction of personal or group identity as well as performance-
oriented folklorists who explore the construction of identity in social interaction, dialogue, and communication. At the opposite pole, we find those
who view identity as a given quality, beyond the reach of individual manipulation. This pole includes both ethnic nationalists who interpret folklore as an expression of a people's soul and postmodern writers who view
Structure (biological or social), Text, or the Site as the origin of identity.
Addressing the question of individual identity, the writings of Jean-Paul
Sartre ([1943] 1956) and Louis Althusser ([1970] 1971) represent the most

radical versions of agentive and given identity. For Sartre, the hallmark of the human condition is one's ability, and radical responsibility, to define oneself; here, the capacity for choice is believed to transform even the most seemingly pre-given feature of character, and identity is ultimately a matter of choice. In contrast, Althusser saw individual identity as a product of bourgeois ideology, and bourgeois ideology itself as an effect of capitalism. In the same way that a policeman's whistle calls forth or "interpolates" reflexive awareness in all that hear it, he argued, the "ideological state apparatuses" of capitalism call into being the illusion of an autonomous personal identity.

While all forms of essentialism (from ethnic nationalism to Robert Bly masculinism) fit at the "given" end of the axis, social constructivism can come in either agentive or given varieties, depending on whether the constructivist sees the social actor or society as the source of the construction. And just as the poles of the affirmative/relational axis interact in a complex manner, a complex mix of agentive and given ideas about identity inform many of the extant scholarly or non-scholarly theories of identity. Writers like Bauman, for example, take the actor's interpretation of identity as an agentive process situated in a given social context. Here, pre-existing cultural identities are actively negotiated and renegotiated through interactions that are situated in the contexts of past social histories, repertoires of expressive resources, and existing social orders and relations of power. Though the question of the origin of identity is a serious theoretical issue, most folklorists do not make their stance on this topic explicit, and their positions must be inferred from their writings. For this reason, we will primarily concern ourselves with the instrumental and regulating versus situational or expressive axis and set aside a larger discussion of the agentive versus given axis. It is worth mentioning, though, that writers who posit institutionalized and regulating identity necessarily construct a realm of bureaucratically given identity, while those thinkers that focus on situational or expressive identity may conceptualize any mix of agency and givenness as the source of identity.

The discussion so far has focused on identities that are totalizing and one dimensional, such as the identity of individuals or ethnic groups writ large. In the real world, however, most identity interpretations are multidimensional, referencing and combining several dimensions of identity (gender, region, class) in one representation. If a simple, one-dimensional interpretation of identity could be represented in the three-space of Figure 1, a multidimensional representation of identity would be understood as a complex whole involving several identities, each of which would be defined along the parameters outlined here. The multidimensional nature of identity will be explored in detail in the next section, but for now it is worth observing that the differences between various ideologies discussed by writers like Hall and Handler turn on the relationship between these dimensions of identity. The unified self of modern Western philosophy is premised on the notion that the various dimensions of identity should hang together in a coherent fashion, while the Indian "dividual" self allows for more flexibility and autonomy among its parts.

Any given statement about identity can be understood in terms of this three-parameter model, and the analysis of identity interpretations can be used to shed light on the interpreter's underlying social theory. If one sees the world in individualistic terms, then one will interpret folklore as the expression of the identity of a unique person defined by affirmative qualities. For the strong individualist, such an identity is only relational inasmuch as it capitulates to or resists larger social pressures. Thus, for example, the expressive culture produced by Oscar Wilde (his writings, his clothing, his carefully groomed public reputation) was intended—and interpreted as—a statement of his unique, carefully elaborated identity, and the same could be said of any other "great artist" in the individualist tradition from James Joyce to David Bowie. In Herder's romantic folklore, identity is affirmative and focused strongly on the level of the (ethnically defined) nation, but present in his writing is a relational critique of the (perceived) decadence of urban German society and the interplay of the urban and the rural. If one's social theoretic impulse is primarily relational and focused on the level of ethnicities and nations, one will interpret folklore in terms of the interaction of social groups. Here, individual creativity may be subsumed under group identity, or the expressive resources of a tradition may be viewed as a vehicle for the blossoming of the individual. Focused on the level of ethnic groups and nation states, Américo Paredes's classic study of Mexican American balladry *With His Pistol in His Hand* (1958) leans toward the relational. While Paredes presents an affirmative vision of Mexican American identity, his vision is colored by a relational awareness that substantive qualities are formed and expressed when social groups interact. Where the Wilde and Herder examples are located firmly at the situational-or-expressive end of the z axis, Paredes discusses both institutionalized and situational identity. Viewing identity as relational and focused on the interplay of the bureaucratic nation state, the ethnic group, and the individual actor, Nagata reveals how the folkways of everyday survival in the modern state involve the creative manipulation of social identity. While recent attention paid by folklorists to the relational and situated negotiation of identity is indeed valuable, our goal here is not to argue for any single model of social life but to explore the different ways in which identity interpretations are made and the underlying ideas about society that they imply.

Wherever they are located on the three axes of this model, all identity interpretations involve a kind of doubling; the person interprets the lore, and then interprets the lore again, projecting the primary interpretation into his/her vision of the social world. Watching *The Importance of Being Earnest* or listening to the "Ballad of Gregorio Cortez," one may note a paradox and interpret it as witty, or one may follow the plot and interpret a character's deeds as brave. Reading these items of expressive culture in terms of identity, one may project that wittiness onto one's mental map and experience it as the uniquely Wilde (or Irish or male or *fin de siecle*) wit; interpreting the bravery in terms of identity, it becomes Mexican American (or working class or male) bravery. Read in terms of identity, beauty is never just beauty. This lovely melody, that stunning outfit, these pretty words become statements of our ethnic pride, our people's ability to find beauty in the context of oppression, or the long and rich tradition of our community. Read in terms of identity, affect is never just affect. These dissonant chords, these ripped jeans, these gentle words become statements of my resistance, our defiance, or their conciliation. For ease of expression, we have represented the interpretation of identity as a linear process in which an interpreter gets an initial meaning and then thrusts it into his/her vision of the social world to see the lore as an expression of identity. In fact, the order of the steps may be reversed (as when a person attends a staged performance of folklore expecting to see an expression of ethnic identity), and most often they occur in a single stroke. The heaviness of heavy metal and the sense that it is the collective property of the subculture emerge together in the musical experience of the metalheads without any intervening steps. The humor of a Wilde *bon mot* and the sense that that humor was uniquely Wilde's are, for individualist Wilde devotees, inseparable. But however the process occurs, the interpretation of identity always makes meaning sociological, uniting a feature of the expressive culture with a conceptualized field of social individuals or social groups.

Both the scholarly error of over-reading and the ubiquity of the notion of identity come from this doubling. For researchers, the danger of over-reading—interpreting a belief or practice as a statement of identity when it is neither intended nor experienced in that way by the participants—is a constant problem. Imputing intention where none is given or taking an insignificant practice as evidence of a hoary tradition are mistakes that almost all students of expressive culture have made at one point or another.

By emphasizing this problem, we don't want to suggest that identity is a useless interpretive framework; rather, we wish to highlight the basic phenomena that make this error possible. Indeed, many pieces of folklore *are* intended and interpreted as statements of ethnic pride, the ability to find beauty in the context of oppression, or the long and rich tradition of particular communities. Performers and audiences (both scholarly and non-scholarly ones) are able to over-read because we recognize the essentially social nature of all conduct and all expressive culture. Because, as we suggested in the introduction, all conduct emerges in a social context and all expressive culture draws on stocks of cultural knowledge, any expressive act may potentially be interpreted as a statement of identity. The error of over-reading comes from making grandiose social claims about random or contingent social acts (the long and rich tradition of buttering toast in a certain way) or from ascribing intention when none is there (the buttering of toast as a statement of ethnic identity).

Of course, the issue of identity would not be so important if individuals merely associated particular identities with value-free qualities or if the interpretation of identity was a strictly individual act of meaning making detached from the social world. This, however, is not the case. While it is obvious that highly institutionalized representations of identity (in identity cards or visas, work permits or legal privileges) are informed by, and even constitutive of, the social order, power relations also play a key role in the situated interpretations of identity in expressive culture. Pre-existing social structures and stocks of cultural knowledge (native social theories, images, icons, and narratives) are the ideological raw material and informing context in which even the newest and most idiosyncratic interpretations are made. And while actors may produce interpretations that resist dominant ideas, none may do so *independently* of the larger social field. That the qualities that become attached to particular groups in identity interpretations are value loaded need not be restated. It is worth stressing, however, that such interpretations of identity gain their valences and meanings through their relationship with a larger social history and social context. Thus, to take the quality "tough" and attach it to a social group may be a positive reinterpretation if that identity has historically been stereotyped "weak" or "overly intellectual" (for example, Jews or gay men), but the same quality may be pejorative if associated with a group that has been depicted as "criminal" or "primitive" (for example, African Americans), and the complex identity interpretations of real-world expressive culture gain their rich, three-dimensional meanings through a network of connections with a larger social universe. Reconfirming, nuancing, adumbrating, resisting, or overturning previous visions, the interpretation of identity is one of the prime battlegrounds upon which ideological struggles are played out.

The Interpretation of Identity in Situated Interaction: Perception and Reflection, Foreground and Background

The discussion so far has focused on identity interpretations in scholarly texts and has tried to illuminate the conceptual apparatus by which such interpretations are made. While these processes are important, the interpretation of identity is more than just the outcome of internal, meaning making activities, and such readings are not the sole possession of academics. On the contrary, they come to light in interaction and are present both within and beyond the confines of the university. To gain the richest understanding of these phenomena, we would need to explore how ideas about identity emerge in all of the varied domains of social life—performances of various kinds, mass-mediated communication, legal proceedings, medical contexts, religious ritual, meditation, and so forth. This is clearly an enormous project, and the remainder of this essay takes a first step in this direction by exploring how identity interpretations are constructed and experienced in face-to-face interactions that involve expressive culture. All of the dynamics we have discussed above still apply in this discussion: the interpretation of identity still projects first-order meanings onto the interpreter's map of the social world, and that interpretive map still entails judgements of scale, agency versus givenness, and so forth. Here, however, our focus shifts from the construction of the conceptual content of identity interpretation to the experience of that content in social interaction. For example, whether we are swapping jokes at a bar, playing music with friends, or watching dancers at a folk festival, ideas about identity may be discussed openly or presented in veiled ways; such ideas may be constructed in language, music, or material culture and may be taken as the focus of attention or shuffled to the distant background of the participant's experience. In the field, we researchers are keenly aware of when the people with whom we work are negotiating identity. But because we are usually so focused on the content of the interpretations (the joke teller's construction of gender, the singer's representation of ethnicity), we are sometimes less aware of how those contents emerge in the immediate experience of the folklore participants. And yet, exactly how these interpretations are experienced is crucial for the overall meaning of the event. Here, we seek to draw greater scholarly attention to these lived meanings and interactional processes, and, following well-established practices in theoretical writing in the humanities, we will illustrate these meanings and processes with an elaborated hypothetical example. While instances of these dynamics can be found throughout the existing literature (including Silverman 1989, Shuman 1994, Walser 1993, Solomon 1994, and Singer 1972), we have chosen to use a hypothetical example in order to present these phenomena in a more systematic manner and to provide illustrations that are directly commensurate with one another. With this analysis in place, we will conclude by suggesting how ideas about identity can be combined with other interpretive frameworks to create rich, multileveled meanings.

We begin by focusing on the audience side of folklore performances, and the first point is that when identity interpretations are made, they can be experienced in several distinct forms. Our hypothetical example will illustrate. Imagine that an American with little experience of foreign cultures has been invited for dinner at the home of a family of native Italians living in Chicago. Watching the grandmother cook, the American might easily see the act of cooking as an expression of Italian identity. In its least problematic incarnation, that interpretation could take the form of a reflective thought in words—a little "voice in the head" saying, for example, "That style of cooking and gesturing looks so Italian." Conversely, the guest might embed his/her interpretation (let us say his) in a perceptual experience without reflectively forming the mental commentary. Just as a person might hear a melody as "lonesome" or "spirited," the guest might "see" the cook's flamboyant hand motions and distinctive knife techniques as imbued with a quality of "Italianness."

When described abstractly, such perceptually embedded interpretations may at first seem strange, but even briefly reviewing our everyday experiences suggests how common these nonreflective, perceptual qualities are (see James [1912] 1967b and Berger 1991). When one watches a sunrise, one doesn't merely see a circular, reddish-yellow blob and then think, "Ah, how beautiful." On the contrary, one embeds the quality of beauty in the sun-image itself. And not only are affective and aesthetic qualities embedded in perception; categories of identity may be experienced in this qualitative and perceptual way. We literally see hand gestures as masculine or feminine, hear the vocal qualities of singers as Balkan or Hawaiian, smell fragrances as Indian or Thai.

Our description of these experiences is liable to misinterpretation, and the nature and content of our claims requires careful explanation. First, we are not saying that there is anything *inherently* masculine about a type of hand movement or any necessary connection between bright, nasal tones and the mountains of Bosnia. Even assuming that a particular perception is veridical (that a particular spice is uniquely used in Thai cooking or a particular type of cutting technique is found on the Italian peninsula and nowhere else), such features would be socially and historically emergent practices, not inherent essences. Alternatively, we are not denying that such interpretations can in fact be veridical. As we suggested in the introduction, anything that a person says or does may be informed by his/her tradition, and particular types of practices are indeed associated with particular societies and cultures. However, the correspondence of an interpretation with an empirically verifiable pattern of practice in a given group is not our concern in this section. Here, we seek only to describe the different forms that identity interpretations may take in lived experience; the first ideas we have suggested are that both perception and reflection are interpretive processes and that culturally derived social categories may be projected into our perceptual experience as qualities on a prereflective basis.

Whether perceptually embedded or reflective, such identity interpretations may be situated in the foreground or the background of the interpreter's experience. This is easiest to see with perceptual interpretations. For example, while our American dinner guest may experience the Italianness of the cook's gestures with great intensity, a Swiss neighbor who has eaten with our hypothetical family many times may experience this same embedded quality but much more weakly. Interpretations formed in reflective thought can also range from the foreground to the background of experience. At first this idea may be surprising, because we usually think of reflection as something that occupies our full attention; in everyday life, however, many thoughts are apprehended with light intensity. Watching an absorbing film, for example, a stray thought about work may vaguely pass through one's mind, garnering a small amount of attention without displacing the movie's powerful images and sounds from the foreground of one's experience. Intently focused on gently folding the egg whites into the cake batter, our Swiss dinner guest may reflect with vague attention that the American's style of turn taking in conversation is characteristic of his country. The question of the intensity with which an interpretation is experienced speaks to the problem of over-reading. Nothing is more embarrassing for the fieldworker than to create an elaborate set of meanings for some custom, only to be told later by his/her research participants that they care little about the practice and rarely give it their full attention. As we shall suggest below, the problem of backgrounded identity interpretations is more complex than it first may seem and requires careful consideration.

Reflective or perceptually embedded, identity interpretations are rarely one dimensional. For example, while it is possible that our American dinner guest may see the cook as simply "Italian," he is more likely to interpret her conduct as illustrative of two or more dimensions of identity—"Ah, the stereotypical Italian *mother* cooking an abundance of food for the family," or "Ah, the *traditional* Italian cook! She uses only the freshest ingredients." It goes without saying that different interpreters may vary in the emphasis they place on any particular dimension of identity (the Marxist guest interpreting the cook as a member of the proletariat, the minister who reads her as Catholic).

Whenever more than one dimension of identity is present, the various facets are organized in a foreground/background structure, and the relationships among them are crucial for the overall character of the interpretation. In our example, the ethnic-gender attribution ("Italian mother") may be foregrounded in the guest's experience, while the features "working class" or "Catholic" may be situated in the further background. Like the goblet and the silhouettes in the famous Rubin's Goblet drawing, the different dimensions of identity form a gestalt—a complex whole in which the various parts color and inform one another. Thus, while our guest may be only dimly aware of the fact that he sees the cook as a member of the working class, this reading may play a key role in his interpretation, coloring the foregrounded attributes of "Italian" and "mother" with a host of meanings and associations. Unmarked categories of identity are often shuffled to the deep background of the identity interpretation; difficult to unearth in interviews and dimly apprehended, such taken-for-granted elements may still be highly significant for the character of the interpretation as a whole. Thus, if our American guest were a cultural conservative, it is likely that he would, by default, read the cook as heterosexual. Such an interpretation would, for our guest, situate the cook in a social space defined both affirmatively by a host of qualities and attributes and relationally in opposition to the concept "gay." Though deeply backgrounded, this reading plays a key role in the overall interpretation. If the reader has any doubt that this reading is present for our hypothetical guest, the reader must only imagine the cook introducing her lesbian partner to the guest (and the guest's subsequent interpretive backfilling) to see the importance of such dimly apprehended dimensions of identity.

Background identity interpretations may take two forms. As Berger has suggested elsewhere (1999), *defining* backgrounds operate like the dark patches in the Rubin's Goblet drawing—informing the foregrounded dimensions of identity and coloring the overall character of the experience. The guest's view of the cook as heterosexual is such an example. *Receding* backgrounds, however, are dimly apprehended conceptions that have little impact on the experience as a whole. Vaguely present but inconsequential, they differ little from genuinely absent interpretations. Region, for example, is a crucial issue in Italian cultural politics, and, for most natives of that country, this factor would rarely be missing when interpreting a fellow

Italian's identity. Given the guest's unfamiliarity with Italy's cultural politics, regional identity would be genuinely absent from his interpretation of the cook. If it was mentioned that the cook was from the northern province of Lombardia or the southern province of Naples, the guest would only use this fact to entrench his interpretation of her as an "authentic" Italian. Slightly nuanced by this receding background, the overall interpretation would change little.

Whether they are located in the foreground, the defining background, or the receding background, perceptually embedded interpretations are often difficult to articulate in words and share in discourse, and issues of power and domination can play a key role here. One would expect that deeply backgrounded interpretations are difficult to describe, but foreground interpretations may also resist explicit articulation. Examples of this kind of explicit denial can be found throughout the ethnographic and cultural studies literature. In his well known work, *Running with the Devil*, Robert Walser (1993) has suggested that gender and sexuality are key issues in the music and culture of heavy metal fans. In some of the subgenres of the style, female characters are markedly absent from the song lyrics or videos. While the "exscription" of women in heavy metal may symbolically resolve the gender contradictions that male metalheads confront in American society, it may also produce homoerotic overtones. Walser suggests that while the images of male bonding in the videos of Judas Priest and the lyrics of the band Accept have clear homoerotic implications, few metal fans would be willing to acknowledge this fact (115–116). In prereflective sense perception, the largely heterosexual and often homophobic audiences literally see the gestures of Priest's singer Rob Halford and literally hear the lyrics of Accept as an expression of the performers's homosexuality; refusing to admit that their heros are gay, however, they resist converting these interpretations from their sensual to their reflective form.

Some of the most vexing dilemmas in the analysis of identity come in teasing out the relationships between defining and receding backgrounds. On the one hand, much critical scholarship (in areas such as Marxism, feminism, or queer theory) is premised on the idea that experiences of expressive culture may be profoundly informed by what we have called embedded and backgrounded identity interpretations; to ignore these taken for granted dimensions of identity (the significance of whiteness for Tim Allen's comedy, for example) is to misunderstand our research participants' experiences and ignore the politics of culture. On the other hand, deciding what dimensions of identity are at play in any given interpretation (and discerning the relative importance of those dimensions) is an extremely difficult task. To read heavy handedly every interaction in terms of race, class, or gender is to risk trivializing the very politics we wish to expose; to assume a priori that we know how our research participants conceptualize race, class, or gender or to assume that they are the only significant dimensions of identity is to naturalize the very ideas we hope to show as historically emergent. The difficulty of converting embedded interpretations into reflective ones produces a related set of paradoxes. One the one hand, scholars from Freudians to Marxists have long known that individuals may actively or passively misinterpret their own experiences or intentionally deceive researchers; on the other hand, to discount the research participants' own descriptions of their experiences and to privilege the researcher's is assume that research participants are nothing more than cultural dupes or bearers of false consciousness. Because the scholarly analysis of identity is nothing more and nothing less than the interpretation of another's interpretation, there is no general, theoretical solution to these difficulties. By emphasizing the problems that confront the researcher, our goal is not to make so pessimistic a critique of the interpretive endeavor as to make scholarship on identity impossible. Indeed, refusing to interpret folklore is itself no solution, because abandoning social research or indulging in interpretive timidity is just another move in the politics of research. We suggest that the way to respond to these dilemmas comes not from theory but from the practice of interpreting expressive culture. By being aware of the dynamics of interpretation and striving to do research that is sensitive to both the problem of power and the experiences of our research participants, the researcher can come to richer, more sophisticated understandings of expressive culture. Our aim, here, is to make those dynamics as explicit as possible.

The Interpretation of Identity in Face-to-Face Interaction: Intention, Communication, and Metacommunication

So far, our discussion has focused on the audience member's individual, momentary interpretation of folklore. Our description can become more nuanced and realistic if we recall that related interpretive practices occur on the part of the performer as well. Observing his/her own actions, the performer may produce a number of reflective or embedded identity interpretations and situate them variously in the foreground, the defining background, or the receding background of experience. For example, having spent an afternoon in the kitchen of a Tibetan neighbor who had recently moved in down the street, our hypothetical Italian cook may become aware of the taken-for-granted elements of her culinary practice and see her own kitchen techniques as distinctively Italian. Observing her own conduct as if at a distance, she may stop and think, "Yes, that is the way we always held the knife in my home town." By the same token, if the cook is busily showing her grandson how to crush garlic or trim artichokes for a rushed workday dinner, the same interpretation may emerge in the background as an embedded interpretation or may not be constructed at all.

Of course, identity interpretations may not merely reflect upon conduct but actually guide it—as when our cook actively exaggerates her kitchen techniques to look "more Italian" for her American guest. From the highly institutionalized interpretations found at folk festivals to the most idiosyncratic displays of identity in everyday life, conduct carried out as a statement of identity has been defined by Milton Singer as a "cultural performance" (1972). Actions guided by prior identity interpretation may be said to be an intentional display of identity, but the complex relationship between action and interpretation problematizes the notion of intention and creates rich dilemmas for the researcher.[7] Ascertaining an actor's intention to perform identity turns on one's ability to distinguish between conduct directed by earlier reflective identity interpretations ("I will now trim the artichoke on the bevel as Italians do"), conduct in which the same interpretation is embedded in the actor's ongoing sensual experience of the action (as when our cook experiences herself preparing food in an Italian way without previously forming a reflective plan), and conduct where identity interpretations are genuinely absent for the actor during the conduct but are imputed by the audience or filled in by the actor retrospectively. Even when we have good reason to believe that an interpretation preceded and guided the conduct, we must still grapple with the problems outlined above and accurately describe the identity interpretation that served as the intention—that is, the vision of the social world implied by the interpretation, the dimensions of identity posited (race, class, gender), the relative foregroundedness/backgroundedness of different dimensions, and so forth.

All of this is further complicated by the fact that the reading of identity is often an interactive process, and the dynamics of interpretation here can be complex. If conduct is intended as a display of identity and interpreted as such by an audience (as in any cultural performance), then that conduct may be said to be a kind of communication about identity. Accompanying discourse about identity (as when the guest and the cook discuss American and Italian styles of cooking while they prepare the meal) or communication about the processes of communication would therefore be metacommunication. Communication and metacommunication about identity may go on simultaneously and take many forms. For example, kinesics, proxemics, and veiled language may be used for implicit, backgrounded, or concealed metacommunication—as when the children in the family interpret their grandmother's conspicuous attention to culinary minutia as an obnoxious performance of identity and catch each other stiffening with embarrassment. Explicit metacommunication about the interaction may be an honest description of the participant's embedded interpretations (as when the guest says to the cook, "You are my ideal of an Italian chef"), and readings of the other's experience may be highly accurate (as when the cook rightly reflects that, as an American, the guest will not like tripe). However, metacommunication may also obscure the actor's own embedded interpretations (as when the guest says that he appreciates the Italian practice of eating organ meats, though in fact he finds the practice both distinctively Italian and repulsive). Likewise, meta-interpretations may misread the interpretations of the other (as when the children misinterpret their mother's genuinely unreflective concern for culinary fine points as a self-conscious display of identity). Turning to higher orders of reflexivity, we add that any metacommunication made by any participant in the event is itself an example of conduct that may be interpreted in terms of identity—as when our guest reads the cook's penchant for observations about her own cooking as distinctively Italian. Such second-order interpretations may be made explicit in the dialogue (a positive spin: "You Italians love to share your traditions with others"), remain as an internal, reflective thought (a negative spin: "These Italians never shut up"), or be embedded in the actor's perceptual experience (as when the guest hears the cook's words of meta-commentary as delightful Italian volubility or annoying Italian chattiness.)

As the literature in our field has shown, the amount of metacommunicative discourse about identity varies from one type of situation to another. In highly dialogic genres of face-to-face expressive culture—such as ritualized insult exchange (Solomon 1994) or public lectures (Singer 1972)—interpretations may be actively negotiated in the event. In other genres of expressive culture, such as highly scripted forms of religious worship, metacommunicative interpretations of identity may be sharply circumscribed or forbidden. Just as the participants may have foreground, embedded interpretations that resist reflective articulation, so too may they have reflective interpretations that are never shared in metacommunicative discourse. Even within those genres that emphasize negotiation, strict limits may be set on the types of identity interpretations that may enter explicit metacommunicative discourse, and once again the issue of power relations enters here. For example, questions of gender, race, or even class may be discussed in the public events of mainstream American society (graduation ceremonies, parades, and so forth); however, sexual orientation is still largely beyond the bounds of explicit metacommunicative discourse there.

In any given event or type of event, what interpretations are made, how explicitly they are made, and who makes them are all outcomes of generic constraint, larger issues of power, and the creative agency of the participants.

Taken alone, any one of the interpretive dynamics that we have described may be familiar to scholars in our field; in fact, most of us could probably illustrate a number of these situations with examples from our own research. Taken together, however, this set of dynamics produces an interpretive field of incredible complexity. If we wish to understand identity issues in folklore, we must grapple with this interpretive field in all of its richness. As we suggested above, identity interpretations project the meaning of the folklore into the interpreter's vision of the social world. That vision amounts to nothing less than the interpreter's implicit folk theory of society, and to study identity in folklore performance means, first and foremost, to unearth that theory. To get a fuller understanding, we must account for the multidimensional nature of identity, the interpretive dilemmas of power, and the different ways that ideas about identity emerge in experience. The situation is made still more complex by the dynamics of communication, the problems of intention, and the issue of metacommunication and generic constraint. It would be impossible to illustrate all of the differing situations that might arise when these phenomena occur in combination. We can, however, suggest some of this complexity by expanding upon the cooking scenarios that we have developed in the last two sections. The example is purely hypothetical, but it suggests some of the richness that can arise in the interpretation of identity in folklore performance.

Maria Lucci is a seventy-three-year-old native of Centro, a prosperous small town surrounded by smaller, poorer villages in central Sicily. In 1961, Maria immigrated to Chicago with her husband (a respectable farmer, now deceased) and her ten-year-old son, Paolo. While Maria speaks only Italian, her son learned English quickly and grew up to be a successful lawyer. One Sunday, Paolo brought his two children (Marco, twelve, and Dina, twenty-one) to lunch at Maria's house. Touting the meal as a "traditional Italian Sunday dinner, an experience you will never forget," Paolo also invited Jack, a wealthy American client with little knowledge of Italy. While Marco sets the table, Paolo explains to Jack that his mother's method of paring the artichokes is typically Italian. "That's the way they did it in the village," he explains. "You don't waste a thing this way, which is important, and you get the best texture." Jack makes an effort to watch, and Paolo, stealing a meatball from the pan, continues that, as a kid, his Mom always gave him the best portions of meat and the largest helpings of pasta. Getting a clean towel from the pantry, Maria adds extra garlic to the sauce and, in broken English, gently scolds Dina for not being more friendly and talkative with her father's guest. Dina smiles and, on her way to washing lettuce in the sink, nudges Marco in the ribs. He quickly gives Maria a hug and says how much he loves his *nonna*'s cooking.

Throughout the entire scene, Maria's actions are the object of intense and complex identity interpretations. We can begin with the cook herself. Maria knows that her son likes to show off his mother's cooking as a display of Italian culinary arts; though she doesn't understand English, she also knows that her son emphasizes his working-class roots and represents the cooking as good peasant food. This is particularly galling to Maria, because, while her husband was a farmer, she came from a well-respected family in Centro. Wanting to accommodate her son's career but sick of being represented as an ignorant farmhand, Maria forms a complex identity interpretation that guides her cooking. Before Paolo and his guests arrive, she thinks to herself, "Whatever Paolo says, I will show his friend that I am Maria Lucci, the daughter of Massimo di Testa, mayor of Centro." In this reflective interpretation, village, family, and class identity are fused in the foreground, while nationality, and perhaps gender, are part of the defining background. The relational/affirmative dimension of the identity interpretation is particularly important here, as the sophistication of Centro (and its most prominent family) is constructed in opposition to the perceived provinciality of its surrounding villages. Guided by this interpretation, Maria's cooking is primarily intended as a display of Italian bourgeois sophistication. She uses fresh towels to illustrate her hygienic standards, and, bowing to her notion that Americans expect Italians to use lots of garlic, doubles up on the fragrant bulb to appeal to her audience. For Paolo, personal identity, ethnicity, and class engage in a complex dance as the scene unfolds. In the explicit metacommunication that preceded the interaction, ethnicity is foregrounded. Alluding to narratives of immigrant upward mobility in America, class is part of the defining background in this framing as well, and this feature briefly rises to prominence during the interaction when Paolo points out Maria's frugality. Ethnicity and class become backgrounded in Paolo's overall experience when he notices his mother's atypical, and to him aberrant, use of the extra garlic and towels. Dividing the social world into family members (a source of embarrassment that must be controlled) and outsiders (people who must be impressed), Paolo reads his mother's behavior as a classic example of Lucci family social sabotage. Such an interpretation is not gendered (his father and uncles, he believes, always did this kind of thing as well), and he tries to hide his frustration with Maria.

For Dina, gender identity, individual identity, and ethnic identity combine in complicated ways as the encounter transpires. A senior English major at a local university, Dina had spent the morning studying for the final in the fifth women's studies class of her college career. At the beginning of the encounter, she cannot help but see Maria's cooking and Paolo's braggadocio as straightforward expressions of traditional gender identities. Having witnessed similar scenes for years and argued with her father about his sexism, the interpretation is automatic and backgrounded. The quality of "stereotypical maleness" is embedded in her perceptual experience of her father's words and gestures; bored, she doesn't even bother with a reflective critique. When Maria tells Dina to be more friendly, however, the young woman realizes something different is going on today. For years, Maria and her son have always impressed upon the children that Americans are more closed-mouthed than Italians; because they wanted to avoid the image of the boisterous Italian family, "don't air your dirty laundry in public" became law in the Lucci household, and Maria always avoided any talk about politeness or propriety in public. When Maria actively comments on Dina's behavior, the granddaughter takes it as a transgression of this quasi-institutional family rule against public metacommunication about identity. Observing Maria's cooking with new interest, Dina sees her conduct as a parody of the "Italian grandmother routine," an expression of unsuspected resistance in Maria's character. Dina's washing of the lettuce is intended as an attempt to perform the role of the "proper Italian daughter," and she nudges her brother to get him to play along. Up to this point, Marco's identity interpretations are largely embedded. He reads his father's usual bragging comments as an expression of his dominating character and sees the simmering resentment in the women's conduct as a familiar expression of their angry personalities. When Dina nudges him in the ribs, Marco knows that it is time to play the good boy, although he isn't quite sure why. Throughout this scene, Jack is oblivious to most of the subtle metacommunication. While he takes Maria's cooking and the boisterous family banter as an expression of Italian ethnic identity, his mind is mostly on the business matters that he and Paolo will discuss later that day.

Variously emphasizing personality, kin group, region, ethnicity, gender, and class, the interpretations found in this example involve multiple dimensions of identity and shift fluidly from foreground to background, reflection to embedded perception, explicit to implicit communication. While a groundwork of partially shared ideas about identity informs the participants' conduct (the image of the boisterous Italian family, the steaming bowl of pasta as an icon of Italian culture), miscommunication, partial communication, and deception are constantly at play here, making it difficult for us to take any single action as a straightforward example of ethnic identity. The scene illustrates the varied ways in which notions of identity can play themselves out in any given situation and suggests how the concepts we have introduced can sensitize the folklorist to the interpretive richness of folklore events. In some cases, it may be difficult for a fieldworker to elicit from his/her research participants this detailed a record of their interpretations, and by no means do we wish to suggest that this kind of experiential transcript is the only valid interpretation of folklore. We do believe, however, that this fluid texture of experiences is the foundation from which folklore events derive their meanings and that such lived meanings can be partially shared between fieldworker and research participant through the standard ethnographic techniques of participant/observation, interview, and so forth. Examining other types of events (such as a play or a musical performance) or focusing on songs, stories, or costumes (rather than the events in which they are experienced), the scholar may find interpretations of identity that do not involve the constantly shifting byplay that we illustrated above. If, however, identity is the issue at stake, the underlying interpretive dynamics will be the same.

Identity in Combination with Other Interpretive Frameworks: The Aesthetics of Identity

Because meaning making is an open-ended process, individual interpretive frameworks are rarely employed in isolation. Identity can be combined with other frameworks to produce complex, multilayered interpretations, and to illustrate we will conclude by exploring the relationship between identity and aesthetics. When these two frameworks are combined, conduct is interpreted in terms of identity, and then the identity interpretation itself is enmeshed with one or more rich, valual qualities and taken as the object of aesthetic judgement. The valual attributes of the interpretation may include those traditionally associated with the term "aesthetics" (i.e., beauty or ugliness), but they may also include a wide range of other value qualities, including but not limited to the affective (such as rage, delight, sadness), the sensuous (luxuriance, pain, numbness), or the stylistic (elegance, coolness, dorkyness). For example, to many audiences in the 1970s, what was enjoyable about David Bowie's performances was not just the musical sounds he created—the delicate vocal timbre, the intricate melodies, the powerful rock and funk grooves. Neither were the aesthetic qualities of the music and the stage show merely seen as an outcome of Bowie's personal identity—an individual who is idiosyncratic, intelligent, creative, and so forth. Further, Bowie was not merely trying to publicly think through or make a general announcement about his identity. On the contrary, the noted performer intended his identity itself to be an aesthetic object. The songs, clothes, and gestures were the media through which his identity was constructed (as a person who was creative but dispassionate, highly individualistic but vulnerable, androgynous and powerful), and that identity itself was presented as the focus of aesthetic enjoyment.

While music and dance may be vehicles for these type of interpretations, the media of everyday face-to-face interaction (conversation, gesture, and clothing) are crucial for the aesthetics of identity. We can get a better understanding of the performer's role in this process by distinguishing between the mundane *presentation* of self and the aesthetic *performance* of self. In Erving Goffman's formulation (1959), all interaction involves a presentation of self in which the actors monitor and direct their conduct to manage the impression that they "give" and "give off" to the other. Situated within the Goffmanian tradition, Richard Bauman (1989) defined performance as heightened activity in which the actor takes responsibility for a competent display of aesthetic conduct. Traditionally, the conduct that has been analyzed as performance has been storytelling, song, or dance, but as a variety of scholars have shown, the stuff of everyday face-to-face interaction—walking (Del Negro 1999, 2004), clothing and gesture (Willis 1975), or the wearing of make-up (Mendoza-Denton 1996)—may be highly aestheticized as well. If the self is *presented* when an actor manipulates the media of face-to-face interaction to achieve instrumental social business, the self is *performed* (in a Baumanian sense) when the actor displays his competent use of the media of face-to-face interaction, sets out his/her presentation of self for public viewing, and offers up the identity that is constructed as an object of aesthetic judgement.[8] Such conduct is highly reflexive. Taken for granted in mundane interaction, norms of behavior and rules of etiquette are brought to the fore in the performance of identity and serve (in conservative performance) as the criteria of evaluation or (in transgressive performance) as the object of critique. Conforming to, elaborating upon, reinterpreting, or flaunting the conventions of interaction, the performer offers up carefully managed conversation, gesture, and clothing to construct an identity that the audience interprets through the lens of aesthetics.

While popular music and everyday social interaction both involve aestheticized identity interpretations, contemporary late night television talk shows are the domain *par excellance* for the performance of identity. Beyond a movie plug or a personal anecdote of dubious veracity, little factual information is exchanged in the celebrity interviews on David Letterman or Jay Leno. Here, the smallest details of conversation, gesture, or clothing are intended to be guides to the actor's identity, and that identity becomes the object of aesthetic enjoyment. An everyday guy with an attitude, a goofy young woman with a hint of sexuality, a cool artist in control of his world, the identities constructed on the Letterman set are meant to be taken as objects of aesthetic pleasure. Such performances are not the sole province of the mass media. Closer to the territory that folklorists usually call home, the identity plays of the singles bar or the village square offer similar delights. When traditionally construed, sound is the medium of music and gracefully crafted melodies are the aesthetic objects; in the museum, paint and canvas are the raw material and compelling images are the thing that is evaluated. For the talk show guest or the barfly, conversation, gesture, and dress are the media and identity is the aesthetic object.

Of course, any form of conduct may serve as the vehicle for highly aesthetic identity interpretations, and comparing the performance of identity in popular music and talk shows highlights different facets of these phenomena. The difficulty of seeing music or dance as a performance of identity comes not in seeing the conduct as aesthetic (for most in the West see music and dance as aesthetic by default), but in recognizing the identity constructions themselves as aesthetic objects. The difficulty of seeing everyday interaction as a performance of identity comes not in seeing interaction as an expression of identity (for most see speech and gesture as the basic entrance to personal identity), but in seeing it as aesthetic. It is because so many of today's celebrities are primarily artists of identity (rather than singers or actors) that they are able to fluidly shift between such a wide variety of genres, from cinema, to music, to dance, to the television talk show. For them, the media are merely the means to a larger aesthetic end.

Of course, in many cultures music is not aestheticized by default, and everyday interaction is not seen primarily as an expression of individual identity. The aesthetics of identity and the performance of self are best thought of as a historically emergent and culturally specific set of interpretive practices, albeit common ones in today's world. Seeking to avoid essentialism, we emphasize that identity interpretations can be combined with other cultural concepts and used to create other, second-order interpretive frameworks. Identity may thus be "theologized" (interpreted in terms of religious ideas) or "scientized," and we cannot begin to explore the range of composite interpretive frameworks that may emerge from such combinations. Critics of commodity fetishism, particularly those in postmodernism, have argued that the aestheticization of identity is a key part of the culture of consumer capitalism, but a fuller inquiry into the articulation of interpretive dynamics with larger economic and social processes is best left for future research. By exploring the aesthetics of identity, we hope to have suggested one way in which our ideas can be applied to contemporary forms of expressive culture, and we encourage scholars to examine the different ways in which identity is combined with other interpretive frameworks in other cultural or historical contexts. In the broadest frame, we hope to have helped make sense of the concept of identity and suggest why this ubiquitous concept requires additional theoretical attention in our field. However one interprets the notion of identity, two things are clear. At least in the near future, identity will remain a relevant concept in both the study of social life and in world societies themselves. And as those societies change, the notion of identity will change as well, serving as a vehicle for the social imagination and as a continuous source of problems and opportunities for folklore studies. In the construction of identity, the world is doubled, and doubled, and doubled again endlessly. Folklorists can do no less, and ask for nothing more, than to interpret those worlds and ask what they mean.

Notes

*

Preface (pp. ix–xv)

1. Though many of these ideas are developed in the essays here, some are presented more completely in our other work. For example, Del Negro 1999 and 2004 present a fully articulated critique of the notions of "folklore," "high art," and "popular culture" and a discussion of the problems involved in the genre approach to folklore studies. Berger 1999 discusses how practice theory and phenomenology can be used in the study of expressive culture to shed light on the dialectics of agency and larger social forces.

Chapter 1. New Directions in the Study of Everyday Life
(pp. 3–22)

1. While the literatures we explore here construct the notion of everyday life in related ways, other authors develop this concept along different lines. In the work of Alfred Schutz, for example (Schutz and Luckmann 1973, [1983] 1989), the everyday is one of many "life-worlds" (or "provinces of meaning"), each of which is characterized by the unique way it structures the relationship between subject and object and the way that a subject dispenses meaning there (1973, 23). In the everyday life-world, the objects that one confronts resist one's needs and desires, time flows only in one direction, and space extends beyond one's immediate sensory field. Everydayness is not associated with the mundane, and highly unique events like a coronation or the signing of a peace treaty are considered to be as much a part of the everyday life-world as are the ordinary practices of the workplace or the home. The everyday life-world is understood in opposition to the life-world of dreams, ecstasies, and fictive states like child's play or theatrical performances, each of which is characterized by its own unique set of relationships between subject and object. The life-world of dreams, for example, collapses as soon as we leave them, and in the life-world of theatrical dramas, one may jump back and forth in time.

2. Similar themes have also been important for folklore's allied discipline of ethnomusicology (see, for example, Blacking 1973 or Crafts et al. 1991).

3. While many scholars in pre-1960s folklore studies had only addressed issues of power implicitly (i.e., by celebrating the expressive creativity of disenfranchised groups), a number of them were explicitly politicized (for example, Hurston [1935] 1994; Botkin 1944; Paredes 1958). Since the transformations of the 1960s, the politics of culture has become central to the field (see, for example, Farrer 1975; Limón

1983; Whisnant 1983; Frykman and Löfgren 1987; Briggs 1988; Goodwin 1989; Cerny and Seriff 1996).

4. Other influences on de Certeau were Annal school thinkers such as Fernand Braudel, who argued that the examination of everyday practices is crucial for understanding the development of human civilization. In *Capitalism and Material Life: 1400–1800* ([1967] 1973), for example, Braudel explores the historical transformation of daily practices in modernity and shows how such practices provide the basis upon which people determine what they can or cannot achieve. Inspired by this school of thought, de Certeau seeks to understand the creative ways in which individuals struggle and navigate through the maze of possibilities and constraints that makes up daily existence.

5. While this research was being conducted, related theories about the dialectics of tradition and innovation in everyday expressive behavior were being developed in American folklore studies (see Hymes 1975b; Toelken 1979, 34). In fact, the connections with folklore studies are not accidental. A careful reading of volume one of *The Practice* reveals de Certeau's awareness of both the classics of European folklore (Vladimir Propp and Antti Aarne; see de Certeau [1974] 1984, 19) and the early statements of performance theory in American folklore (Richard Bauman and Joel Sherzer; see de Certeau [1974] 1984, 81, 217 n.4). Likewise, in volume two of *The Practice* de Certeau et al. describes the methodology of folklore research as "the socioethnographic analysis of everyday life" and explicitly cites these methods as one of the bases of their project ([1980] 1998, 7).

6. Another key source of insights into the relationship of microlevel practice and larger social forces is Dorothy E. Smith (1987). Reacting against what she sees as the unsociological excesses of microlevel oriented research, she argues that we must not merely "problematize the everyday world"; that is, we must not simply ask how activities and situations are accomplished in the ethnomethodological sense of the word. Grounded in Marx's materialist philosophy, she insists that larger social forces are not immediately observable in any given situated context and only become apparent when we look at the organization of practices across contexts. Further, such forces impinge upon situated activity in ways that the participants themselves do not always recognize. Smith calls for research that discovers, rather than assumes, the ways in which macrolevel social organization shapes microlevel social practice. Such work seeks to develop a "relation[ship] between the sociological subject and a (possible) sociology . . . in which the latter may become a means to disclose to the former the social relations determining her everyday world" (Smith 1987, 98).

7. Taking everyday life as a concept constructed largely through opposition, we take our cue here from the work of Mike Featherstone (1995). Exploring a range of ideas that extends from ancient Greek mythology and philosophy to nineteenth-century social theory, Featherstone suggests that everyday life is constructed in opposition to what he calls "the heroic life." In these representations, the repetitive, taken-for-granted routines of the everyday world, Featherstone argues, are typically associated with women, caregiving, and biological reproduction and contrasted with the danger-seeking, adventurous lives of warriors, artists, or intellectuals. The latter groups differentiate themselves by displaying the qualities of the legendary Hellenic heroes or manifesting the Nietzchean ideal of *vornehmheit,* an ethos of personal distinction.

Within cultural studies, the tension between everyday life and more spectacular forms of culture has also been an important theme. For arguments about the need for cultural studies research into everyday practices, see Miller and McHoul 1998 and Willis 1991.

8. The town of Sasso and all of the people mentioned here are real, but the names have been changed to protect the anonymity of the research participants.

9. See Berger 1999, 251–261 for a discussion of the relationship between relativistic and critical perspectives in ethnographically based research. Additionally, see Fiske 1992 on the importance of ethnography in cultural studies.

10. For a detailed discussion of these ideas, see Del Negro 1999, 10–20; 2004.

Chapter 2. Theory as Practice (pp. 23 –40)

1. For a valuable discussion of the relationship between these rather diverse thinkers, see Paul Rabinow's introduction to the *Foucault Reader* (1984, 3–29).

2. For a discourse-centered approach to the politics of data construction that parallels my own practice-based account of theory building, see Briggs's discussion of representation as an active, situated, and political achievement (1993a, 389–390).

3. For an intriguing discussion of the philosopher's ruminations about the status of his/her writing table, and a thoroughgoing defense of the empirical study of history against the attacks of a then-burgeoning anti-empirical strain in Marxism, see E. P. Thompson (1978, 6).

4. Both the English word "essence" and the ancient Greek *eidos* are used in the English translation of *Ideas I*. Kohák explains that in the original German, *eidos* and the German word *Wesen* are both used, and that the two mean roughly the same thing in the early sections of the work. However, in the later sections, Kohák states, they come to be subtly differentiated, and he notes that Husserl "tends to use *Wesen* when he is speaking of a principle or a typical way of being as exemplified and seen in an instance, and to use the term *eidos* when speaking of it in isolation" (197, note 12).

5. The phenomenological notion of *eidos* has affinities with the psychological notion of gestalt. For a discussion of the influence of gestalt psychology on phenomenology, particularly the phenomenology of Maurice Merleau-Ponty, see James Schmidt (1985, 38–39).

6. For a rich discussion of Rubin's Goblet and other multi-stable diagrams that is used to introduce fundamental concepts in phenomenology, see Ihde [1977] 1986.

7. This is not to say, of course, that the *eidetic* description can fail to describe the structure of the participant's experiences; the demands of phenomenological ethnography require theory to be based in experience. While theory need not agree with the participant's (sometimes flawed) reflective descriptions of their experiences, it must still agree with the experiences themselves.

8. While focusing more on the folktales per se and less on the subject's situated engagement with the tales in experience, Max Lüthi's analysis of European folktales illustrates an explicitly phenomenological approach to the structure of a body of folklore ([1947] 1986).

9. Though it is beyond the bounds of the present discussion to work out the complex relationships between transcendental and existential phenomenology, it is worth noting that Merleau-Ponty saw existential ideas in many of Husserl's writings. For a rich analysis of the intricacies of his existentialist reading of Husserl, as well as a thorough discussion of Merleau-Ponty's critique of the privileging of the *eidetic* over the factual and the contingent, see Schmidt 1985.

10. For a critique of orthodox Marxism from the phenomenological tradition that foreshadows many of the ideas of contemporary neo-Marxism, see the political essays collected in Maurice Merleau-Ponty's *Sense and Non-Sense* ([1948] 1964).

11. Ketner is correct, therefore, in suggesting that we can abstract data from "unique and nonrepeatable situations" (1973, 120) in order to make generalizations. My goal here is not to disprove Ketner but to extend his argument by suggesting

that such *eidetic* generalizations are locked in a dialectic with "unique and nonrepeatable" data, and that this dialectic has the potential to transform the meaning of those generalizations without invalidating their abstract structure.

12. As a kind of social science fiction, Jorge Luis Borges's *Labyrinths* ([1962] 1964) suggests that, even with the data at hand, closure might not be possible. Positing an enormous but finite library, Borges suggests that for closure to occur, we would need a complete command of the literature. However, a finite amount of knowledge that is greater than the scale of human comprehension is, for the purposes of practice, infinite, and a command of the literature would still be impossible. Even if the literature could be mastered, theory building would still be a social and political process constrained and enabled by our intellectual history.

Chapter 3. Horizons of Melody and the Problem of the Self
(pp. 43–88)

1. On the different senses of the term "horizon" in phenomenology, see Ihde 1976, 38–39, 46 n.8.

2. See chapter 4, note 1, for a discussion of our (my and Del Negro's) usage of the term "aesthetics."

3. On the cultural basis of the notions of composition, performance, and improvisation, see Nettl 1974 and Sawyer 1996.

4. Defining the different dimensions of any given perceptual modality is a complex issue. Not only must one be careful to distinguish the dimensions of perceptual experience (for example, pitch, dynamic, etc.) from the dimensions of the physical stimulus that evokes them (frequency, amplitude, etc.), one must also recognize that several different features of the physical stimulus may combine to evoke a single perceptual quality—for example, dynamic envelope and overtone structure combine to inform our experience of timbre. Further, Ruth Stone has observed that the very terms used to describe the different dimensions of auditory experience may be culturally specific (1982, 76–78). Unless otherwise indicated, I will use the phrase "perceptual dimension" to indicate a dimension of perceptual *experience* and will assume that such dimensions have some relationship, however complex, to one or more features of the physical world.

5. Here, my usage differs from the standard terminology in the field. On traditional uses of the terms "inner and outer horizons" in phenomenology, see Dreyfus 1992, 34, 241–242, or Kockelmans 1994, 22.

6. It is perhaps worth emphasizing at the outset that I intend no value judgements with the terms "gross" and "fine." There is nothing inherently better about music with fine details or worse about music with gross details.

7. In academic music studies, the term "text" is traditionally used to refer to the words to which a line of music is set. In popular music, those words are referred to as "lyrics." To follow the practices of my research participants and to avoid an overlap with the broader humanistic usage of the word "text," I will employ the term "lyrics" here.

8. By taking individual musical details in isolation, the discussion so far may have led some readers to consider the focusing of attention to be an unproblematic affair and to question whether sound does indeed have a horizonal structure. When a highly trained listener intensely attends to a solo performance of a piece that he/she knows well, that listener may be able to easily focus attention on even very fine features. Taking this case as a model, such a person may imagine that all small-scale perceptual features are fully present for experience at all times. But I believe that if one carefully examines the structure of experience, one discovers that when a given

fine detail is foregrounded, others are backgrounded. While, as Ihde shows (1976, 40), it is possible to expand the ratio of focus to fringe, it is rarely if ever the case that *every* feature of the sound emerges in a fully focal manner. Further, listening to duets, trios, or larger ensembles—or attending to performances that are strongly multisensory—so many phenomena are present, each with its own complement of features and details, that even the most sophisticated listener will experience the sound as possessing a graded, horizonal structure.

9. Here and throughout, the terms "romantic" and "connoisseuristic" are meant in a value-neutral way; no critical judgements are intended regarding the musics or aesthetic ideologies that I discuss.

10. "What is time, then? If nobody asks me, I know; if I have to explain it to someone who has asked me, I do not know" *Confessions* XI, 14.

11. In two different works (1966, 226; 1979, 60–61), Gibson develops a *reductio ad absurdum* critique of humuncular reasoning in visual perception that is strikingly similar to Merleau-Ponty's. Like phenomenological approaches to perception, Gibson's ecological theory is a critique of mentalistic accounts of the senses, and as a result the parallels between ideas in Gibson and those in phenomenology are many. Though it is far beyond the scope of this study to tease out all of the points of contact between these bodies of work, it is worthwhile to observe that Gibson's analysis of the occluding edge and related phenomena parallels Husserl's notion of horizons and his famous die example.

12. Ihde also uses a hypothetical example of a person taking in a sweeping vista (1976, 40). His example, however, is used to illustrate the shifting ratio of focus and fringe, whereas I am interested here in the relationship of perspective and self-experience.

13. It is worthwhile to emphasize that this example is not meant to stand for some generalized "everyday" experience of the self. While the "self in the head" is something that many people have encountered at one time or another, "everyday life" is not, as Del Negro and I show in chapter one, a sphere of activity identical in all cultures. Comparing across different societies, or comparing different groups within a given society, the forms of conduct in which people commonly engage are so diverse that it would be rash to posit a single "everyday" form of activity, let alone a single mode of self-experience. While the domination of experience by visual perception is something that may be very common in our species, the mountain view example has a number of features (the only slight appearance of aural phenomena, the complete absence of reflective thought) that make it distinct from a universal "everyday" structure of experience, if such a thing could be imagined at all. I have specified these features in order to facilitate a comparison with the meditation example and to show that the perspectival organization of phenomena constitutes a form of self-experience, independent of the experiential modality that presents them.

14. Bermúdez explains that this feature of perception is commonly referred to as the "egocentric frame of reference" (1998, 152).

15. It is worth noting that, in both examples, the perspectival sense of "here" was reinforced by virtue of a feature of perception explored in the first section of this chapter: while the attentional field of any given sensory modality is weighted toward certain values, we may partially resist these weightings and focus attention in different ways within a given horizon. This feature holds true for both the mountain view and meditation examples, and in both cases the weighting is spatial. In the mountain view example, I find it easiest to focus my vision on objects that are a few feet away, while I must make an effort to attend to those that are extremely close or far. In the meditation example, it was easiest to attend to points near the center of the tactile array, although with effort I was able to attend to points at the fringe.

What differs in the two examples are the factors that inform the weighting. In the mountain view example, the optical limits of the eye make attending to very near or very far objects difficult and weight the spatial field. In the meditation example, that weighting was imposed by the initial act of organizing attention. Intending to "focus on my breathing," I established a focus and fringe that were strongly sedimented in the perceptual field. Thus, while I was able to attend to points on my abdominal muscles distant from the focus, this refocusing required effort, and I experienced these points as far relative to the more or less stable background of the sedimented field. I do not know what would have happened if I would have persisted in this effort to attend to phenomena at the fringe. It may be that enough active attention to those muscles would have reconstituted the field with a new focus point, or it may be that the proprioceptive stimulation produced by the motion of the diaphragmatic breathing would have been too weak to constitute a field there. In either case, the act of shifting focus from near and easily grasped phenomena to distant and more difficult to grasp phenomena helped to reinforce the sense of here and self.

16. Notions similar to these are also common outside analytic philosophy. For example, the idea that thought and language are interdependent can also be found in anthropology, folklore studies, semiotics, and linguistics. Specifically addressing the issue of language and the self, writers from Louis Althusser ([1970] 1971) to contemporary deconstructivists (for example, Lee 1993) have suggested that language serves to "position" the subject and that the naming function of language doesn't merely describe but in some way actually creates the self.

17. For sake of clarity and brevity, I have focused on Bermúdez's critique of capacity circularity, but he also suggests that there is a second paradox inherent in the traditional view of self-consciousness (14–16). This problem arises from the fact that the traditional view holds that mastery of the first person pronoun accounts for the ability to conceptualize the self, but that the linguistic rule that constitutes this mastery makes reference to the first person pronoun. Creating a vicious circle by presupposing what it seeks to explain, the traditional view possesses what Bermúdez calls "explanatory circularity."

18. In the fantasy that began this chapter, the failure of the street sign to reveal fine details when inspected closely and the failure of the mountains to take up greater visual space when approached were meant to illustrate what would happen if Gibsonian phenomena like looming and optical flow ceased to function.

19. As in other locations, the points of contact between Bermúdez's analytic approach to questions of mind and phenomenological treatments of these issues are striking. The discussion of horizons and time in Husserl's Second Meditation ([1931] 1960, 44) is strongly consonant with Bermúdez's thinking. Similar themes can also be found throughout Gibson 1979.

20. This idea—that in perception, we are aware that there is more to any given object than our immediate experience of it—connects with both Husserl's discussion of the horizon of objects in the die example ([1931] 1960, 44), and Bermúdez's discussion of the nonconceptual viewpoint (1998, 168).

21. I would like to acknowledge Mary Bucholtz (2001, personal communication) for suggesting this term.

22. This idea—that a type of self-experience can be generated when forces external to the person strongly guide or limit his/her perceptual experience—was inspired by Mihaly Csikszentmihalyi's important observation that the loss of self in flow activities cannot occur when the requirements for action that a situation places on the person are so great as to be overwhelming or so limited as to be "boring" ([1975] 2000, 42–54). Shifting the emphasis of these ideas, I have read Csikszentmihalyi to mean that some kinds of requirements for action placed on the individual

by the world can lead to particular types of self-experience, and this interpretation led to the discussion above. For a fuller discussion of Csikszentmihalyi, see the next section of this chapter.

23. For a discussion of Csikszentmihalyi's overarching theory of the self, see Csikszentmihalyi 1988, 17–21; 1990.

24. This is not to say that Csikszentmihalyi's work is dismissive of lived experience or disengaged with phenomenology. In the preface to the twenty-fifth anniversary edition of *Beyond Boredom and Anxiety* ([1975] 2000), Csikszentmihalyi explicitly acknowledges the importance of phenomenology in the development of his thinking (xiii), and much of the text is a phenomenological critique of mechanistic approaches to psychology. Further, Berger and Luckmann are cited in a passage about the self to show how this psychic structure is a key part of social life (42). However, the notion of the self construct in these passages is defined in terms of its psychic functions rather than its structure in lived experience. A slightly different relationship with phenomenology is articulated in Csikszentmihalyi's 1990 book *Flow* (25–26, 247).

25. This is not to say Csikszentmihalyi envisions flow as a strictly bodily phenomenon. In *Flow* (1990), Csikszentmihalyi devotes a chapter to flow in "mental" activities like the solving of crossword puzzles and the composition of poetry. What Csikszentmihalyi argues is that during flow states, thought about the self, not thought in general, is absent from experience.

26. Here, it is important to see that the entities to which Tagg's terminology refers are elements of musical forms, not elements of the experiential field. Tagg uses the word "figure" to refer to the primary melody in a composition and the word "ground" to refer to the musical accompaniment. While it may be implied that melody and accompaniment are often placed in a foreground/background relationship in a listener's perceptual experience, to my reading, Tagg's usage of this terminology refers specifically to the musical forms themselves, not to their locations in the focus/fringe/horizon structure of lived experience.

27. Hesmondhalgh seems to read Tagg in the same way. Interpreting the passage from Tagg's article that I have just quoted, Hesmondhalgh writes that, "Tagg seems to be suggesting that it is the act of immersion in music at parties which expresses a particularly strong version of collectivism" (263).

28. Allowing for a variety of political meanings to be associated with the loss of self in rave and treating those meanings as an empirical reality to be discovered (219), Tagg clearly recognizes the importance of this issue. Further, it should be noted that throughout his work, Tagg strongly recognizes that the same musical forms may be read in different ways. For example, see Tagg's discussion of the cultural basis of the interpretation of sound symbolism in music (1990, 5).

Chapter 4. The Role of Reflexivity in the Aesthetics of Performance (pp. 89–123)

1. Just as the aesthetic effect of a song or a story is difficult to describe, so too is the notion of "aesthetics" highly resistant to theoretical formulation. While it is well beyond the scope of this chapter to define this concept, we are able to articulate the kinds of experiences we have in mind when we use this word. It is common for scholars to talk about the "meaning" of an individual act or item of expressive culture, and by *aesthetic* we (Berger and Del Negro) refer to an experience of meaning as it is enmeshed with some valual quality—affect, style, desirability, and so forth. Such a definition includes the qualities traditionally associated with the word "aesthetic" (beauty and ugliness) but does not draw distinctions between the different

domains of the valual; further, this definition emphasizes the links between those qualities and other dimensions of meaning in experience. By *aesthetic response* and *aesthetic effect* we simply mean experiences of meaning-value constituted by a person as he/she engages with expressive culture.

2. Several factors have gone into our choices of examples for this article. Northeast Ohio and central Italy have been longstanding field sites for us, and our familiarity with these regions has provided a rich source of materials for discussion. More importantly, however, we have chosen to explore these highly divergent examples to emphasize the fact that reflexivity is central to all performance and communication, independent of the media, genres, or world areas involved. Limited to neither music nor bodily display, popular culture nor traditional folk custom, reflexivity is, we believe, an issue whenever an individual takes responsibility for displaying artistic competence.

3. On the reception of *Verbal Art as Performance* in the intellectual history of folklore, linguistic anthropology, and related disciplines, see Rudy 2002 and Bauman 2002.

4. For a different analysis of the role of reflexive language in subject positioning, see Silverstein's notion of indexical creativity (1976, 34).

5. Inspired by French approaches to literary theory, another group of researchers sees reflexive language as not merely positioning the subject but actually constructing it. For an example of such an approach, see Lee 1993.

6. Originally approaching performance theory from the perspective of theater studies, Richard Schechner (1985) engages with the issue of reflexivity in a different fashion. Analogous to the folklorists' discussions of reflexive language is Schechner's sophisticated analyses of framing. Schechner's comparative work on theater and ritual illustrates how different types of framing constitute different types of "performance systems" (ritual, theater, historical re-enactments, theme parks; 1985, 95) and how the subtle meanings of performance are established through the use of multiple levels of framing (92–93, 280). Focusing on space rather than language, his work shows how the physical setting in which an event occurs—the totalizing environment of the "village" or "town" in historical re-enactments, the traditional theater with its framing proscenium arch (94–96), the complex spaces of experimental theater (266–270, 302–307)—establishes the performative frame.

Further, Schechner's interpretation of the idea of framed behavior has interesting implications for the problem of subject positioning. Building on the work of Gregory Bateson and Victor Turner, Schechner suggests that the performance frame is essentially unstable, producing a situation in which "multiple selves coexist in an unresolved dialectical tension" (6). While Schechner does not explore the microlevel mechanisms of reflexive language and reflexive consciousness through which these selves interact, his emphasis on the ludic and flexible nature of subject positioning is consonant with the approaches we wish to develop here.

7. See Sawin 2002 for a related discussion of the need for an audience-centered approach in performance studies.

8. This dialectical model of subject positioning is consistent with the notion of the "decentered," as distinct from deconstructed, subject (see, for example, Giddens 1979, 38–48), but we feel that the term "decentered" has problematic implications in the contemporary scene. "The subject" only needs to be removed from the center of analysis in the intellectual context of an idealism that views the lone individual as the root of all meaning. In the contemporary academy, however, few scholars subscribe to such an acultural and dehistoricized perspective, and the term "decentered subject" has antihumanistic connotations that we feel run counter to the themes of agency and interpretation we wish to emphasize here. On the role of

poetics and performance in the intellectual history of the subject, see Bauman and Briggs 1990.

9. Jakobson's work has been fundamental to the analysis of reflexive language. See his discussion of shifters and his exploration of the reflexive relationships between message and code in "Shifters, Verbal Categories, and the Russian Verb" (1971).

10. While Jean-Paul Sartre believed that Husserl was unable to save phenomenology from solipsism ([1943] 1956), the problem of solipsism is tangential to our present concerns. Husserl's aim in the Fifth Meditation was not to construct an argument that would defend phenomenology against the charge of solipsism but to rigorously describe lived experience and discover in that experience the apodictic certainty that other subjects exist. Whether or not Husserl's descriptive method is a successful response to these criticisms, his descriptions of our experience of the other and the intersubjective nature of the world are valid in the terms that Husserl intended—as rigorous descriptions of experience. Our goal here is not to address the problem of solipsism but to use those descriptions as a grounding for the larger arguments about reflexivity and aesthetics that we develop below.

11. Such an interpretation follows what James Schmidt has called Merleau-Ponty's "existentialist Husserl" (1985, 36). Throughout, our reading of Husserl has been informed and inspired by Hammond, Howarth, and Keat 1991, as well as Schmidt 1985 and Kohák 1978.

12. This is, of course, to arrive at Mead's social subject from a bodily and experiential, rather than a linguistic, route.

13. For an existentialist approach to these issues, see Merleau-Ponty's discussion of pairing in child development ([1945] 1981, 354).

14. This, of course, raises the problem of how one can know if a particular other body is a subject. Husserl addresses this issue by distinguishing between the animate bodies of genuine subjects and mere "pseudo-organisms" (such as robots), suggesting that the activities of genuine other subjects are "harmonious" ([1931] 1960, 114). Here, we are only concerned with achieving an effective phenomenological description of what it means to experience the other as a subject, and the difficulties of the problem of "pseudo-organisms" are beyond the bounds of our present concern.

15. Here the notion of attention is understood in a phenomenological fashion. Attention must not be seen as a substantial thing, an entity whose deployment causes the physical world to become "experience." Interpreted phenomenologically, the notion of attention accounts for the fact that experience usually contains multiple phenomena at once and that these phenomena emerge with a greater or lesser degree of clarity and intensity (for a fuller discussion of this point, see Berger 1999, 303–304, note 3). Taken in this way, our discussion of the organization of attention can be understood as an analysis of the ways in which subjects arrange phenomena relative to one another in experience. For a parallel argument about the notion of consciousness, see James 1967a.

16. For the inverse point—that what is true of artists is also true of all persons engaged in everyday interaction—see Caton 1993, 328–329.

17. On the role of reflective and reflexive thought in jazz improvisation, also see Paul F. Berliner's landmark study *Thinking in Jazz: The Infinite Art of Improvisation* (1994). On this topic, as well as on the relevance of Silverstein's work on metapragmatics for understanding jazz and music performance in general, see also Ingrid Monson's *Saying Something: Jazz Improvisation and Interaction* (1996).

18. As Berger has argued elsewhere (1997, 1999), the organization of attention can be understood as *social practice* in the practice theory sense of the term. In Giddens's view ([1976] 1993, 1979, 1984), "practice" is any conduct that comes about through a duality of social context and the agency of its practitioner. Informed by

the contingencies of the performance event, the ideologies of the player's music scene, and the player's own agentive involvement in the event, the organization of attention is an exemplar of Giddens's notion of practice.

19. Jane C. Sugarman's powerful work on song in Prespa Albanian weddings (1997, 263–285) is particularly relevant to these issues. Basing her study on rich ethnographic data, Sugarman shows how the singers' choice of songs, elaboration of song texts, use of vocal techniques and melodic devices, and control of physical demeanor serve as indicators of their emotional states and their involvements with the performance. Drawing on ideas from Judith Irvine, Sugarman depicts such signals as "metacommunicative commentary" (265) on the song and the singer's engagement with it. Most importantly, Sugarman reveals how the participant's affect, metacommunication, and levels of engagement in the event are deeply informed by culturally specific ideas about gender and performance in Prespa Albanian culture.

Interpreted in the language we have developed in this chapter, Sugarman's analysis of singing and interaction in these events (especially the *konak*, an all male social gathering) describes what we would call an "organization of attention in events" specific to Prespa Albanian culture, while her comparison of male and female styles of metacommunication there illuminates what we will shortly call an "ideology of attention" and an "aesthetic of reflexivity."

For a more detailed discussion of the organization of attention in Ohio's Rock and Jazz scenes, see Berger 1999.

20. Both of these kinds of framing are examples of Michael Silverstein's "reflexive calibration" of metapragmatic signs (1993, 50). In his formulation, signs that frame or comment on other signs can be "calibrated" to their semiotic objects in a variety of ways. In reflexive calibration, the framing signs occur simultaneously with the signs they frame and achieve their framing function in an implicit manner. Silverstein provides two examples: the use of rhyme and meter to frame a piece of text as poetry (Jakobson's "poetic function" [1960]), and the use of prosody, contour, gesture, and so on to frame speech in face-to-face conversation. Although Silverstein primarily addresses himself to language and does not give names to these two different kinds of reflexive calibration, his two examples correspond to what we have called "embedded" and "accompanying" metacommunication.

21. Because of the sensitive nature of other data collected during this research, the town's name and the identities of the various participants in the research have been obscured.

22. This situation is similar to Hymes's "perfunctory performance" (personal communication from Hymes to Bauman, quoted in Bauman 1977, 26–27).

23. Sugarman's work illustrates related dynamics in a different Mediterranean performance event. Exploring Prespa Albanian weddings, she shows how demeanor and comportment (eye contact, gesture) serve as indicators of the participant's attention to the event and how these are carefully controlled in women's performances to project an image of propriety (1997, 269).

Chapter 5. Identity Reconsidered, the World Doubled (pp. 124–157)

1. Throughout this paper, we will use the term "identity interpretation" to refer to a situation in which an actor experiences a stretch of behavior (her own or someone else's) as an expression of identity.

2. See Hall 1996, 602. For a classic intellectual history of the notion of the great chain of being, see Lovejoy 1964.

3. It is worthwhile noting that Dorson's "A Theory for American Folklore"

(1959) offers a complex view of folklore in the age of the mass media. While his condemnation of modernity's commercialization of folklore is unwavering, Dorson was optimistic about folklore's survival within the belly of the beast, and he even encouraged folklorists to study the interplay between folklore and popular culture (211).

4. For an explicit discussion of the relationship between folklore and symbolic interactionist approaches to identity, see Bauman 1989.

5. It is important to keep in mind that while institutionalized identity generally represents the interest of the powerful and the situated negotiation of identity is often a "weapon of the weak," these relationships may be reversed and must always be interpreted within their unique social contexts. Thus over the course of history one finds ample evidence of governments coercively regulating the identities of their citizenry. For our purposes, one of the most striking examples occurred in early-twentieth-century Turkey, when the government coerced its citizens into Europeanizing their names as part of a large-scale campaign of Westernization and modernization (Türköz 1998). But government policies can also be designed with the intent of *correcting* structural inequalities, as in the affirmative action programs of the United States, and, to a degree, in the Portal case itself.

For a powerful discussion of the state and ethnic identity in a different cultural context, see Silverman 1989.

6. By this definition, identity interpretations in artistic behavior only become institutionalized and regulating when an expressive genre is adopted by an institution (such as when law or strict, non-negotiable custom are codified in proverbs) and when the identity interpretations found in those expressive forms are experienced by actors as quasi-autonomous and legislative of behavior.

7. In interpretive sociology, the literature on intention and action is both deep and rich, and our discussion here was inspired by the writings of Alfred Schutz ([1932] 1967) and Anthony Giddens (1979, 41–43, 55–59).

8. Building on the work of Richard Bauman and Judith Butler, Patricia Sawin (2002) has developed a related but distinct notion of the performance of self. In Sawin's reading, Butler shows that an individual's gender identity is not an underlying essence but an embodied social process confirmed and reconfirmed by its enactment in day-to-day conduct. Comparing this vision of quotidian, gendered performance with Bauman's ideas about the performance of expressive culture, Sawin finds more similarities than differences. Everyday gendered conduct, she argues, is often judged on Bauman's criteria of competence and often possesses an aesthetic component. Both are emergent, enacted, and informed by culture, and Sawin sees a smooth continuum between the two senses of the word performance. While we agree that both everyday behavior and framed, expressive conduct share many qualities, our notion of the performance of self takes Bauman in a different direction and emphasizes the distinct interpretive dynamics that occur when identity interpretations are aestheticized.

Works Cited

*

Abrahams, Roger D. 1977. Toward an enactment-centered theory of folklore. In *Frontiers in folklore,* edited by William R. Bascom. Boulder: Westview Press.

Allen, Ray. 1991. Shouting the church: Narrative and vocal improvisation in African American gospel quartet performance. *Journal of American Folklore* 104:295–317.

Althusser, Louis. [1970] 1971. Ideology and ideological state apparatuses (Notes towards an investigation). In *Essays on ideology.* London: Verso.

Babcock, Barbara. 1977. The story in the story: Metanarration in folk narrative. In *Verbal art as performance,* edited by Richard Bauman. Rowley, Mass.: Newbury House Publishers.

———. 1980. Reflexivity: Definitions and discriminations. *Semiotica* 30:1–14.

———. 1987. Reflexivity. In *The Encyclopedia of religion,* edited by Mircea Eliade, volume 12. New York: Macmillan.

Bakan, Michael B. 1999. *Music of death and new creation: Experiences in the world of Balinese Gamelan Beleganjur.* Chicago: University of Chicago Press.

Bateson, Gregory. 1972. A theory of play and fantasy. In *Steps to an ecology of mind.* San Francisco: Chandler.

Bauman, Richard. 1972. Differential identity and the social base of folklore. In *Toward new perspectives in folklore,* edited by Américo Paredes and Richard Bauman. Austin: University of Texas Press.

———. 1977. *Verbal art as performance.* Rowley, Mass.: Newbury House Publishers.

———. 1983. Folklore and the forces of modernity. *Folklore Forum* 16:153–158.

———. 1986. *Story, performance, and event: Contextual studies of oral narrative.* Cambridge: Cambridge University Press.

———. 1989. Performance. In *The international encyclopedia of communications,* edited by Erik Barnouw. Oxford: Oxford University Press.

———. 2002. Disciplinarity, reflexivity, and power in *Verbal art as performance:* A response. *Journal of American Folklore* 115:92–98.

Bauman, Richard, and Charles L. Briggs. 1990. Poetics and performances as critical perspectives on language and social life. *Annual Review of Anthropology* 19:59–88.

Ben-Amos, Dan. 1972. Toward a definition of folklore in context. In *Toward new perspectives in folklore,* edited by Américo Paredes and Richard Bauman. Austin: University of Texas Press.

Bendix, Regina. 1997. *In search of authenticity: The formation of folklore studies.* Madison: University of Wisconsin Press.

Benedict, Ruth. [1934] 1959. *Patterns of culture.* Boston: Houghton Mifflin.

———. 1946. *The chrysanthemum and the sword: Patterns of Japanese culture.* Boston: Houghton Mifflin.

Berger, Harris M. 1991. Armloads of crystals: A general theory of music and emotion. Master's thesis, Indiana University.

———. 1997. The practice of perception: Multi-functionality and time in the musical experiences of heavy metal drummers in Akron, Ohio. *Ethnomusicology* 41: 464–488.

———. 1999. *Metal, rock, and jazz: Perception and the phenomenology of musical experience.* Middletown and Hanover: Wesleyan University Press and University Press of New England.

Berliner, Paul F. 1994. *Thinking in jazz: The infinite art of improvisation.* Chicago: University of Chicago Press.

Bermúdez, José Luis. 1998. *The paradox of self-consciousness.* Cambridge, Mass.: MIT Press.

Blacking, John. [1969] 1995. Expressing human experience through music. In *Music, culture, experience: Selected papers of John Blacking,* edited by Reginald Byron. Chicago: University of Chicago Press.

———. 1973. *How musical is man?* Seattle: University of Washington Press.

Borges, Jorge Luis. [1962] 1964. *Labyrinths: Selected stories and other writings,* edited by Donald A. Yates and James E. Irby. New York: New Directions.

Botkin, Benjamin. 1944. *A treasury of American folklore: Stories, ballads, and traditions of the American people.* New York: Crown Publishers.

Bourdieu, Pierre. 1977. *Outline of a theory of practice,* translated by Richard Nice. Cambridge: Cambridge University Press.

Braudel, Fernand. [1967] 1973. *Capitalism and material life: 1400–1800,* translated by Miriam Kochan. New York: Harper and Row.

Briggs, Charles L. 1988. *Competence in performance: The creativity of tradition in Mexicano verbal art.* Philadelphia: University of Pennsylvania Press.

———. 1993a. Metadiscursive practices and scholarly authority in folkloristics. *Journal of American Folklore* 106:387–434.

———. 1993b. Generic versus metapragmatic dimensions of Warao narratives: Who regiments the performance? In *Reflexive language,* edited by John A. Lucy. Cambridge: Cambridge University Press.

Bronner, Simon J. 1996. Folklore movement. In *American folklore: An encyclopedia,* edited by Jan Harold Brunvand. New York: Garland Publishing.

Brunvand, Jan Harold. 1978. *The study of American folklore.* New York: W. W. Norton.

Butler, Gary. 1992. Indexicality, authority, and communication in traditional narrative discourse. *Journal of American Folklore* 105:34–56.

Caton, Steve C. 1993. The importance of reflexive language in George Herbert Mead's theory of self and communication. In *Reflexive language,* edited by John A. Lucy. Cambridge: Cambridge University Press.

Cavicchi, Daniel. 1998. *Tramps like us: Music and meaning among Springsteen fans.* Oxford: Oxford University Press.

Cerny, Charlene, and Suzanne Seriff, eds. 1996. *Recycled, re-seen: Folk art from the global scrap heap.* New York: Harry N. Abrams.

Clifford, James, and George E. Marcus, eds. 1986. *Writing culture: The poetics and politics of ethnography.* Berkeley: University of California Press.

Coffin, Tristram Potter, and Hennig Cohen, eds. 1966. *Folklore in America*. Garden City, N.Y.: Doubleday.

——. 1973. *Folklore from the working folk of America*. Garden City, N.Y.: Doubleday.

Cohen, Anne, and Norm Cohen. 1974. A word on hypothesis. *Journal of American Folklore* 87:156–160.

——. 1975. When all is said and done, we make hypothesis too. *Journal of American Folklore* 88:417–418.

Crafts, Susan D., Daniel Cavicchi, Charles Keil, and the Music in Daily Life Project. 1991. *My music*. Middletown and Hanover: Wesleyan University Press and University Press of New England.

Csikszentmihalyi, Mihaly. [1975] 2000. *Beyond boredom and anxiety: Experiencing flow in work and play*. Twenty-fifth anniversary edition. San Francisco: Jossey-Bass Publishers.

——. 1988. The flow experience and its significance for human psychology. In *Optimal experience: Psychological studies of flow in consciousness,* edited by Mihaly Csikszentmihalyi and Isabella Selega Csikszentmihalyi. Cambridge: Cambridge University Press.

——. 1990. *Flow: The psychology of optimal experience*. New York: HarperCollins.

de Certeau, Michel. [1974] 1984. *The practice of everyday life,* volume 1, translated by Steven Rendall. Berkeley: University of California Press.

de Certeau, Michel, Luce Giard, and Pierre Mayol. [1980] 1998. *The practice of everyday life,* volume 2: *Living and cooking,* translated by Timothy J. Tomasik. Minneapolis: University of Minnesota Press.

Dégh, Linda. [1962] 1969. *Folktales and society: Storytelling in a Hungarian peasant community,* translated by Emily M. Schossberger. Bloomington: Indiana University Press.

Del Negro, Giovanna P. 1997. *Looking through my mother's eyes: Life stories of nine Italian immigrant women in Canada*. Toronto: Guernica.

——. 1999. "Our little Paris": Modernity, performance, and the *passeggiata* (ritual promenade) in a central Italian town. Ph.D. diss., Indiana University.

——. 2004. *The Passeggiata and popular culture in an Italian town: Folklore and the performance of modernity*. Montreal: McGill-Queen's University Press.

Del Negro, Giovanna P., and Harris M. Berger. 2001. Character divination and kinetic sculpture in the central Italian *passeggiata* (ritual promenade): Interpretive frameworks and expressive practices from a body-centered perspective. *Journal of American Folklore* 114:5–19.

Dorson, Richard M. 1952. *Bloodstoppers & bearwalkers: Folk traditions of the Upper Peninsula*. Cambridge, Mass.: Harvard University Press.

——. 1959. A theory for American folklore. *Journal of American Folklore* 72:197–215.

——. 1978. Editor's comment: We all need the folk. *Journal of the Folklore Institute* 15:267–269.

——. 1981. *Land of the millrats*. Cambridge, Mass.: Harvard University Press.

Dreyfus, Hubert L. 1992. *What computers still can't do: A critique of artificial reason*. Cambridge, Mass.: The MIT Press.

Dundes, Alan. 1965. What is folklore? In *The study of folklore,* edited by Alan Dundes. Englewood Cliffs, N.J.: Prentice-Hall.

——. 1975. Metafolklore and oral literary criticism. In *Analytic essays in folklore*. The Hague: Mouton.

Evans-Pritchard, Deirdre. 1989. The portal case: Authenticity, tourism, traditions, and the law. In *Folk groups and folklore genres: A reader,* edited by Elliott Oring. Logan: Utah State University Press.

Farrer, Claire, ed. 1975. *Women and folklore.* Prospect Heights, Ill.: Waveland Press.

Featherstone, Mike. 1995. The heroic life and everyday life. In *Undoing culture: Globalization, postmodernism, and identity.* London: Sage Publications.

Feld, Steven. [1982] 1990. *Sound and sentiment: Birds, weeping, poetics, and song in Kaluli expression.* 2d. ed. Philadelphia: University of Pennsylvania Press.

Felski, Rita. 2000. The invention of everyday life. *New Formations* 39:15–31.

Fine, Elizabeth C. 1984. *The folklore text: From performance to print.* Bloomington: Indiana University Press.

Fiske, John. 1992. Cultural studies and the culture of everyday life. In *Cultural studies,* edited by Lawrence Grossberg, Cary Nelson, and Paula A. Treichler. New York: Routledge.

Foley, John Miles. 1992. Word-power, performance, and tradition. *Journal of American Folklore* 105:275–301.

Frykman, Jonas, and Orvar Löfgren. 1987. *The culture builders: A historical anthropology of middle class life,* translated by Alan Crozier. New Brunswick: Rutgers University Press.

Geertz, Clifford. 1973. *The interpretation of cultures.* New York: Basic Books.

———. 1983. "From the native's point of view": On the nature of anthropological understanding. In *Local knowledge.* New York: Basic Books.

Gibson, J. J. 1966. *The senses considered as perceptual systems.* Boston: Houghton Mifflin.

———. 1979. *The ecological approach to visual perception.* Boston: Houghton Mifflin.

Giddens, Anthony. [1976] 1993. *New rules of sociological method: A positive critique of interpretive sociologies,* 2d. ed. Stanford: Stanford University Press.

———. 1979. *Central problems in social theory: Action, structure, and contradiction in social analysis.* Berkeley: University of California Press.

———. 1984. *The constitution of society: Outline of the theory of structuration.* Berkeley: University of California Press.

Glassie, Henry H. 1982. *Passing the time in Ballymenone: Culture and history of an Ulster community.* Philadelphia: University of Pennsylvania Press.

Gleason, Philip. 1983. Identifying identity: A semantic history. *Journal of American History* 69:910–931.

Goffman, Erving. 1959. *The presentation of self in everyday life.* New York: Doubleday.

Goodwin, Joseph P. 1989. *More man than you'll ever be: Gay folklore and acculturation in middle America.* Bloomington: Indiana University Press.

Hall, Donald E. 1980. *Musical acoustics: An introduction.* Belmont, Calif.: Wadsworth Publishing.

Hall, Stuart. 1996. The question of cultural identity. In *Modernity: An introduction to modern societies,* edited by Stuart Hall, David Held, Don Hubert, and Kenneth Thompson. London: Blackwell.

Hallowell, A. Irving. 1976. Ojibwa ontology, behavior, and world view. In *Contributions to anthropology: Selected papers of A. Irving Hallowell,* edited by Raymond D. Fogelson et al. Chicago: University of Chicago Press.

Hammond, Michael, Jane Howarth, and Russell Keat. 1991. *Understanding phenomenology.* Oxford: Basil Blackwell.

Handler, Richard. 1988. *Nationalism and the politics of culture in Quebec.* Madison: University of Wisconsin Press.

——. 1994. Is "identity" a useful cross-cultural concept? In *Commemorations: The politics of national identity,* edited by John R. Gillis. Princeton: Princeton University Press.

Herder, Johann Gottfried. [1764–67] 1992. *Selected early works, 1764–1767,* translated by Ernest A. Menze with Michael Palma. University Park: Pennsylvania State University Press.

Herndon, Marcia, and Norma McLeod. 1980. *Music as culture.* Darby, Penn.: Norwood Editions.

Hesmondhalgh, Dave. 1995. Technophrophecy: A response to Tagg. *Popular Music* 14:261–263.

Hurston, Zora Neale. [1935] 1994. *Mules and men.* New York: HarperPerennial.

Husserl, Edmund. [1913] 1962. *Ideas: General introduction to pure phenomenology,* translated by W. R. Boyce Gibson. New York: Collier Books.

——. [1929] 1964. *The phenomenology of internal time-consciousness,* translated by James S. Churchill and edited by Martin Heidegger. Bloomington: Indiana University Press.

——. [1931] 1960. *Cartesian meditations: An introduction to phenomenology,* translated by Dorion Cairns. The Hague: Martinus Nijhoff.

Hymes, Dell. 1975a. Breakthrough into performance. In *Folklore: Performance and communication,* edited by Dan Ben-Amos and Kenneth Goldstein. The Hague: Mouton.

——. 1975b. Folklore's nature and the sun's myth. *Journal of American Folklore* 88:345–369.

Ihde, Don. 1976. *Listening and voice: A phenomenology of sound.* Athens: Ohio University Press.

——. [1977] 1986. *Experimental phenomenology: An introduction.* Albany: State University of New York Press.

Jakobson, Roman. 1960. Closing statement: Linguistics and poetics. In *Style in language,* edited by Thomas A. Sebeok. New York and Boston: John Wiley and Sons and the Technology Press of MIT.

——. 1971. Shifters, verbal categories, and the Russian verb. In *Selected writings,* volume 2: *Word and language.* The Hague: Mouton.

James, William. [1890] 1981. *The principles of psychology.* Cambridge, Mass.: Harvard University Press.

——. [1912] 1967a. *Essays in radical empiricism.* Gloucester, Mass.: Peter Smith.

——. [1912] 1967b. The place of affectional facts in a world of pure experience. In *Essays in radical empiricism.* Gloucester, Mass.: Peter Smith.

Jansen, William Hugh. [1959] 1965. The esoteric-exoteric factor in folklore. In *The study of folklore,* edited by Alan Dundes. Englewood Cliffs: Prentice-Hall.

Judas Priest. 1976. Victim of changes. *Sad wings of destiny.* RCA AYK 1–4747.

Kapchan, Deborah A. 1994. Moroccan female performers defining the social body. *Journal of American Folklore* 107:82–105.

Keil, Charles, Angeliki V. Keil, and Dick Blau. 1992. *Polka happiness.* Philadelphia: Temple University Press.

Ketner, Kenneth Laine. 1973. The role of hypothesis in folkloristics. *Journal of American Folklore* 86:114–130.

———. 1975. Hypothesis fingo. *Journal of American Folklore* 88:411–417.

Kirshenblatt-Gimblett, Barbara. 1975. A parable in context. In *Folklore: Performance and communication,* edited by Dan Ben-Amos and Kenneth S. Goldstein. The Hague: Mouton.

———. 1983. The future of folklore studies in America: The urban frontier. *Folklore Forum* 16:175–234.

Kockelmans, Joseph J. 1994. *Edmund Husserl's phenomenology.* West Lafayette, Ind.: Purdue University Press.

Kohák, Erazim V. 1978. *Idea and experience: Edmund Husserl's project of phenomenology in "Ideas I."* Chicago: University of Chicago Press.

Korson, George Gershon. 1943. *Coal dust on the fiddle: Songs and stories of the bituminous industry.* Philadelphia: University of Pennsylvania Press.

Kratz, Corrine. 1990. Persuasive suggestions and reassuring promises: Emergent parallelism and dialogic encouragement in song. *Journal of American Folklore* 103:42–67.

Lawless, Elaine J. 1992. "I was afraid someone like you . . . an outsider would . . . would misunderstand": Negotiating interpretive differences between ethnographers and subjects. *Journal of American Folklore* 105:302–314.

Lee, Benjamin. 1993. Metalanguages and subjectivities. In *Reflexive language,* edited by John A. Lucy. Cambridge: Cambridge University Press.

Lefebvre, Henri. [1947] 1991. *The critique of everyday life,* volume 1: *Introduction,* translated by John Moore. London: Verso.

———. [1967] 1990. *Everyday life in the modern world,* translated by Sacha Rabinovitch. New Brunswick: Transaction Publishers.

———. 1987. The everyday and everydayness. *Yale French Studies* 73:7–11.

Limón, José. 1983. Western Marxism and folklore: A critical introduction. *Journal of American Folklore* 6:34–52.

Lovejoy, Arthur O. 1964. *The great chain of being: A study of the history of an idea.* Cambridge, Mass.: Harvard University Press.

Lucy, John A. 1993. Reflexive language and the human disciplines. In *Reflexive language,* edited by John A. Lucy. Cambridge: Cambridge University Press.

Lüthi, Max. [1947] 1986. *The European folktale: Form and nature,* translated by John D. Niles. Bloomington: Indiana University Press.

Magliocco, Sabina. 1993. *The two Madonnas: The politics of festival in a Sardinian community.* New York: Peter Lang.

Marriott, McKim. 1976. Hindu transactions: Diversity without dualism. In *Transaction and meaning,* edited by Bruce Kapferer. Philadelphia: Institute for the Study of Human Issues.

Marx, Karl. [1867–94] 1974. *Capital.* London: Lawrence and Wishart.

Mead, George Herbert. [1934] 1967. *Mind, self, and society.* Chicago: University of Chicago Press.

Mead, Margaret. 1928. *Coming of age in Samoa: A psychological study of primitive youth for Western civilization.* New York: William Morrow.

Mendoza-Denton, Norma. 1996. *"Muy Macha":* Gender and ideology in gang-girls' discourse about makeup. *Ethnos* 6:47–64.

Merleau-Ponty, Maurice. [1945] 1981. *Phenomenology of perception,* translated by Colin Smith. London: Routledge.

———. [1948] 1964. *Sense and non-sense,* translated by Hubert L. Dreyfus and Patricia Allen Dreyfus. Evanston: Northwestern University Press.

———. [1964] 1968. *The visible and the invisible,* translated by Alphonso Lingis and edited by Claude Lefort. Evanston: Northwestern University Press.

Miller, Toby, and Alec McHoul. 1998. *Popular culture and everyday life.* London: Sage Publications.

Monson, Ingrid. 1996. *Saying something: Jazz improvisation and interaction.* Chicago: University of Chicago Press.

Moore, Robert E. 1993. Performance, form, and the voice of characters in five versions of the Wasco Coyote Cycle. In *Reflexive language,* edited by John A. Lucy. Cambridge: Cambridge University Press.

Nagata, Judith A. 1974. What is a Malay? Situational selection of ethnic identity in a plural society. *American Ethnologist* 2:331–350.

Narayan, Kirin. 1995. The practice of oral literary criticism. *Journal of American Folklore* 108:243–264.

Nettl, Bruno. 1974. Thoughts on improvisation: A comparative approach. *Musical Quarterly* 60:1–19.

Oring, Elliott. 1994. The arts, artifacts, and artifices of identity. *Journal of American Folklore* 107:211–247.

Paredes, Américo. 1958. *With his pistol in his hand: A border ballad and its hero.* Austin: University of Texas Press.

Paredes, Américo, and Richard Bauman, eds. 1972. *Toward new perspectives in folklore.* Austin: University of Texas Press.

Parmentier, Richard J. 1993. The political function of reported speech: A Belauan example. In *Reflexive language,* edited by John A. Lucy. Cambridge: Cambridge University Press.

Phair, Liz. 1998. Polyester bride. *Whitechocolatespaceegg.* Matador records. CDP 7243 8 53554 2 4.

Pirkova-Jakobson, Svatava. 1956. Harvest festivals among Czechs and Slovaks in America. *Journal of American Folklore* 69:266–280.

Pocius, Gerald L. 1991. *A place to belong: Community order and everyday space in Calvert, Newfoundland.* Athens: University of Georgia Press.

Pred, Allan Richard, and Michael John Watts. 1992. *Reworking modernity: Capitalisms and symbolic discontent.* New Brunswick: Rutgers University Press.

Propp, Vladímir. [1928] 1968. *Morphology of the folktale,* 2d. ed., translated by Laurence Scott and edited by Louis A. Wagner. Bloomington: Indiana University Press.

Rabinow, Paul. 1984. Introduction. In *The Foucault reader,* edited by Paul Rabinow. New York: Pantheon Books.

Radway, Janice. 1984. *Reading the romance: Women, patriarchy, and popular literature.* Chapel Hill: University of North Carolina Press.

Roberts, Warren E. 1988. *Viewpoints on folklife: Looking at the overlooked.* Ann Arbor: UMI Research Press.

Rose, Tricia. 1997. Never trust a big butt and a smile. In *Feminist television criticism: A reader,* edited by Charlotte Brunsdon, Julie D'Acci, and Lynn Spigel. New York: Oxford University Press.

Rudy, Jill Terry. 2002. Toward an assessment of *Verbal art as performance:* A cross-disciplinary citation study with rhetorical analysis. *Journal of American Folklore* 115:5–27.

Said, Edward W. 1979. *Orientalism.* New York: Vintage Books.

Sartre, Jean-Paul. [1943] 1956. *Being and nothingness: An essay on phenomenological ontology,* translated by Hazel E. Barnes. New York: Philosophical Library.

Sawin, Patricia E. 2002. Performance at the nexus of gender, power, and desire: Reconsidering Bauman's *Verbal art* from the perspective of gendered subjectivity as performance. *Journal of American Folklore* 115:28–62.

Sawyer, R. Keith. 1996. Semiotics of improvisation: The pragmatics of musical and verbal performance. *Semiotica* 108:269–306.

Schechner, Richard. 1985. *Between theater and anthropology.* Philadelphia: University of Pennsylvania Press.

Schmidt, James. 1985. *Maurice Merleau-Ponty: Between phenomenology and structuralism.* New York: St. Martin's Press.

Schutz, Alfred. [1932] 1967. *The phenomenology of the social world,* translated by George Walsh and Frederick Lehnert. Evanston: Northwestern University Press.

———. 1976. Fragments on the phenomenology of music. *Music and Man* 2:5–72.

Schutz, Alfred, and Thomas Luckmann. 1973. *Structures of the life-world,* vol. 1, translated by Richard M. Zaner and H. Tristram Engelhardt Jr. Evanston: Northwestern University Press.

———. [1983] 1989. *Structures of the life-world,* vol. 2, translated by Richard M. Zaner and David J. Parent. Evanston: Northwestern University Press.

Sherzer, Joel. 1987. Poetic structuring of Kuna discourse: The line. In *Native American discourse: Poetics and rhetoric,* edited by Joel Sherzer and Anthony C. Woodbury. Cambridge: Cambridge University Press.

Shuman, Amy. 1993. Dismantling the local. *Western Folklore* 52:345–364.

Silverman, Carol. 1989. Reconstructing folklore: Media and cultural policy in Eastern Europe. *Communication* 11:141–160.

Silverman, Sydel F. 1975. *Three bells of civilization: The life of an Italian hill town.* New York: Columbia University Press.

Silverstein, Michael. 1976. Shifters, linguistic categories, and cultural description. In *Meaning in anthropology,* edited by Keith H. Basso and Henry A. Selby. Albuquerque: University of New Mexico Press.

———. 1993. Metapragmatic discourse and metapragmatic function. In *Reflexive language,* edited by John A. Lucy. Cambridge: Cambridge University Press.

Singer, Milton. 1972. *When a great tradition modernizes: An anthropological approach to Indian civilization.* New York: Praeger Publishers.

Smith, Dorothy E. 1987. *The everyday world as problematic: A feminist sociology.* Boston: Northeastern University Press.

Solomon, Thomas. 1994. *Coplas de Todos Santos* in Cochambamba: Language, music, and performance in Bolivian Quecha song dueling. *Journal of American Folklore* 107:378–414.

Stoeltje, Beverly. 1988. Gender representations in performance: The cowgirl and the hostess. *Journal of Folklore Research* 25:141–153.

Stoeltje, Beverly, and Richard Bauman. 1989. Community festival and the enactment of modernity. In *The old traditional way of life,* edited by Robert Walls and George Shoemaker. Bloomington: Trickster Press.

Stone, Ruth M. 1982. *Let the inside be sweet: The interpretation of music event among the Kpelle of Liberia.* Bloomington: Indiana University Press.

———. 1988. *Dried millet breaking: Time, words, and song in the Woi epic of the Kpelle.* Bloomington: Indiana University Press.

Stone, Ruth M., and Verlon L. Stone. 1981. Feedback, event, and analysis: Research media in the study of music events. *Ethnomusicology* 25:215–226.

Sugarman, Jane C. 1997. *Engendering song: Singing and subjectivity at Prespa Albanian weddings.* Chicago: University of Chicago Press.

Tagg, Philip. 1990. Reading sounds (Music, knowledge, rock & society). *Recommended Recorded Quarterly* 3:4–11.

———. 1994. From refrain to rave: The decline of figure and the rise of ground. *Popular Music* 13:209–222.

Tedlock, Dennis. 1972. *Finding the center: Narrative poetry of the Zuni.* New York: Dial Press.

Thompson, E. P. 1978. *The poverty of theory and other essays.* London: Merlin.

Thoms, William. [1846] 1964. Folklore. In *The study of folklore,* edited by Alan Dundes. Englewood Cliffs: Prentice-Hall.

Titon, Jeff Todd. 1995. Text. *Journal of American Folklore* 108:432–448.

Toelken, Barre. 1979. *The dynamics of folklore.* Boston: Houghton Mifflin.

Tönnies, Ferdinand. [1887] 1963. *Community & society,* translated and edited by Charles P. Loomis. New York: Harper and Row.

Türköz, Meltem. 1998. The distribution of amnesia: Family names and ethnicity in Turkey. Paper read at American Folklore Society Annual Meeting, October 30, Portland, Oregon.

Turner, Victor. 1969. *The ritual process: Structure and anti-structure.* Chicago: Aldine Publishing.

van Leeuwen, Theo. 1999. *Speech, music, sound.* London: Macmillan.

Walser, Robert. 1993. *Running with the Devil: Power, gender, and madness in heavy metal music.* Middletown and Hanover: Wesleyan University Press and University Press of New England.

Whisnant, David E. 1983. *All that is native and fine: The politics of culture in an American region.* Chapel Hill: University of North Carolina Press.

Willis, Paul. 1975. The expressive style of motor bike culture. In *The body as a medium of expression,* edited by Jonathan Benthal and Ted Polhemus. New York: E. P. Dutton.

Willis, Paul, with Simon Jones, Joyce Canaan, and Geoff Hurd. 1990. *Common culture: Symbolic work at play in the everyday cultures of the young.* Boulder: Westview Press.

Willis, Susan. 1991. *A primer for daily life.* London: Routledge.

Winters Bane. [1993] 2001. Wages of sin. *Heart of a killer.* Century Media CMR 7979–2.

Woodbury, Anthony C. 1987. Rhetorical structure in central Alaskan Yupik traditional narrative. In *Native American discourse: Poetics and rhetoric,* edited by Joel Sherzer and Anthony C. Woodbury. Cambridge: Cambridge University Press.

Yoder, Don. 1963. The folklife studies movement. *Pennsylvania Folklife* 13:43–56.

———. 1976. *American folklife.* Austin: University of Texas Press.

Index

*

Abrahams, Roger D., 5, 20, 21–22
Aesthetic of reflexivity, xiii, 89–90, 95, 117–21, 165n1, 168n19
Agentive/given identity, 138–39
Akron (Ohio) heavy metal scene, 49–50, 104. *See also* Heavy metal music; Rock music
Akron (Ohio) jazz scene, 103–7. *See also* Jazz music
Alienation, 6
Althusser, Louis, 138–39, 164n16
Anti-disciplines, 7
Ascribed/achieved identity, 138
Attention: attentional self, 76, 78–79, 82–83, 100–101, 164n22; ideology of attention, 103, 106–10, 115, 116, 168n19; organization of attention in an event, 103–6, 116–17, 167n18, 168n19; organization of phenomena, 103; phenomenological meaning of, 167n15; reflexive attention, xii–xiii, 91, 100–106
Audience, 94–95, 108–10, 117, 144

Babcock, Barbara, 90–91, 93, 94
Bakan, Michael, 81
Bauman, Richard: on data/theory dialectic, 24; definition of performance, 15, 30, 155; on differential identity, 131–32, 139; on framing performance, 90–92; interest in

everyday-life study, 5; on reflexive consciousness, 96, 103, 121; *Verbal Art as Performance* (1977), xii, 15, 90–96
Ben-Amos, Dan, 30
Bendix, Regina, 131
Benedict, Ruth, 37
Berliner, Paul, 107
Bermúdez, José Luis: nonconceptual point of view, 73–74, 164n20; on self-consciousness, xii, 46, 61–62, 72–75, 164n17, 164n19; on somatic proprioception, 69–70, 73; on thought/language interdependency, 71–72
Birmingham school, 7–8
Blacking, John, 86
Body: comportment, 119–21, 168n23; fatigue/endurance in musical performance, 50, 104–5; intersubjectivity and, 97–99, 113–14, 167n14; meditation and, 65–67; self-perception and, 61–64, 68–70, 163n15; sound perception, 48–49
Borges, Jorge Luis, 161n12
Bourdieu, Pierre, 6
Braudel, Fernand, 160n4
Briggs, Charles L., 24, 161n2

Capitalism, 29–30, 33–34, 139
Caton, Steve C., 96, 100

Cavicchi, Daniel, 16–17
Class, 11–13, 17, 18–19, 21–22. *See also* Marx, Karl
Cleveland (Ohio) hard rock scene, 104, 108. *See also* Rock music
Cleveland (Ohio) jazz scene, 82, 103, 106–7. *See also* Jazz music
Coffin, Tristram P., 130
Cohen, Anne, 24
Cohen, Hennig, 130
Cohen, Norm, 24
Context, 11, 25–27, 95
Critical theory, 19–20, 147–48, 156
Csikszentmihalyi, Mihaly, 79–81, 164n22, 165nn24–25
Cultural performances, 149
Cultural studies, 7–8, 160n6

De Certeau, Michel, 6, 20, 160nn4–5
Decentered subject, 166n8
Descartes, René, 64, 128
Detail claustrophobia, 59
Detail vertigo, 53, 55–56, 58–59, 82
Di Roma, Rosa, 119–21
Dialectics, 32–33, 94–95
Differential identity, 131–32, 136, 139
Disinvoltura, 117–21
Dorson, Richard, 129–30, 136, 168n3
Doubling, 141–42, 157
Dundes, Alan, 131
Durkheim, Emile, 131

Eidos: gestalt psychology and, 162n4; seeing/seeing as, 27–28; theory building and, 25, 29–32, 161n7; translation of term, 161n4
Empiricism, ix–x
Ensemble texture, 83–86, 165nn27–28
Epoché (brackets), 97, 167n10
Erikson, Erik, 128
Ethnic identity, 137, 140
Ethnography, 19–20, 37, 104, 125
Ethnopoetics, 24, 35–36
Evans-Pritchard, Deirdre, 132–33, 136–37
Everyday life: contextual factors of, 11; critical perspective on, 8–10, 19–20, 160n7; cross-cultural concepts of,

163n13; defined, 3–4, 159n1 (chap. 1); economic factors in, 12–13, 17–19; in folkore studies, 4–6; as framework for interpreting practice, 10, 19; ideology and, 11–12; production of society in, 6–8, 10, 21–22; social taxonomy and, 13–14, 17–19
Expressive culture, x–xi, 8, 14–21. *See also* Performance
Expressivity, 46–47, 54–55, 162n8

Featherstone, Mike, 14, 160n7
Felski, Rita, 4, 9, 13, 21
Flow, 79–81, 164n22, 165nn24–25
Focus, 47–50, 59, 162n8. *See also* Detail vertigo
Folk groups, 131
Folklore (field of study): communication approach, 124–25; concept of, x; data/theory dialectic, 24–25, 32–40; "everyday life" concept in, 4–6; identity concept in, 129–34; ideological labels in, 21; material culture, 5, 121–22; metatheory in, 23–25; neoromantic tradition in, 4, 7–8; politics of culture, 159n3; theory building in, 30–32
Foregrounding, 47–48
Foucault, Michel, 7, 25
Frames, 14–15, 92, 166n6, 168n20
Fringe, 47–48, 55, 162n8

Geertz, Clifford, 127
Gender, 11–12, 17–18, 119–21, 168n23, 169n8
Giard, Luce, 7
Gibson, J. J., 46, 72, 163n11, 164nn18–19
Giddens, Anthony, 6, 25, 167n18
Gleason, Philip, 126, 128
Goffman, Erving, 5, 15, 155
Grounded aesthetic, 8

Hall, Stuart, 128, 140
Hallowell, A. Irving, 126
Handler, Richard, 126, 128, 132, 140
Heavy metal music: connoisseuristic interpretation in, 58–59; death metal style, 104; gender/sexuality issues,

147; melodic metal style, 54, 56; social patterning in, 84–86; underground bands, 49–50, 104
Herder, Johann Gottfried, 129–30, 140
Here/there, 69–70
Heroic life, 14
Hesmondhalgh, Dave, 83–86, 165n27
Horizon: defined, 44; fantasy example of, 43–44, 164n18; focus/fringe/horizon structure, 47–49; horizonal grading, 54–55, 162n8; inner vs. outer horizon, 48–49, 53–54, 56, 58–60, 162n5; melodic horizon, 45
Hume, David, 61–62
Humunculus, 63–65, 68, 70, 76, 163n11
Husserl, Edmund: *Cartesian Meditations* (1931), 96–103, 164n19; on *eidos*, 29, 161n4; on *epoché* (brackets), 97–98, 167n10; existentialist reading of, 161n9, 167n11; on horizon, 44–45, 164nn19–20; on intersubjectivity, 97–99, 113, 167n14; on self-awareness, xiii–xiv; transcendental phenomenology of, 32, 64–65
Hymes, Dell, 15

Identity: affirmative/relational parameter of, 135–36, 140; agentive/given identity, 138–39; ascribed/achieved identity, 138; cross-cultural perspectives, 126–28, 140; definition, 126; differential identity, 131–32, 136; doubling, 141–42, 157; ethnic identity, 137–38, 140; in folklore studies, xiii, 129–34; foreground/background perceptions of, 145–48; historical perspectives, 128; institutionalized/situational parameter of, 135–39, 142, 169nn5–6; as interpretive dynamic, 148–54; as interpretive framework, 124–26, 134–37, 135 (fig. 1); metacommunicative expressions of, 149–54; national identity, 128–30, 133–34, 136, 140; as perceptually embedded/reflective, 144–48; presentation/performance of, 155–56; society and, 128–31; subject positioning, 93–95, 112, 166n8;

transcendental subject, 95. *See also* Self
Ideologies of everyday life, 11–12
Ihde, Don, 47, 162n8, 163n12
Individualism, 83–86, 128, 140
Instrumental culture, 14–15, 20–21
Intention, 82, 148–49
Intersubjectivity: body and, 97–99, 113–14, 167n14; identity and, 128; performance and, 102–3, 108–10, 113–14, 121; phenomenology of, 97–103
Intertextuality, 24

Jakobson, Roman, 95–96
James, William, 46, 61
Jansen, William Hugh, 131
Jazz music, 103–10. *See also* Akron (Ohio) jazz scene; Cleveland (Ohio) jazz scene
Johnston, Jeff, 112
Judas Priest (heavy metal band), 50, 53, 56, 147

Kant, Immanuel, 75
Kapchan, Deborah, 119
Kendall, Martha B., 96
Ketner, Kenneth Laine, 24, 161n11
Kirshenblatt-Gimblett, Barbara, 4
Kohák, Erazim V., 27
Korson, George, 130
Kratz, Corrine, 93–94
Kuhn, Thomas, 25

Language, 71–73, 77, 92, 94, 164n16
Lefebvre, Henri, 6–7, 13
Loss of self: attention and, 82–83; in collective experience, 85–86, 165n28; in flow, 79–81, 164n22, 165n25; in meditation, 67; reflexive thought and, 81–82; study methodology for, 61, 86–88; visual/auditory perception and, 83
Lüthi, Max, 161n8

Magliocco, Sabina, 5
Marriott, McKim, 127
Marx, Karl, 27, 29–30, 33–34, 160n6, 161n10 (chap. 2). *See also* Class

MUSIC/CULTURE

A series from Wesleyan University Press

Edited by George Lipsitz, Susan McClary, and Robert Walser

My Music
by Susan D. Crafts, Daniel Cavicchi,
Charles Keil, and the Music in Daily
Life Project

Running with the Devil:
Power, Gender, and Madness
in Heavy Metal Music
by Robert Walser

Subcultural Sounds:
Micromusics of the West
by Mark Slobin

Upside Your Head! Rhythm and Blues
on Central Avenue
by Johnny Otis

Dissonant Identities: The Rock 'n' Roll
Scene in Austin, Texas
by Barry Shank

Black Noise: Rap Music and Black
Culture in Contemporary America
by Tricia Rose

Club Cultures: Music, Media,
and Subcultural Capital
by Sarah Thornton

Music, Society, Education
by Christopher Small

Listening to Salsa:
Gender, Latin Popular Music, and
Puerto Rican Cultures
by Frances Aparicio

Any Sound You Can Imagine:
Making Music/Consuming Technology
by Paul Théberge

Voices in Bali: Energies and Perceptions
in Vocal Music and Dance Theater
by Edward Herbst

Popular Music in Theory
by Keith Negus

A Thousand Honey Creeks Later:
My Life in Music from Basie to
Motown—and Beyond
by Preston Love

Musicking: The Meanings of
Performing and Listening
by Christopher Small

Music of the Common Tongue:
Survival and Celebration in African
American Music
by Christopher Small

Singing Archaeology:
Philip Glass's Akhnaten
by John Richardson

ABOUT THE AUTHORS

HARRIS M. BERGER is Associate Professor of Music in the Department of Performance Studies at Texas A&M University. He is the author of *Metal, Rock, and Jazz: Perception and the Phenomenology of Musical Experience* (Wesleyan, 1999), and his articles have appeared in the journals *Ethnomusicology, Popular Music, Journal of American Folklore,* and *Journal of Folklore Research.* With Michael T. Carroll, he co-edited *Global Pop, Local Language* (University Press of Mississippi, 2003), an edited volume on the politics and aesthetics of language choice and dialect in popular music around the world. Berger received his B.A. in Music from Wesleyan University, and his M.A. and Ph.D. in Folklore/Ethnomusicology from Indiana University.

GIOVANNA P. DEL NEGRO is Assistant Professor of English at Texas A&M University. She is the author of *Looking Through My Mother's Eyes: Life Stories of Nine Italian Immigrant Women in Canada.* Her work on performance, identity, and *piazza* strolling has appeared in the *Journal of American Folklore* and *Midwestern Folklore,* and she is currently the convener of the Mediterranean Studies Section of the American Folklore Society. Her book *The Passeggiata and Popular Culture in an Italian Town: Folklore and the Performance of Modernity* (McGill-Queen's University Press) will be published in 2004. Del Negro received a B.A. in Sociology from Concordia University, an M.A. in Popular Culture from Bowling Green State University, and a Ph.D. in Folklore and American Studies from Indiana University. She is currently conducting ethnographic research on women's stand-up comedy in San Francisco, Houston, Montreal, and London.